Elvis LIVE AT FIVE

ALSO BY JOHN PAXSON

BONES

A GOLDEN TRAIL OF MURDER

A Novel By
John Paxson

Thomas Dunne Books
St. Martin's Press ⚜ New York

THOMAS DUNNE BOOKS.

An imprint of St. Martin's Press.

www.stmartins.com

ISBN 0-312-28557-4

First Edition: August 2002

10   9   8   7   6   5   4   3   2   1

FOR LUCREZIA

ACKNOWLEDGMENTS

A fiction is a product of imagining, and the imaginings in this fiction are mine, so I take full responsibility for them. But a fiction is also a knot of a million strings, and a number of very good people helped me tie that knot.

Shauna LaRussa was critical to the original act of creation, while Amanda Paxson offered unflagging support and encouragement. Marie Connors brought a gentle and sentient eye to the process, and Joe Connors—as he has throughout—kept the language honest.

David Boyd, Dena Wackwitz, and Joe Summey offered smart ideas, unquestioning friendship—and proof that Texas is home to some of the finest people there are.

John Baxter and Michael Crean in London offered a glimpse of that odd universe inside a microchip, while Katharine Kidde in New York cajoled, critiqued, and persevered to prove she is without peer in the universe of literary agents. And Marcia Markland at St. Martin's was there at the beginning, never lost faith, and finally put it all on the line. Thank you, Marcia.

The other real players in this small fiction are too numerous to name. They are the journalists I've worked with through three decades who catch history on the fly—and get it mostly right.

Elvis LIVE AT FIVE

*I*T IS dark and cold this morning in London. Midwinter, and a soft rain is smearing against the windows of the flat where I'm living. The tide is in and the broad, muddy wash of the Thames is high. But no boats are on the river yet—it's too early. A police car hurries across a bridge, its bright lights bouncing off the black water in a distorted slash of slanting blues and whites.

I'm up because of the nightmares that infect what little sleep I can manage. It's been that way for weeks now, maybe months: I'm losing track of time. And it's getting worse. I'd thought the move to London might help, that three thousand miles of ocean between me and America might soften the images and ease the terror. But it's been just the reverse. The ocean seems to be acting like some giant magnifying glass, snapping into grotesque focus the awful things I have run from in America.

It is dark and cold this morning in London and I can't sleep because I have a story to tell. I realized that a few hours ago as I was searching through the television channels. It was an image from the BBC that hit me like a hammer in the chest: thousands of hollow-eyed refugees huddled around bonfires at night in heavy snow, soldiers with rifles pushing into the crowds of bewildered and terrified people, a dark-haired reporter shouting into the camera, steam pouring from her mouth as she spoke. I had the sound down—but I didn't need the reporter's useless words to understand the pictures. They washed across me like an acid bath. Thousands of men, women and children in a long snaking line of misery and fear stumbling through the winter snows of Nebraska—American men, women and children being force-marched through a living nightmare, the shock lines of terror on their faces as plain as the American flags on the uniforms of the men with the guns.

I sat here last night watching those silent images and felt myself and all the things I believe in dying. For that refugee column was no isolated event, no one-time aberration, but a part of a contagion that is sweeping my country like the malignant cells of a cancerous tumor. It is everywhere—in Los Angeles and San Diego, in Washington and Dallas, in Seattle and Brownsville. It is spreading—and it is killing as it spreads.

I am haunted with nightmares because I am a large part of the reason that contagion is out there. My shadow is on the trampled snows in Nebraska—and countless other sites of despair and anger and hatred across America. My finger is on the triggers of the soldiers' rifles; it is my face that reflects in the frightened eyes of the refugees.

As the images from the BBC poured through the room, I realized that it is I more than anyone else who created these nightmares. I realized as well that if they are ever to end, it is I who must stop them.

I turned off the box—killed the pictures—and watched the river. And I realized this morning what must be done. My hope—my only hope—is that people might listen to a story. It is a story of joy and despair, of courage and cowardice, of genius and brute stupidity. And it is a story of hubris. Only by telling it in its full can there be any chance that we will escape the growing darkness.

I prepare to tell this story hoping it may be believed by some, knowing it will be disbelieved by many others. Yet it is a true story. A story that must be told. I have come to understand in a profound way that my very survival depends on telling this story. Your survival, too.

CHAPTER ONE

IT WAS a conversation with a dead movie star that got it all started. The first time I ever laid eyes on Duncan Gelder, the man who was to loom so large in my own future, he was having a chat with Marilyn Monroe. And even though Marilyn had been dead for longer than most could remember, it wasn't a one-sided conversation: Marilyn was talking back. That's what stopped me, jarring me out of an otherwise normal day. If I'd only known then, had some hint. But life is seldom that generous.

I heard it as I was walking down the hallway toward the television newsroom. It was coming from one of the small video-editing rooms. "I love you, Duncan Gelder." A woman's voice—breathy, sultry—somehow familiar.

"And I love you." A man's voice answering—tentative, a little nervous—but a man's voice nevertheless.

The conversation was so odd and so out of place that I slowed to listen. As I passed the door, the woman spoke again. "Are you sure Duncan loves me?" That was the line that got me. I knew that voice—everyone knew that voice. The problem was, as far as I knew, Marilyn Monroe was still quite dead.

"Duncan loves you more than love itself," the man was saying.

Marilyn purring. "How much is that?"

I eased open the edit-bay door. In the dim blue light, a large man with a thick neck and ratty thinning hair had his arms out wide, an ice-cream bar in one hand. He was talking to a television set. "This much," he was saying, "Duncan Gelder loves you this much."

Marilyn Monroe was gazing back from the screen, her eyes dancing, her mouth drawn into a half-smile. "Ooh, I like that." She puckered her red lips and blew a wet kiss. "That's for my baby Duncan."

"Friend of yours?" I said, quietly.

The man's large bulk jerked in surprise, and he fumbled at the buttons on the console in front of him, freezing Marilyn's image on the screen. He swiveled around awkwardly in the chair, a startled expression on his face. His T-shirt had bits of chocolate on it.

"Interesting conversation," I offered.

"Marilyn Monroe," he said, hunching his shoulders uncomfortably toward the television set and blinking his thyroidal eyes as though they were hurting him. He squeezed off a tight, embarrassed grin that showed too many teeth in a crowded mouth.

I looked from him to Marilyn and back. "Quite a toy. What is it?"

The man licked self-consciously at a drip of ice cream running down his thumb. "Old movie shots. Things like that."

"I'm Nick Upton, by the way, the news director here. And you're . . . ?"

"I know," said the man, rising slightly in his chair.

"Your name is . . . ?"

"It's Gelder. I mean I'm Duncan. Duncan Gelder." His words were as clumsy as his body. "With a G. Gelder. I'm a new freelancer."

I recognized the name: his résumé and audition tape had come across my desk a week or two before. I'd liked his work and I remembered wondering at the time what kind of mother—or father—would load a kid with a name like Duncan Gelder. From Gelder to Gelding wasn't much of a step. Schoolyards must have been nasty places for a kid with a name like that. "So Marilyn, huh? You do that yourself?"

Gelder nodded shyly.

"Pretty sophisticated for this place."

"Spare-time stuff," said the man with a dismissive shrug. "Something I play around with at home. I brought it in to see how it'd look on this equipment."

I nodded. "And it's old movies edited together, something like that?"

"Something like that."

My experience in edit bays had usually been with pictures of car crashes, fires and too-cute animals. Marilyn Monroe was a first. "Play it again?"

Gelder seemed to brighten at that suggestion and turned in his chair, entering a series of keystrokes on the board in front of him. Marilyn's face collapsed into a grid of small colored squares and the screen went to black. "I go through her old movies," the man said over his shoulder, "and pick out words, intonations, facial gestures I can use." His clumsiness—both physical and verbal—had disappeared the second he turned back to his machines. He hit another button and the woman's face appeared again full frame on the monitor.

"I script up a conversation and then build up her video and audio." Gelder gnawed absently at the ice-cream bar. "It's all computerized. Mixed media. I time it out so her pauses match what I'm saying. It makes it sound like we're talking but there's no real interaction—it's just a tape playing." He entered more keystrokes and Marilyn's face came to life.

"Well, hi there, Duncan," said Marilyn Monroe, her eyes shining with flirty sexuality. "What brings you by today?" It was eerie how real Marilyn seemed—almost as though she were sitting in front of a TV camera next door. The quick, omnivorous eyes, the glossy red lips, milky skin and platinum hair. Beautiful. But eerie.

Duncan Gelder was also watching the face. "I thought I'd drop off these flowers," he said to the monitor.

The shot pulled out to show Marilyn from the waist up, her

heavy breasts puckering out of a narrow red-sequined gown. Next to her on the screen, a tall-looking dark-haired man with wide shoulders, an angular face and a heavy five-o'clock shadow handed her a bunch of roses.

"Guy looks like you," said Gelder without turning.

That surprised me and I caught myself running my hand across my chin, wondering if he really did look like me. I realized I had no good notion of precisely how I appeared to others. I'm tall—better than six three—and I have dark hair and a heavy stubble but beyond that mirrors—even the television cameras—tell me little. I suppose it's the same for most people.

Marilyn held the roses to her nose and breathed in their scent. "Lovely roses, Duncan." She looked back up at Gelder from the screen. "You're so sweet. I love you, Duncan Gelder."

"And I love you." Gelder was working without a script: he'd obviously said the lines so often that they were committed to memory.

The camera came in close: Marilyn's face had taken on a pouty, teasing look. "Are you sure Duncan loves me?"

"Duncan loves you more than love itself."

"How much is that?"

"This much," said Gelder, holding out his arms again as he had when I'd first come across him. "Duncan Gelder loves you this much."

"Ooh, I like that." The puckered lips again and a wet kiss blown from the television screen. "That's for my baby Duncan."

"Thanks, Marilyn," said Gelder.

Marilyn pushed out her chest and arched her eyebrows in a frowning question. "Are you busy tonight, Duncan?"

"I'm never too busy for you."

Marilyn seemed to be thinking something over: she cast her eyes down and nibbled the end of her tongue, then looked back up. "I want you tonight," she whispered. Her eyes were hollow—and her voice was hungry. I wondered silently if I was the only one who felt the sexual energy jumping off the screen.

Gelder's voice next to me again: "Eight o'clock?"

CHAPTER TWO

MARGARET WARES hunched into the dressing-room mirror, trying with both hands to steady the silver lipstick tube and draw its red line for a third time across her mouth. She knew better than to be nervous, knew it was amateurish to get the shakes over a five-minute interview on a lunch-time television show no one watched—an interview done by a weatherman, at that—but she was having a tough time with it.

She checked the line and rubbed her lips together. Close. Why was it she could address an audience of hundreds of academics—intellectual peers—without so much as a single nervous twitch, but would break into sweats anytime a television camera was even in the neighborhood? Maybe it was the issue of control, she thought to herself as she blotted the lipstick with a tissue and picked at the corner of her mouth with her little finger. You have at least a hope of controlling situations if you're face-to-face with people, but there's no way you can control the impersonal, passive stare of the camera. It doesn't care if you make a fool of yourself. To paraphrase a famous newsman: the dumb thing never even blinks.

Knuckles rapped on the dressing-room door and a muffled voice said "three minutes." The woman ran both hands through her dark-red hair and bent into the mirror a final time, rubbing at the slight circles under her blue eyes, picking at the corner of her mouth again and giving her lipstick one last critical look. Not great, she thought, not great. Too nervous, too tired, too old.

The man who was going to interview her might possibly pass for handsome if the only evidence used was taken from

Marilyn licked her lips. "I'll put something on .

Gelder hit a button and the glamorous image fro
screen. "That's the end of it."

I didn't know quite what to say. The whole thin
beginning to feel awkward, like I'd stepped into son
else's fantasy—or fetish—and needed to step back
quickly. In twenty-some years in the news business—mos
it in television—I'd run into more than a lifetime's share
oddities. But nothing quite like this.

Gelder seemed to sense my uneasiness. "I do it with other
stars, too," he said lightly, his crowded mouth squeezing out a
friendly smile. "Everyone's doing it these days. The audio's the
tough part, but I think I've about got that licked. I've got
some other stuff, too. It's a lot neater. Lot more cutting edge. I
mean it's even beyond that. Maybe you'd like to see it sometime?" I offered a noncommittal shrug.

In the dark background, Marilyn was gazing out from the
television screen with a startled look on her face. The video
rictus had caught her with her mouth beginning to open, her
eyes widening toward surprise, as though she'd been silenced
just as she'd been about to say something truly important.

the neck up. His face was square, angular and well-proportioned. He had a head of thick dark hair that seemed to be all his own and if it was dyed, it was a pretty good job. The rest of him, though, reminded Margaret of a pair of rolled up socks. A small pair.

The man barely noticed as they led Margaret onto the television stage and miked her, arranging her in one of two gray cloth-covered office chairs against a wall covered with an enlarged photo of the Dallas skyline. She was surprised by how hot the lights were. She ran a finger across her upper lip and felt a sheen of moisture. Someone offstage said "one minute."

"So, Missus Warren," said the man, turning to her finally in a regal sort of way, his glance lingering a long extra moment on her chest. "Welcome to the show." Up close, she realized he was even more made up than she—a bottled suntan had been shoveled onto his face and his eyebrows were filled in with dark pencil. He switched on a TV grin. Perfect white teeth.

"And I'm delighted to be here," said Margaret, though she wasn't and worried it was obvious. But she had books to sell and pompous little weathermen with good teeth and television talk shows were one of the tools. "It's actually not Missus Warren but Ms. Wares. Margaret Wares."

"Ms.," said the man, drawing out the word and rolling it in his mouth. "I'll be sure to get that right. Why don't we just relax and have some fun." His eyes washed across her chest again.

An announcer's voice came up on a speaker somewhere. Margaret felt her stomach go sideways as a pair of large studio cameras rolled into position in front of the set. A stage director in scuffed jeans and a faded ponytail was counting down the seconds on his fingers. At *one* he dropped his arm and pointed silently toward the stage.

"And a lovely Dallas Wednesday noontime to all of you," said the host into a camera about five feet in front of him. "It's the middle of the week, middle of the summer. The weekend's just a couple of days away, huh? How 'bout that? I'm Iso

Bahr and today we've got a real special treat for you. You may not realize it, but in just a few weeks this nation will be commemorating the twenty-fifth anniversary of the passing of a truly great American. August sixteenth, nineteen seventy-seven. A black day for Americans. The day Elvis Presley died. And we have one of this country's leading experts here with us today to talk about that man. I'd like you to give a big hometown welcome to Margaret Warren. She's a Ms." At that Bahr arched his eyebrows slightly. "Now, some of you may know her from a column she writes every now and then for the paper. Others of you may know she's a professor. What most of you probably don't know is that there's another side to this handsome young lady, the side that is an accomplished author. Margaret Warren's new book, *Elvis, the Making of a Myth*, is going to climb to the very top." Bahr held up the book in his small fist as the second camera pushed in for a tight shot.

I was watching it all from the back of the control room at the other end of the station. That's a perch I take pretty much any time we're on the air. With a chair that's friendly to my tall frame and the various intercoms and telephones that let me talk to the studio and to the newsroom, it's a good spot to keep an eye on the air product, and on the people putting it there. It's also a good spot to hide out. The room's dark, people are busy and unlike the newsroom, where my office walls are glass and at least one set of eyes is always watching, here I can pretend to be alone.

At the front of the room, Jolene Pool, who was directing the show, called a shot change and the face of Margaret Wares filled the large central monitor that dominated the room: blue eyes, prominent cheekbones and full lips framing an enigmatic smile, as though the woman knew some small secret that no one else was in on. An intriguing face.

Jolene called another shot and Iso Bahr's face filled the screen. "So Miss Warren, Margaret if I may. First about you. You're a college professor?"

"It's Wares, actually, Margaret Wares."

"Of course, of course," said Bahr. "You're a teacher?"

Margaret Wares nodding. "A college professor."

"University of Texas?"

"That's right, Iso. UT-Dallas."

"English, right?"

"Actually, it's semantics."

"Semantics," said the weatherman, rolling the word like it was an exotic new taste he couldn't exactly place. "And we all know your occasional column in the *Tribune*, 'On Words.' You've been writing that what, a couple of years now?"

"Six, actually," said the woman.

The weatherman nodded. "Okay, now Elvis. The King. What was he really like?"

In her uncomfortable chair on the hot, claustrophobic set, Margaret felt a moment of panic at the question, as if any one human could describe another in the twenty-five seconds or so television allowed for answers. For in-depth answers. She decided to push it away. "Complex, Iso, a tremendously complex human being."

"Interesting," said Bahr, nodding her on.

"A country boy who became a big-city icon. A natural talent so great that geography and economics couldn't keep him down." Margaret felt herself hitting her stride and began to relax. "A son of poverty who became a son of America." Margaret switched into autopilot at that point. The nerves were gone, she wasn't worried about lipstick or sweat. She was back on comfortable home turf.

It was quiet in the control room, most faces turned up to the central monitor where Iso Bahr was listening and nodding his head. A slight scowl told people he was hearing what his guest was saying but was not completely convinced she knew what she was talking about. He'd copied the look from Mike Wallace.

At the front console, Jolene Pool fiddled with a headset that made her look vaguely like an air traffic controller, which, in a way, she was. "Camera two," she said into the tiny mike that hung off a thin plastic tube in front of her mouth, "camera two, give me a slow push on her face. Ready camera two . . . take two."

Margaret Wares from the knees up filled the large screen. A dark tailored jacket and slacks and a white blouse set off with a blaze of color from a gold-and-blue silk scarf.

Jolene was studying the picture and talking to the camera operator. "Keep it slow, two, fluid. That's it. Let's stop it when we get full face. . . ."

". . . was when he joined the army," the woman was saying. "I mean, it's hard today with our post-Vietnam sensibilities and all of that to imagine how his enlistment delighted this country. Well, let me back up on that. Certainly not all of the country. Even then, there was a growing antiwar movement, certainly. But his enlistment delighted his people, his constituency, shall we say. I mean, this man represented the farm boys who were going off to fight this war. He was an icon to them, the sort of man who—"

"That's interesting, interesting," said Bahr, cutting her off in midsentence. The red tally lights blinked. Iso Bahr paused to let the cameras catch up with him and fixed his guest with his best *60 Minutes* stare. "Was Elvis an alien?"

"What the fuck did he just say?" shouted Jolene as the whole sleepy control room instantly came to life. "Ready one—take one!"

Margaret Wares's startled face full frame in the monitor, her mouth half open in astonishment.

Jolene shot an angry glance over her shoulder at me. "Boss, you've gotta do something with this moron." She turned back to the console. "Okay, everybody settle down. We've been Iso-ed. Two—camera two—listen to me, pull out wide. Wide two-shot. More. That's it. Two, ready two and—take two. And, good-bye *Noon Show.*"

I watched the spectacle unravel and wondered to myself what sort of coupling could create a man like Iso Bahr. The IQ of a warm day protected by a self-assurance that was so strong he didn't even realize how dim his own bulb could be. I'd inherited him two years before when I moved to Dallas after self-destructing in the big markets on the West Coast. But despite icy glares from angry directors—and shows that occasionally fell to dust on the air—had no intention of getting rid of him. The man might have the personality of a doorknob, but for some unexplainable reason, audiences loved him. In television that meant job security. And though I'd never admit it to another soul, I considered him something of a secret weapon. Bahr was one of the most inexhaustible talkers I had ever met. With little more than a one- or two-word idea to go on, he could babble like a brook for hours. In television, where you fill endless chunks of nothing with anything you can get your hands on, a guy who could talk like that was money in the bank. The only problem was you couldn't always be sure what was going to come out of his mouth.

On the set, Bahr was wrapping it up with a nonchalant patter, while Wares sat across from him with a look of bewilderment on her face. Jolene rolled credits and the show finally, mercifully, came to a close.

I was back in my office off the newsroom talking on the phone and gnawing at a ham sandwich when Margaret Wares showed up at my door. Through the glass walls, I could see more than a dozen people studiously pretending not to watch.

"You're the man in charge of this station?" she said, her voice sharp as a knife, her blue eyes tight and angry.

"The news part," I said, rising politely as I put down the phone and tried to swallow an over-sized bite. "Nick Upton."

"You've got a problem, Mr. Upton," she said, almost spitting the words. She was still in her camera makeup, which served to exaggerate the angry lines around her eyes and mouth.

"You're right," I said calmly. "I apologize for that." She was better looking in the flesh than on TV—the blue of her eyes was almost electric and the small, enigmatic twist to her mouth that I'd noticed on the air gave her expression an edge of good humor that showed through even in the midst of her anger. I glanced at her hands. No wedding ring on her slender fingers. Interesting woman. "Want me to fire him?" I asked.

The words seemed to stop her and she took a half-step backward.

"He can be a problem," I said, grinning to take some of the heat out of the encounter. "We try to keep it bottled up but sometimes it just spills out. Maybe you'd like to sit down?"

She shot me a withering look. "That was embarrassing out there. Elvis, an alien? I'm there with a well-researched book on a genuine American phenomenon, and this little toad is leering at me, getting my name wrong, trying to look down my blouse"—she rolled her eyes at this—"and asking if Elvis was from outer space. What incredible garbage. That's the kind of place you run here?"

"Sadly, it is sometimes," I said, making a conscious effort to establish eye contact and not, under any circumstance, look at her breasts—though now that the subject had been raised, it was almost impossible. "What can I say? You have my apologies." It didn't seem like the time to point out the obvious—that she was on television because of Elvis and the power of that single word, and not because of anything to do with her own academic brilliance. "So Elvis, huh? Hotter than a depot stove these days. How's your book selling?"

Margaret Wares either didn't hear me or chose to ignore me. "Maybe you should warn your guests."

"Makes for better television if we don't."

The woman stared at me for a beat as the words sank in. "Don't ask me back," she said, turning from the room and slamming the door behind her.

I sat there as she marched back across the newsroom and disappeared out the main entrance, with the staff again pretending they weren't watching. Later that day, I caught myself writing out the name 'Maggie' in cubed block letters and thinking about blue eyes and smiling lips. It got me through most of an otherwise interminable budget meeting.

CHAPTER THREE

MARGARET WARES was not the only storm to hit that week. The second came a few days later—and this was a real one.

Throughout a long Friday afternoon there had been plenty of warning that bad things were coming as the horizon to the west of the city grew dark with angry black clouds piling up, north to south, as far as people could see. Folks said later the light that afternoon was funny—a kind of sickly lime green. By four the ominous mass had begun to churn and a little after four thirty the sirens started going off across Dallas and Fort Worth warning that tornadoes were on the way.

It was controlled bedlam at the TV station. I'd been moving nonstop back and forth among the newsroom, the set and the control room for a couple of hours as the anchors and Iso Bahr broke into the afternoon programming to warn of the storm's approach. We were using multicolored Doppler radars, real-time satellite images, split screens, computer-generated modeling graphics—every whistle and bell we could pull out of our kit bag to make it look like we were on top of the story as the storm cells intensified and moved east toward the city. Well before the sirens went off, I had to gamble on a decision: whether to commit to the danger of sending people and valuable equipment out into the path of the storm to get shots of it coming in or hold them back in the relative protection of the station until the worst had gone by. It's not that there weren't volunteers—the younger reporters and cameramen were crazed to get out of the building and into the action. But I knew the dangers only too well and was stalling.

Once—just once—I'd guessed wrong on the risks of sending people into a dangerous news story. I'd paid for it every single day since. A dead-hot summer day, a cloudless sky under a smothering sun, the air so dry you could almost hear it gasping. A cigarette flicked casually from a car in Topanga Canyon had sent a rolling wall of flames into the Hollywood Hills.

As a younger man, a man so righteously full of himself he was bursting, I had sent a television crew out to cover the fire. The reporter was young, female and inexperienced and didn't want to go. The cameraman was a veteran of a hundred fires and—I thought—knew what he was doing. It should have been all right. Should have been. Three empty words. The winds changed, the fire veered and the two ran for their lives. I caught the paramedics' call on the news desk radio scanner: the cameraman was singed. The young reporter was badly burned. She held on for two long, agonizing, endless days at the UCLA Medical Center. Three days after that, I was a pallbearer at her funeral. I didn't know it then, but that funeral was my exit ticket from LA.

Now, as the storms bore down, I finally struck a cautious compromise: five volunteers out with the less expensive—and less reliable—microwave units, the rest of the staff held back along with the satellite trucks until after the front had passed. I accepted that the other stations in town would be less timid in committing their people and would probably beat us on the story—but after the fire in the hills, I didn't intend ever again to make a decision that would turn me into a pallbearer.

A couple of the younger people who still hadn't figured out the fragility of their own souls were the first out the door, laughing and making jokes about oral sex and giving those who'd stayed behind a clumsy thumbs-up. Two older reporters who'd been around a bit—both of them men—left the building quietly, their faces serious.

The first twister touched down on Texas Bob's Best Little Fordhouse dealership in Fort Worth, tossing the immaculate new cars into the air like toys thrown around by an angry child, blowing out the floor-to-ceiling glass of the showroom in a concussive burst and twisting the blue- and white-aluminum walls and roof into shrapnel. Luckily both employees and customers had been herded into an underground storm bunker and didn't get hurt.

The tornado jumped over a restaurant next door and slammed into a red-brick fire station, collapsing it inward like a pile of wooden blocks. A woman in the dispatch office was crushed to death by a nine-ton ladder truck that came through a reinforced steel and brick wall.

The twister jumped back into the sky for half a mile before coming down a last and fatal time on a neatly manicured block of stucco homes and green lawns and leaving behind a swath of splintered beams, broken glass, strewn insulation and three grotesquely mangled bodies.

The newsroom assignment desk caught the Fort Worth call on the police radio scanner and moved microwave trucks and reporters in that direction. The anchors interrupted a game show to say a twister was on the ground and reporters were on the way. Anxious eyes watched the newsroom monitors to see if the other stations in town would beat us to the first pictures.

The second and third twisters came in north of the city across two suburban developments. Valley Ranch, where the Dallas Cowboys trained, lost a shopping mall, a grade school auditorium, a stretch of mobile homes—and three citizens. Plano fared better: one block of houses down, the roof torn off a retirement home. No dead.

When the worst had passed, I ordered out the rest of the microwave units and the satellite trucks. We were in full-disaster programming now, two anchors—a gentle middle-aged African-American man whom I liked and an icy blonde in her early thirties whom I could barely stand—were working the phones and reading news items as they came in. Iso Bahr was in position nearby against a blue screen updating the radar images as the storm front moved east toward Rockwall, Greenville and Sulphur Springs. A hard-luck night ahead for those towns.

I slipped into the noisy control room: reporters' faces on the monitors beginning to get their live shots up from the scenes of carnage, cameras panning hurriedly across acres of rubble, firemen in Day-Glo orange and green talking soberly about dead and injured, anchors interrupting with questions. Everyone remarking how much it sounded like a freight train. Jolene in her air controller's headset shouting camera cues, hissing orders at the half-dozen assistant directors scattered around her—and in the middle of it all taking a phone call from her mother. She was the calmest person I had ever seen in the middle of a disaster.

"Mr. Upton?" A quiet voice next to me in the confusion. "Maybe you have a second?"

I turned to see a pair of thyroidal eyes, patchy hair and a busy mouth—the man with Marilyn. The man with the bad name. Duncan Gelder. "Why aren't you in edit?"

"I just got here and thought maybe you'd want this." He held out a video cassette about the size of a pack of cigarettes. "I think it might be pretty good."

I shot him a quick questioning glance.

"Some storm shots," he said, his mouth working overtime in some private conversation. "May be pretty good."

"Cue it up. Edit three."

Gelder smiled. "On my way."

"Bring edit three on-line!" I yelled toward the front of the control room. "Might be something there."

A technician hit a couple of switches and one of the dozens of screens on the wall came to life with a blurred image of tape in rewind. The rewind stopped, the screen firmed up and the pictures began to play.

"Holy fuck!" yelled Jolene, putting down the phone to watch the screen. "Ready edit three! Bring it up. And—take edit three."

A voice from somewhere else: "What is this shit?"

"Awesome," yelled Jolene. "Keep it coming. Don't let it stop!"

A tornado in the distance, snaking and swirling, its head buried in the dark gray clouds, its tail whipping back and forth across houses and electrical lines, sparks and small explosions erupting with each hit, a car whirling into the air.

Jolene was shouting to make herself heard above the noise: "Cue the anchors. Amateur video, just in. Amateur video. Exclusive. Let it run, let it fucking run!"

The picture did a slow zoom forward until the whole frame was filled with the churning tail of the twister as it dug through the city. Another car flying into the air. Something, maybe a human body, catapulting through the screen and out of the shot. Gasps in the control room.

"Great fucking stuff," said a voice reverently.

The view pulled back again and the whole room watched mesmerized as the tail of the tornado clawed down toward the earth, glanced across the roof of one building and dropped down on another that seemed to explode with the weight.

"Where'd we get this?" said Jolene over her shoulder.

"Gelder, the new guy."

"Unbelievable. He gonna get a raise, boss?" Scattered laughter.

"Where the fuck was he?" said another voice.

"Water tower, looks like."

"Guy must have balls the size of grapefruits."

The tape continued to roll as the twister mowed through a block of houses like a giant churning foot kicking through a miniature landscape. At the end of the block, the picture zoomed in until the twister filled the whole screen. Wood and metal flying, a washing machine caroming through the shot and off the screen, and then the tornado hopping toward the sky, dirt and debris raining down from it. The camera followed it upward until it disappeared back into the black clouds that had spawned it. The tape went to black. Scattered applause and cheers in the control room.

"Camera one—take one!" yelled Jolene. "Edit three rerack that tape—we just got us an Emmy!"

The faces of the two anchors filled the screen. "Wasn't that something?" said the black man, arching his eyebrows slightly to show emotion. "Unbelievable" answered the white woman coolly, careful not to spoil her poise or her pose with an unpracticed facial expression.

I went looking for Gelder later that evening after we'd gotten through the heavy part of the disaster and back into regular programming.

"Nice work," I said, sticking my head into the open door of the edit bay.

Gelder turned from his monitors—the same monitors where we'd watched Marilyn: "Thanks."

"You went up on a water tower?"

Gelder shrugged. "Some new stuff I've been playing with."

"With a tornado coming in?"

Gelder wiped a crumb from his T-shirt, a shy look in his large eyes.

"Well," I said, "it may have been stupid but you got the picture." Even as I said the words, though, I had a jarring off-center feeling that things weren't as they seemed. Had Gelder—the king of cut and paste—cut and pasted a tornado? That would be a tough one. Once it's out there, how do you retract a picture? I couldn't pull it back if I wanted. And in my line of business, you didn't ask a question when you knew you wouldn't like the answer. "It was the lead on the network tonight. New York liked it a lot."

"Thanks."

"You might even make some money from it."

"I could use that."

I glanced at the silent monitors. "How's Marilyn?"

Gelder smiled. "Haven't had time to ask her. I've been on a new project."

"Same thing?"

"Not really," he said. "I think I may have mentioned it to

you. A lot more cutting-edge. Something I've been working on for about a year. I've got a little bit of it here. Maybe you'd like to see it? It's better than the tornado."

That got my attention. "Better than the tornado?"

Gelder's toothy grin widened into a large smile. "Ten times better. Maybe a hundred. Can I show you?"

I nodded and settled into a padded chair, grateful to be off my feet for the first time in the better part of twelve hours. Watching Gelder get his machines ready, I wondered idly why it was that the business attracted such oddballs. For some reason, I thought of the tall woman in Chicago who couldn't keep her hands off the men she was editing with. Strange that her face would swim up from my memory—I hadn't thought about her in years. In the middle of an edit, I'd suddenly feel her nails crab-walking up the side of my thigh. She did the same thing with every guy she cut with. She'd stop if they squirmed, but after a while there'd be the nails again. Or the guy in the small station in Idaho where I'd started out. He had a drinking problem that went undiscovered until people showed up for work Sunday morning to find him passed out with an empty vodka bottle on the control console and a porn movie broadcasting out to the sleepy little town. The man was fired, though there'd been no complaints at all about the unusual Sunday morning programming. I wondered where they were now almost twenty years later—whether they were still out there washing around in the sad video diaspora moving restlessly up and down the dial, eternally convinced that the next job would be the sweetheart.

"Ready," said Gelder, and I straightened up. "So what I've got is something new. I guess maybe you can see for yourself whether it works." Gelder turned a knob and keyed in a series of commands on the console and the screen came to life.

"Hi there. My name's Elvis Presley." And it was very much Elvis Presley—the soft mouth turning to the edge of a sneer, the dark hair falling rakishly over his eye. He had on a dark shirt under a white sports coat and was holding a guitar loosely at his side. "Duncan Gelder and I conjured up this trick with televisions and computers to show the world just exactly what can be done when smart people go to work with smart tools."

With that, Presley looked down and strummed the strings of the guitar, humming a few bars from "Love Me Tender." He looked back into the camera. "We thought you might enjoy a small demonstration of just how far the age of computer technology has advanced. What you're actually seeing is my good friend Duncan transformed by the magic of little digital ones and zeros into me, Elvis Presley. Like it?"

With that the image paused, Presley's face frozen on the screen.

I glanced at Gelder, looked back at the screen and then at Gelder again. "Marilyn part two?"

Gelder seemed surprised by the question. "Not at all," he said quickly, defensively. "I mean Marilyn's just cut and paste. This is new. Completely new."

"It looks like the same thing."

Gelder seemed pained at the comment. "It's a universe apart. Marilyn was just clips that I put into a sequence that made it look like she was real and interactive. This is the real thing."

"Elvis is dead."

"Well, okay, not that real obviously. But it's television real."

"No clips?"

Gelder was shaking his head. "No clips at all. I mean, this thing for all intents and purposes is a real Elvis Presley sitting there. I mean, he says whatever I want him to say, moves however I want." Gelder's voice was getting higher, his words coming out rapid-fire. "I mean this is cutting edge. This could revolutionize television—"

The stream of words was interrupted by a newsroom desk assistant who poked his head into the edit bay to say they'd just found another dead in Plano and ask if they should go on with a special report.

"I'll be right there," I said, rising from the chair. "Nice job, Duncan."

"You actually like it?" His voice was almost childlike.

"I like it," I said and though the tone probably sounded patronizing, I did in fact like it. What I could understand of it. "We'll talk more," I said, easing my way out of the tight room.

Chapter Four

My eyes were locked on the television set as I struggled to keep my mind blank, my reactions under control. The screen sat there inert and stupid, the red, blue and yellow color bars as dumb and uncommunicative as a beach towel while the droning audio-test signal poured from its electronic throat with the irritating insistence of a car alarm.

"Take it, take it!" Jolene had her director's voice on and it was sharp and in command. The screen sat there unchanging and the woman's tone grew more urgent. Sweat was beading Jolene's flushed face now and her matted blond hair had fallen across her eyes. "Take it! Take it! Take it!" The television sat passive and unresponding. Jolene was almost screaming now, her words coming so fast they were a single sound: "Takeittakeittakeittakeittakeit!" No change on the TV. "Oh, God!" Her eyes locked on the dark ceiling, her damp back bowed and tensed, her jaws grinding. "Take-it-take-it-take . . . oh, oh my God. . . . oh fuck . . . oh fuck . . . oh take . . . it. . . . take . . . oh . . . Jesus!" Jolene's naked body bent into a long wild spasm, her eyelids flickering, her mouth opening and closing as small screams built in her throat and pushed out through her clenched teeth. The spasm gradually died away but then came on again suddenly with more force than before. Her back arched and her whole naked body shuddered. The woman let out a moan, held it for an instant, and collapsed onto my sweaty chest.

The two of us lay in silence for a time, catching our breath and wits, our mingled sweat cooling in the night air. My gaze was on the idling TV set at the foot of the bed, my mind spinning randomly through a hazy kaleidoscope of tornadoes, breasts and camera shots.

Jolene rolled onto her back and looked at the ceiling. "Jesus."

"Yeah." It was the best I could manage after a day of storms and a night of sex.

"I think it's the tornadoes," she said.

"What's the tornadoes?"

"Me coming that hard."

"Electricity," I said.

"I always come harder during storms."

"You came?"

"You're a fuck," she giggled and rolled from the bed, her thin body reflecting pale blue in the light from the television as she disappeared into the bathroom. I punched the pillow and sat up, pulling the limp sheet over my waist.

"We did good today," Jolene said, her voice muffled by a half-closed door. "Where'd you disappear to?"

Duncan Gelder's face swam into my mind. "Meeting."

"Important?"

"Elvis Presley."

"That storm video was fucking great." The toilet flushed.

"Thank Gelder."

Jolene came back into the room carrying her clothes and sat on the edge of the bed. "Ran on network about a ton of times," she said, hooking her bra together and twisting it around and arranging herself into it. "I can't believe he got those shots."

I was staring at the TV set and didn't answer.

"What's up with you?" the woman asked, pulling on a pair of jeans and smoothing her hair.

"What'd you say?"

"That I can't believe he got those shots." Jolene glanced toward me uncertainly. "You mad at me or something?"

"Sorry about that. Just thinking."

"That's a change."

I shot her a dirty look—a friendly dirty look—and she laughed. "Oops, Jolene," she said teasingly. "Rule number one, don't bite the boss. Fuck the boss, but don't bite the boss."

I threw the pillow but she ducked the shot, giggling.

"No, it's the damned color bars," I said.

Jolene followed my gaze toward the TV set. "Color bars? So? They're color bars. What about them?"

"It's the middle of the night and that's what our station's running—color bars. We shouldn't be."

"Sounds like somebody's not too smart," she said, throwing me a teasing look that explained precisely who wasn't too smart.

I shrugged. "The network canceled its overnight show. Not much I can do about that. It's not my job anyway. I run news, not programming."

"All the networks canceled," said Jolene, "but the others seem to have managed to do something about it." She gave me a quick peck on the cheek, then threaded her slender hands through my hair and gave me a deep, hard kiss on the mouth. "God, that was good tonight. Have to fly. When do I see you again?"

"Call my secretary."

Jolene gave my head a push. "You're a shit."

"Pray for storms," I said, smiling.

"Ready director," said Jolene, "and take director."

I lay there after she'd gone, thinking about her, about the storms, about the color bars. The truth was, I preferred to keep things casual between us, had managed it that way for the six months or so we'd been seeing each other, and didn't have a good reason to change it. The woman was fine to be around, great in bed—but commitment was the last thing I wanted. I sensed she was hungry for it—but I wasn't ready to give it. Not yet, maybe not ever.

My mind brushed against the Hollywood fire but I forced myself to move on. We'd done okay today on the tornadoes. Not great, but okay. We weren't first on the air from the scene—I'd been too tentative—but Gelder's video was the best in town and it was ours exclusively. When we finally got there, we'd been in all the right places, done all the right things, more or less, and nobody had gotten hurt. Nobody had gotten hurt.

I picked up the remote and surfed through the middle-of-the-night offerings. The big station across town was in a rerun of an afternoon talk show. A good-looking middle-aged woman with short platinum hair, creamy lips and huge breasts was solicitously interviewing a set of giantly obese twin sisters and flashing smirking looks to the audience. I noticed the camera angles: they shot her from the side to get her chest in profile. Cynical but smart.

The independent station was in an old Elvis movie. Jesus, Elvis again—the dead man seemed to be everywhere. Twenty-five years dead and he's still selling. I thought about Margaret Wares, the lady with the book, the one who'd been Iso-ed. Electric blue eyes. The enigmatic mouth. Bahr trying to look at her breasts. Me trying not to look at her breasts. I let my mind spin on it, undressing her in my head, building a picture of what she'd look like naked, but Elvis started singing on the television and I thought of Duncan Gelder and the odd excitement in his eyes as he played the Elvis tape, the near-mania in his description of it. I wondered if he actually had something there, or if he was just nuts, suspecting I knew the answer. I switched back to my own station. Color bars.

I called the news desk and listened as the assignment editor took me through the latest news wires and police scanners: one more dead from the tornadoes; two drunk teenagers dead in a midnight car wreck on the tollway. A fire at a carpet store, probably arson.

I hung up and flipped back through the channels. The blonde had produced the fat twins' husbands: identical twin brothers, both as thin as tuning forks. Elvis in a cowboy outfit was on a hayrack singing to a group of ranchers. I switched back to my station: color bars.

I was almost asleep when the phone brought me around. The assignment desk, but this call wasn't about drunken teenagers. The kid running the overnight desk had had a call from the station manger, Angus O'Dell. He'd said to wake me up and tell me to be in his office at nine the next morning. A Saturday morning. I switched on the light and checked the clock. A little before two. Bad time for a call like that. Any time's a bad time for a call like that. I ran through it again with the kid, but nothing more than that. O'Dell's office, 9:00 A.M.

I put the phone down feeling a familiar ache growing in my gut, any notion of sleep gone for the rest of the night. There'd been calls like that before in my life, so I had a pretty good guess what this was all about. I'd been at the station a couple of years now—and that's just about the life span of a news director, especially a news director in a shop where the audience numbers are going down instead of up.

I lay back on the bed rubbing my eyes. Those fucking numbers: they had so little to do with what I did, yet I lived—and died—by them. The problem wasn't my station but the network. No one was watching it so there was nobody out there to watch us. I could put a naked nun on the six o'clock news but if the lead-ins from the network weren't good, if the network shows right before mine weren't strong, no one would be watching, and I'd be screwed. And my lead-ins sucked. The big station across town had an hour of Oprah before its six o'clock show and they were golden. They were printing money. I had cartoons—CARTOONS. We had four-year-olds for an audience. Walter Fucking Cronkite couldn't have found a viewer at my shop—and there wasn't one thing on the face of this mud-colored planet I could do about it.

Fuck it, I thought bitterly—I know it's not me, it's the system they've created. The network sucks, and the station's too cheap to do anything about it. It's not me—but in the end it would be me. It had been me before—many times before. It's one of the rungs on the loser's ladder down. A quick meeting with the boss—"sorry but it's the business and there's nothing I can do"—and back on the street looking for the next spot down the dial. I got up and poured myself an economy-sized Scotch, knocking back about half of it in the first tip of the glass. Though I'd been here before, it still hurt like a burn.

CHAPTER FIVE

AFTER A half dozen of the worst hours I'd had in a couple of years, I made my way reluctantly to the station manager's office. I wondered how O'Dell would handle it. The man seemed to me a decent sort—as decent as a former TV-ad salesman could be. He'd always treated me fairly. Always? What's always? I'd been there two whole years. I realized as I paused at his door that I barely knew the man. That's TV—all top, no bottom.

I walked in to find O'Dell studying the Dallas skyline, his back to two men sitting stiffly in leather chairs at a glass coffee table.

O'Dell turned and the men rose. One of them, a tall man with a balding head and a tired black suit that seemed about two sizes too large was a stranger to me. I recognized the other, a short man in a gray business suit with creases that could cut paper. People around town—and behind his back—called him the Blender King. To his face, he was Clare Leese—Mr. Clare Leese—one of the fattest wallets in the city.

O'Dell came over and offered me his hand in a solemn way. "Nick, glad you could make it. Sorry for the short notice. I suspect you know Mr. Leese?" I dipped my head slightly in recognition. "And this," said O'Dell nodding toward the tall bald man, "is Alan Haldeman. I don't think you two have met before. Mr. Haldeman is here from Cleveland. Gentlemen, let me introduce Nick Upton. He's our news director here. Shall we all sit down?"

"I don't think that's necessary," said Leese. "This is going to be quick." His voice was slightly nasal with an East Texas twang redolent of piney woods and cypress swamps. "Mr. Upton, let me cut to the chase here. I am the new owner of this station. Mr. Haldeman is the new station manager. Mr. O'Dell will be leaving later today." On those words O'Dell turned back toward the windows and his shoulders seemed to sag in on themselves.

I looked around the room and blinked, as though the act might somehow clear my eyes of a particularly strange hallucination. But nothing cleared.

"You will stay on," Leese continued, "at least in an interim capacity, to run the news department as Mr. Haldeman transitions in. Let me be crystal clear about this: this is business from now on. This television station has been underperforming for years. We intend to jettison its mom and pop practices and grow it to its full potential. Are we clear so far?"

I looked quickly around the room: my fired boss, the bad suit from Cleveland, and Clare Leese, the little blender king with the narrow mouth and the wide wallet. Clear so far? You bet it was clear so far, as the feeling of relief spread like wine through my bloodstream. I didn't need to use the "take this job and shove it" lines I'd been rehearsing most of the night. I wasn't headed down the dial—at least not yet. Maybe not for a long time if I played it right. You bet it was clear. Somebody for some reason had thrown me a life preserver. I stifled an impulse to jump into the air cheering and instead gave Leese a shallow nod.

"Good," said Leese, briskly. "By this time Monday, I will require from you a plan for reducing staffing in the news operation by twenty percent with a parallel reduction in your part of the operating budget. Mr. Haldeman will draw up the figures for the other parts of the station. While you reduce staff, you will also generate fresh ideas. New approaches. This station is stale. The programming is stale. The news is stale. That has to end and end now. You will find there is plenty of money for smart innovation. There will be no money for perpetuating mediocrity. Are we clear?"

O'Dell threw a forlorn glance over his shoulder. I gave Leese another tight nod.

"Excellent," said Leese, ignoring O'Dell and fixing my gaze with his gray eyes. "I'll see you here Monday at 4:45 sharp. Please come prepared. And not a word of this to anyone." Leese held the door open.

Outside in the corridor, I leaned back against the wall trying to collect myself, trying to bring some sense to what I'd just gone through. O'Dell fired? Station staff cut by twenty percent? I did some quick arithmetic. I'd have to fire two-dozen people. That would be ugly. I actually liked some of them. But I was still working. I still had a job. What had Leese said? "You'll stay on, at least in an interim capacity." We'd see about that. Interim my ass.

I pulled myself together as well as I could and walked slowly back to my office. Despite Leese's orders to keep it quiet, word had obviously gotten around that something bad was in the air: the few weekend people who were in treated me as though I were radioactive, and conversation in the newsroom stopped as I walked through.

Back in my office, I closed the door and rummaged through a filing cabinet looking for staff lists and budgets. I'd dodged a big one this time—and this time I intended to make things work. The newsroom was pretending they weren't watching.

CHAPTER SIX

SORRY, LET me get that thing," said Duncan Gelder, reaching past me to unlock the metal door that led into the garage. "It's a little Stone Age here but it works." He disappeared inside and then popped his head out. "You're tall, aren't you? Watch your head. Careful."

I had to duck down to make it through the door. As I straightened up, Gelder said presto and hit a switch, bathing the room in bright light.

I have to say I was surprised: a two-car garage in a middle-of-nowhere suburban tract in Dallas had been taken over completely by what looked like a television studio. Steel shelves against one wall were piled with more than a dozen television monitors. Stacked across another wall were racks and racks of computers—old laptops and desktops, dozens and dozens of them, all shapes and sizes and all connected together by thick knots of cable and power cords twisting across the concrete floor. Against the third wall, some sort of video-edit system. Overhead, stage lights on steel brackets. In a far corner, a simple bar stool against a blue cloth background, three small TV cameras on tripods in front of it.

"I call it the Cave," said Gelder, his face an odd mix of shyness and excitement and his busy mouth working overtime. "Man, I'm glad you came. I didn't think you would. I mean people say they'll do things and then they never do, huh?"

I nodded, thinking to myself how right he was. I'd had no intention of being here. But that was before the new station owner had planted himself like a gallstone in my life. Clare Leese had me on the ropes. I'd laid off the staff as he'd ordered and cut the budgets. But he still wanted more—and was making it clear that if I didn't deliver, I'd be toast. For weeks now I'd been combing through audition tapes looking for fresh anchors and reporters and had begun bringing people in for interviews. I'd ordered dozens of possible new programs to look over and had even started pirating the signals of big stations around the country to see what I might be able to copy. In the midst of all of that, Gelder had pressed me again to take a look at his stuff and at that stage I figured what the hell.

I took a few steps into the middle of the room and turned in a slow circle. What the hell indeed. When Gelder had mentioned he was working on something new, I'd imagined a laptop computer and a TV set. Nothing like this. Nothing nearly like this. "You built this?"

"From bits and pieces."

"And it's what, exactly?"

"Sort of a TV studio," said Gelder in a tone that had hints of both apology and pride. "I mean, it's nothing like you have at the station or anything like that. It's sort of a homemade production studio. I tried setting it up in the house but there wasn't enough room so I moved it out here to the garage."

"How'd you know how to do all this?"

"School," said Gelder, with an odd shrug, as though it was something to be ashamed of. "I did English Lit for a while but that was boring so I got into computing with a little TV on the side. After school, I tried but I guess I didn't really fit into the corporate world, so I've been working pretty much on my own."

I looked around the room again. The television gear was familiar enough to me but the rest of the stuff was a mystery. "What's with all the computers?"

"Maybe I can show you?" said Gelder eagerly, settling himself on a wooden chair at a console in front of the wall of monitors. "I control it from here. Watch." With that he hit a series of switches and the room seemed to jump to life, the dozens of computers booting up with the peculiar groans and hisses of hard drives coming up to speed. On another wall, color bars materialized from the black lifeless depths of the television monitors and the room settled back into a low electronic hum. Gelder hit another series of buttons and Marilyn Monroe exploded into life on the screens above.

"Well, hi there, Duncan. What brings you by today?" The same beckoning eyes, milky skin, the full lips. Gelder hit a button and her image froze.

"Old stuff," he said dismissively. Another series of keystrokes and the black-and-white image of Groucho Marx swam into view. "Hey, Duncan baby! What are you doing, huh?" Groucho's mustache, the cigar in his hand. "So'd you hear the one about . . ." Gelder hit a switch and Groucho froze in midsentence.

"Impressive."

"Not really," said Gelder. "I've got Groucho, Chico and Harpo in the memory banks. You ever realize Oprah is Harpo backward? Wonder why that is?"

"How'd you get all this?"

"Sort of collected it over the years. It all came in used, most of it broken. I fixed it."

"And it's basically what?"

"Basically a TV studio merged with a computer studio. Mixed media." Gelder ran a hand distractedly through his thin tangled hair. "You get some pretty amazing results when you merge the two. Like those computers?"—he gestured with his arm toward the wall—"you put them all together and they're running a huge amount of memory. You know much about computers?"

I didn't and admitted as much.

"Fair enough," said Gelder. "I'm probably running a million times the memory you've got at the station, something like that. Not great, but pretty good."

"Quite a bit," I managed, nodding as though I knew what Gelder was talking about. "And that's how you make Marilyn?"

Gelder pursed his lips thoughtfully and shook his head. "Marilyn's easy. You could do her basically with a laptop. Everybody's doing that these days. No, the key to the new stuff I wanted to show you is speed. I've sort of managed to push the speed up to a place a lot of people haven't gotten to yet. They'll get there but they're not there yet. You want to sit down on the stool, maybe?"

I glanced dubiously around the room.

"Just a little demonstration," said Gelder. "It won't hurt." With that, he led me across to the stool, hooking a small mike to my collar and adjusting the blue cloth in the background. He turned on a series of spotlights and the rest of the studio dropped into shadow. "Have to hold still for just a second while I line some things up." Gelder wheeled up a large black box and positioned it so it was head-on to me. He hit a switch and a grid of lights flashed out of the box, covering me and the blue background with hundreds of tiny red squares.

"I look bad in plaid," I said, feeling preposterous.

"You won't for long," said Gelder, ignoring my obvious discomfort. He positioned the three cameras in a semicircle around me and fussed with the focus rings. "That's got it. Won't be a minute now."

I watched Gelder's form disappear into the darkness toward the console. The spotlights were uncomfortably bright, and I was beginning to wonder if this wasn't some sort of twisted practical joke.

Gelder's voice from the darkness: "Say something, anything."

"One, two, three," I offered, uneasily. "Something like that?"

"Just talk."

"About what?"

"Anything. Talk about the weather."

"The weather?"

"Just make something up," said Gelder, laughing. "How about those tornadoes we had last month?"

"Okay, how's this? A line of tornadoes rolled through Dallas—"

Gelder cut in. "You can move. I mean it's not like you have to be a statue. Move your arms, gesture, try to act normal."

I tried again, feeling foolish. "A line of tornadoes moved through Dallas a couple of weeks ago." I ran my hand through my hair. "Eight people were killed. Authorities say it was the most intense line of tornadoes seen in this part of Texas in more than forty years. How's that?"

"Good," said Gelder's voice from the darkness. "Keep going."

Fine. Might as well make this interesting. "And a weird freelance editor got some great shots of the storm." I rubbed at an itch on my nose. "Everybody wondered how he did it. Turns out he had a complete mental breakdown and decided to climb to the top of a water tower to get a better look." I laughed at my own words and the absurdity of the situation and brought my hands together in front of me. "How's that?"

Silence for a moment. Then Gelder's voice: "That's a wrap, boss. Why don't you take your mike off and join me."

Gelder was hunched over the console. "One more edit," he said, more to himself than to me, and entered a series of key-strokes. The computers along the far wall were humming. "Got it," said Gelder. "You ready?"

"I guess. Ready for what?"

"Here, take the chair."

The wall of monitors was sitting in black. Gelder leaned over and hit a button. The sounds of Elvis Presley's "Heartbreak Hotel" boomed through the small room and a large television screen jumped to life with a montage of Elvis pictures. The music and the pictures ran for ten, maybe twelve seconds before freezing on an old black-and-white photo of Elvis's head and shoulders, his fifties hair hanging rakishly toward his eyes. The music faded and an announcer's voice came up: "Ladies and Gentlemen, tonight, live, close, personal—and in your home—Elvis Presley."

A smooth dissolve from the frozen picture and there, live on the screen, Elvis Presley—the rakish hair, the heavy pouting mouth, the mysterious hooded eyes playing with the camera.

"A line of tornadoes moved through Dallas a couple of weeks ago," Elvis said and ran his hand through his black hair. I felt my stomach turn over and my head go light: those were my words, my actions, barely five minutes before.

"Eight people were killed." The face of Elvis, the voice of Elvis—the precise sound, the timbre, the intonation. Elvis Presley—live and in person on the screen. Yet they were the same words I had spoken just minutes before—my words, my gestures, all somehow translated, transported into the body and the voice of Elvis Presley. It was surreal—and somehow frightening.

"Authorities say it was the most intense line of tornadoes seen in this part of Texas in more than forty years." Elvis offered a sneered laugh. "How's that?"

"Good," said Gelder's voice off-camera. "Keep going."

"And a weird freelance editor got some great shots of the storm." Elvis brought his hand up, rubbing at his nose, his diamond pinky ring catching the light in a brilliant rainbow of colors. "Everyone wondered how he did it. Turns out he had a complete mental breakdown and decided to climb to the top of a water tower to get a better look." Elvis pinched off a half laugh at the camera and brought his two hands together in mock prayer.

The picture froze, music rolled . . . "Love Me Tender." The announcer's voice: "Live, close, personal—and in your home—Elvis Presley." More music, the picture faded to black and the garage dropped into silence.

I sat there stunned.

Gelder was hovering over my shoulder. "You like it?"

My eyes were still locked on the now-blackened monitor, my mind searching for some rational explanation for what I'd just experienced. "What was that?"

"Elvis," said Gelder, his pinched voice about two steps down from hysterical.

"But that was me." I found myself looking uncertainly from the monitor to Gelder and back to the monitor.

"Television," said Gelder.

I sat there eyeing the dark screen and trying to make some sense of what I'd just witnessed. All the words, all the actions, all the body movements had been mine. But without argument, it had been Elvis Presley on the screen. Elvis Presley as alive and real as I'd ever seen him. Maybe even more alive and real. It hadn't been like an old movie where the characters were somehow larger than life and a touch unreal. It hadn't even been like the old television clips of Elvis performing or being interviewed. My brain was insisting that it had just seen Elvis Presley, alive, sitting there on a stool and talking. Elvis Presley. I turned to Gelder. "You invented this?"

A small look of alarm on Gelder's face. "Well, no, not really. It's not an invention—more like a refinement. I mean most of the technology's already out there. They've had animation programs for years—reanimation, actually. But it's never been very lifelike, if you know what I mean. The body's always too jerky. Movement's wrong. And the sound's terrible. I mean nobody's ever figured out how to do the audio—until now. I speeded it all up to a point where I could do something new."

"You sure did that," I said, my mind beginning to accept what it had just witnessed. "That's one of the most amazing things I've ever seen."

Gelder's smile came back. "Television and computers. Neat, huh?" He hit a button and Presley came back to life.

"Turns out he had a complete mental breakdown and decided to climb to the top of a water tower to get a better look." Elvis caught the camera with the half laugh again and brought his hands together. Gelder pushed a button on the console and the face froze above us on the wide screen.

I looked from the monitor back to Gelder. "So how'd you do it?"

"Long or short explanation?" said Gelder, his eyes shining.

"For the intellectually challenged."

Gelder smiled, his busy mouth working like he was having a separate conversation with himself. "Basically, I've given the computers every image I could find of Elvis, and every sound he ever made that was recorded. The computers study the way he looks and moves, the way he talks—talking is the hard part, actually. I mean, video's easy. The eye isn't as quick as the ear. You can give someone an image of Elvis and if it's only say eighty percent accurate the eye won't notice it. But the audio's the hard part, getting the voice just right. The ear hears a lot better than the eye sees. That's what everybody's been having problems with, but I think I've got it licked."

Gelder paused and I nodded him on.

"So the computer basically synthesizes a new video and audio Elvis. When I put you on the stool, the computer sized you up and substituted the image and sound of Elvis. That grid of red lights over you was kind of like a road map for the computer, to tell it what you were doing. When you moved your arm, the computer saw it and made Elvis's arm move. The speed's the critical thing. The computer has to be able to work fast enough to keep up with all of that."

"Sort of like a Max Headroom? Or Steve McQueen in those car commercials? Forest Gump? Something like that?"

A dubious look from Gelder. "Well, not really. I mean this is pretty different. Those are just sort of tricks. I mean they lay in heads and things like that. It's like retouching photos, only they're doing it with moving pictures. This is fundamentally different. I mean, we're synthesizing a real human here. Or electronically real, anyway." Gelder paused and looked around. "The others are one-shot deals. This thing is sort of self-replicating."

"Sorry?" I said, giving him a blank look.

"Self-replicating. I mean that crap you see with McQueen or Gump, that stuff, it's really labor-intensive. It takes them weeks and weeks to build a few seconds. This thing does it automatically. Feed in the raw material and, bingo, out comes the image. It can go on for days, as long as the computers keep running."

"So you could continue this for half an hour, something like that?"

Gelder nodded. "Half an hour, half a day."

I stepped back and thought about what I'd just seen, my eyes on the face of Elvis, but my mind on Clare Leese. "What sort of costs are there?"

"Costs?" said Gelder.

"What does it cost you to do this?"

Gelder looked confused. "Well, there's the gear I guess but that's mostly free. I mean it was all broken and stuff. There's the electricity. That's a cost but I hadn't really thought about it much."

I was doing the mental calculations even as he spoke. No denying that Elvis was hot right now and no denying that Gelder's images had amazed me. And if they amazed me they'd probably amaze others. Others like a television audience. And I could do it mostly for free. Maybe Leese would like that. Television and computers. Not bad. I glanced up at Elvis and back at Gelder. "What do you think about putting Elvis on TV?"

CHAPTER SEVEN

THE MEETING Monday morning with Clare Leese in his new corner office—O'Dell's corner office—was to be quick and to the point. At least that was my plan, and it was a plan I intended to stick to even though the hangover I was carrying made the notion seem almost impossible.

I'd well and truly fallen the night before, smack through the narrow glass lips of a Scotch bottle. I was paying for it this morning: the world had a liquid gauze over it that seemed to blur all edges and erase every third or fourth word to the point where I had trouble making sense of even the simplest conversation. Nevertheless, I had to perform, present Leese with the latest budget numbers and convince him that I had enough new ideas that I deserved to hold on to my job.

By firing two dozen people and trimming news coverage to the bone, I'd hit his numbers—barely, but I'd hit them. I figured if he was okay with my latest numbers, I'd walk him through some of the new reporter hires I had in mind. Then I'd spring the idea of filling that black hole that sat like an ugly scab on our Friday-Saturday overnight. Gelder's Elvis would be part of that solution. I figured that by adding a few other programs and selling a few commercials, we could fill the whole night. No more color bars. We wouldn't make money—but we wouldn't lose any either. And if Elvis took off? Who knows.

I walked in to find the short man pacing back and forth with a copy of the morning paper in his hand, his gray eyes twitching with a frosty look. He threw the paper on his desk and gave it a malevolent glare. "So who's Margaret Wares," he said in a biting voice, "and what'd we do to piss her off?"

Somehow my fumed brain remembered Margaret Wares— the great-looking redhead with the electric-blue eyes, the great-looking redhead Bahr had humiliated on the set. But the newspaper? I didn't know anything about a newspaper. "Sorry, boss? Margaret Wares?"

Leese picked up the paper and pretended to study it. "Margaret Wares, it says here. The *Tribune*'s media columnist." Leese pronounced *media* like it had a bad taste. "Ring a bell?"

I nodded lamely, my head pounding. "I didn't know about media columnist. I knew she had a column once in a while. Writes on the derivation of words, things like that. Bahr interviewed her a while back, before you took over. She wrote a book on Elvis."

"That must have been stimulating," said Leese dryly. "Well, she seems to be paying us back for it. May I read you a line or two?" He glanced at me and shook his head. "You've got to take better care of yourself."

I shrugged my shoulders, silently cursing myself for the bout with the bottle: I'd been such a wreck when I got up, I hadn't even glanced at the paper and had no clue that a newspaper column would be landing in my face.

"She writes pretty well," said Leese. "Let me quote her: 'A recent national survey found that Americans have more faith in used-car dealers than in television journalists. My own experience suggests that mentioning car dealers in the same sentence does them a grave injustice. For its mendacity, banality and vulgarity, local television deserves to have its own place in the honor roll of purely loathsome professions.'" Leese looked up from the newspaper. "You with me, Mr. Upton?"

I nodded and kept my mouth shut.

"But wait," said Leese, "there's more. I'll just skip down to the good part. Is that all right with YOU?" Leese gave me a smile that wasn't in the least friendly. " 'KVGO, the perennial also-ran that inhabits the very bottom of television's slimy pond, didn't get there by accident. It earned it. Its news programs are, in a word, a joke. The main evening anchors bring about as much liveliness and intellectual insight to their work as department store mannequins—and are just about as interesting to watch. The station's small weatherman appears to be there only for the unintentional comic relief he brings. He is one of those true mathematical rarities—a man for whom both shoe size and IQ are a single-digit number. Put it all together and you have a station that is nearly incapable of presenting accurate and timely information. KVGO's motto is: 'News for You from the News Pros.' I would suggest it should be 'If It's News to You, It's News to Us.' "

Leese glanced up from the paper with a cold look in his eyes. "Department store mannequins? Comic relief? What, exactly, did Mr. Bahr say to this woman?"

"She'd written a book about Elvis and was talking about the psychology of the man, that sort of thing. Bahr asked her if he was an alien and she got a little upset."

"A little upset? Yes, Mr. Upton, I'd say she got a little upset." He looked back down at the newspaper. "It continues. 'There are very few bright spots when you look around the local television market. Perhaps it's the effect of so many consultants and spin doctors. Or perhaps it's that television in the new millennium attracts to its profession the worst and dullest rather than the best and brightest. Whatever the reason, the reality is this: your time would be better spent doing *absolutely nothing* than watching television, especially KVGO. It's the city's perpetual loser, and there's no mystery why.' " Leese sat down heavily at his desk.

"Maybe I should call her?"

"Don't," snapped Leese. "Maybe she'll forget about us."

I remembered how the woman barged into my office to demand an explanation. "I doubt it."

"Me, too. Should we fire Mr. Bahr?"

"His numbers are too good."

"How good?"

"Extremely," I said.

"How good's extremely?"

"Best we have."

"Fine." Leese curled the newspaper into a tube and dropped it into a waste basket. "Let's do budgets."

"I thought maybe we could also talk about a programming idea?"

"That's Mr. Haldeman's department."

"I may have found a way to fill the Friday-Saturday hole. And make money."

"Fair enough," said Leese, "but let's do your budget first. Where I come from, you figure out if you can buy the gas before you plan a road trip. Show me your numbers."

THREE WEEKS later the new boss called a station meeting.

At the head of the conference-room table, Leese and Alan Haldeman were in low-voiced conversation and either didn't notice or pretended not to notice the people as they drifted in and took their places around the table. I sat to one side, casually studying the two men and eavesdropping on other conversations as they lapped like waves through the room.

I'd had very little to do with Haldeman since Leese came on the scene. As far as I could tell, he spent most of his day behind closed doors going over schedules and finances. Word around the halls was he was a bit of a prick, bright enough but not very original, more concerned with what appeared on the ledgers than on the screen. He'd cut the programming department almost in half to meet Leese's budget numbers.

At the far end of the mahogany table, Iso Bahr was flirting with an assignment editor—Felicity—whose hair color seemed to change weekly and whose single social triumph was a session of oral sex with a famous local quarterback nearly fifteen years before. Or so she claimed. Bahr himself was known around the station as a serial philanderer, though he made a continuing public spectacle of doting on his wife and the four kids he'd parked in a giant house with a pool on the far-northern outskirts of town. As usual, he was already in full set makeup, though it was hours to air. I suspected the little weatherman was like a lot of others in the business—ego on the outside, fright and insecurity on the inside. They wore the heavy makeup like armor.

Nearby, the salt and pepper anchors, whom Wares had described as department store mannequins, were studiously ignoring each other. Another dozen or so people from sales, from production, from finance, were eating donuts and stirring coffee cups. Duncan Gelder was working on a Danish and sprinkling crumbs on the mahogany. At the far end of the table, Jolene was talking to a man from the sports department. No sign of acknowledgment from her that we were more than just professional colleagues. We kept it low-key and liked to pretend no one knew. True secrets in a TV station, though, are about as rare as original ideas and I suspect we were high on the gossip chart. She looked particularly good in an expensive tailored pants suit and her blond hair was pulled back into a severe bun. Above her a wall of TV monitors sat in black.

"Okay, let's do this," said Leese in a curt voice and the low buzz of conversation quickly subsided. "I'm pleased to see the turnout this morning. Before we get started, I thought it would be useful to open this up for questions any of you might have." Leese made a show of looking around the table. "Now, any of you have any questions— any problems—with where we've come in the last couple of months? If so, now's your chance to get 'em out, get 'em on the table." The words may have invited comment, but the tone of voice didn't and the room remained as quiet as an empty box.

"Fair enough," said Leese. "The business here today is to announce some changes to our Friday night/Saturday morn-

ing programming. It's actually Saturday mornings we're having trouble with. Midnight onward."

"Maybe we could sell color bars?" said someone brightly to
a scattering of laughter. Leese scowled and the room shut up.
I suspected it was a novel experience for Leese to have someone talk back to him. And I knew it was a novel experience
for this crowd to be expected to remain quiet, even if the guy
was the boss and owner. The learning curve for both sides
was going to be more of a cliff than a slope.

"All right, fine," said Leese. "Let's get on with it. Mr. Upton
here has come up with what we think is a workable solution.
Mr. Upton?"

"It's a simple plan," I said, pushing some papers out in
front of me. "Basically, we're going to fill the hole. Midnight
Friday we're rerunning the five o'clock news on tape."

"We get residuals?" asked the black anchor good-naturedly.
Polite laughter in the room. It always surprised me how def-
erentially people in the business treated anchors, as though
they were rare South Pacific flowers that would wither if they
weren't watered and fussed over properly. The truth was most
were just normal human beings who had lucked into a pretty
good gig.

"No residuals," I said. "Just more fame. That takes us to one
A.M. One to two we're in a rerun of the 'Hallinger Hour.'"

"A political talk show's dull TV," said the black anchor.

"But free in rerun use," I said. "We don't pay for it and we
can put some ads into it, make some money. That gets us to
two. After Hallinger we have an hour of programming from
Unicorn."

"Unicorn?" Iso Bahr looking startled. "That's a schlock
house." Noisy agreement from around the table.

I brought it back under control. "It's cooking, gardening,
things like that."

" 'This Old Mouse,' " said someone and the room erupted in
laughter.

"And almost free," I pointed out.

"That gets us to three," said Jolene quietly from her end of the table.

"Three o'clock we rerun the half hour news from eleven," I said.

"Three-thirty?" prompted Jolene. "Half hour to go?"

"Public access," I said, and the place seemed to explode with voices.

"Fat bald women with tattoos," said someone.

"Your dildo and you," said another to general laughter.

"Elvis Presley," I said—and the room slowly quieted, faces turning to look in my direction. "Elvis Presley." I let it play for a beat or two and glanced at the far end of the room. "Jolene, if you'll do the honors?"

The woman stood and turned out the lights, slipping a cassette into a tape machine.

"We've been experimenting for the past few weeks with a new concept," I said. "Something that hasn't been seen on TV before. Jolene?"

The director hit a button.

A bright countdown on the television monitor, white numbers flashing across a rolling blue background. At two the screen went to black. A brief pause in the darkened room, then the deep tones of a professional announcer as a still photo of Elvis materialized on the screen: "Ladies and gentlemen. Today KVGO-TV takes you to the next step in television. It is, quite simply, a quantum leap into the future, and it will take television to a place it's never been. Ladies and gentlemen—Elvis Presley."

The photo faded to nothing and suddenly—there was Elvis. The sequins of his white suit glittered in the stage lights and his dark eyes danced with energy. Elvis alive and on the screen. A nervous throat-clearing from somewhere in the conference room.

Elvis grinned. "Hi there, folks." The deep voice, the casual syrupy Southern drawl. "I'm Elvis Presley. But you probably know that, don't you?" A shy smile as he brought his hand up and rubbed his studded collar, a diamond ring catching the light and throwing off a burst of color. "Clare Leese and Nick Upton asked me to drop by. Sorry it had to be on videotape. But they said they were thinking about us all doing a television program together. Well, it sounds like a pretty good idea."

Elvis moved in his chair and swung his gaze to the left, a strand of hair falling into his eyes. The shot changed as a camera to his left brought his face into a close-up view. "So, we should all get acquainted. Again, my name's Elvis Presley and I used to be a singer." A soft deferential chuckle. "I did a little television here and there. Maybe you remember Ed Sullivan?" A slight smile before his face grew serious. "Now, you know and I know that I died a few years back."

The forms around the conference table were as still as park benches. Iso Bahr had a look of outright incredulity on his face.

"I don't want you to be uncomfortable about this. Dying's the natural part of living. I did both of them." Elvis grinned from the screen. "I suppose I lived better than I died, but that's history, isn't it? Anyway, I'm interested in coming back and doing some television. Nick Upton over there at the head of the table, and Duncan Gelder there, said they might have some ideas."

Several heads swiveled to glance at me and Gelder and then looked back at the screen.

Elvis ran a finger along his lower lip. "But we should probably do some explaining. I mean most of you look like you've seen a ghost."

A nervous ripple of self-conscious laughter in the room.

"I'm not a ghost, and I'm not an impersonator. But I've got to tell you, I'm just amazed at the number of people out there today impersonating me. And some are sooooo bad." Elvis wrinkled his nose and laughed and the room laughed, too. "Anyway, I'm not an impersonator. This hand"—he raised his hand and rotated it slowly in front of him—"this hand is my hand. This voice you hear is my voice. This hair"—he pushed the lock of unruly hair from his eye—"this hair is my hair. I'm Elvis, brought to you courtesy of television and some new and pretty good computers."

With that Elvis stood up and the camera shot changed to show him full form as he walked slowly across the stage. "I don't want to get too technical. Heck, I don't understand it myself. I never even owned a laptop." The casual grin again. "But what Nick and Duncan here have done is they took all of my old pictures and all of the things I've said and sung and they put them into a computer. Now they have a gimmick where they can basically turn pretty much anyone into me. Even you, Iso."

Iso Bahr started like he'd been hit with a spark and looked around embarrassed. Elvis laughed. "That's right. Even Iso Bahr can be Elvis Presley." Quiet laughter in the room.

Elvis sat back down. "Now, my two new friends have made it so I'm pretty alive. And I guess that's the point of the television we'll be doing. It's gonna be me up there on the screen with a studio audience asking questions, all of it live. Maybe I'll sing once in a while, something like that, but basically it's a new kind of talk show."

The shot changed to a close-up of Elvis's face. "Three-thirty Saturday mornings. We're gonna do some television." The shot widened and Elvis waved his hand. " 'Til Saturday, friends. Rock and roll."

The screen went to black. Jolene switched the lights on and the room sat in stock-still quiet for a moment before erupting into a welling surge of animated voices.

I glanced at Leese and then back at the room. "Three-thirty Saturdays," I said rising and heading toward the door. The rest of the room stood with me. "See you on the TV." Across the sea of excited faces, Jolene caught my eye and winked.

Chapter Eight

Hello, my name is Elvis." The stagehand peered uncertainly into the camera, his bearded face tattooed with red-lighted squares from the projector in front of him. "My momma back home in Tennessee sent me this letter . . ."

"Cut! Cut it!" I stared at the man, feeling an unreasonable anger at his inability to pretend to be someone else. "Elvis isn't from Tennessee. Where'd you get that?"

The stagehand squirmed on the wooden stool. "Man, I wasn't even born."

"Next."

Felicity, the assignment editor with the quarterback in her past, stepped forward from a small knot of newsroom people. Her hair was ginger red this week. She grinned self-consciously and tugged at her short black skirt as she climbed onto the stool, crossing her legs demurely and hooking a high heel over a wooden rung.

I patted her on the shoulder. "Okay, Felicity. It's just an audition. You okay?"

The woman nodded nervously.

"Felicity's up next," I said toward the back of the studio where we had relocated all the equipment from Gelder's garage. "You ready?"

Gelder entered a command on a keyboard. The woman's image appeared on the monitor in front of him, covered in the matrix of tiny red-lighted squares, and a wall of computers spun into life. Gelder hit another button and the assignment editor's form dissolved into a series of blue and yellow skeletal lines and then firmed up into the image of Elvis Presley.

Back onstage, the three cameras dollied in. I pointed toward Felicity and stepped backward out of the shot.

The woman looked at the head-on camera, looked at me, looked back at the camera.

"Talk," I whispered.

She moved her mouth as though about to speak but no sound emerged.

"Just start talking. Anything. Say 'Hi, my name's Elvis.'"

The woman glanced at me again and back at the camera. Twenty seconds passed, maybe thirty, as she sat there frozen. Finally her mouth started working and she uttered a small, squeaky hi. With that, she broke into tears, jumped from the stool and ran from the set.

"Fuck." I sat down dejectedly on the edge of the stage.

"Troubles?" Iso Bahr in heavy camera makeup fresh from the noon weather show was hovering nearby. "I saw her act," he said. "Not quite ready for prime time."

I nodded miserably. We'd been at it for a couple of days now and it wasn't working. People were either too stupid for the role, or too nervous. I glanced across at Bahr. "I don't think I've ever seen so many people in a television station afraid of a camera."

"That's why we get the big bucks, boyo," he said. "Not everybody can do it."

"I'm amazed. I thought we were in the TV business."

"Only a few of us are, Nick," said Bahr, pompously.

"Think you could do it?"

Bahr took a dramatic step backward and pulled a look of surprise from his practiced list of ready-made facial expressions. "Me? Iso as Elvis?" He shook his head. "Not in my contract."

"As a favor?"

Bahr pursed his mouth and shook his head. "There's no favor clause in my contract."

"It's public access. No commercials. Experimental. Nobody's making money."

"It's a ventriloquist's dummy."

"May make television history."

Bahr seemed to pause at that. "I'd have to talk to my agent," he said.

Once the idea was out there, it actually didn't take Bahr that long to make up his mind. A few hours later, he sidled up to me in a hallway and asked, casually, if the job was still open. I realized he'd only wanted an invitation. I nodded and it was a done deal on the spot: our small weatherman would be KVGO's Elvis, the hidden heart and soul of the King of Rock and Roll.

Over the following days, speculation around the station had it that Bahr actually saw it as a chance to prove he was, in fact, the King—the only one with the natural genius and God-given talent to pull it off. It caused a lot of snickering. I wasn't among those laughing: a lot was on the line with this show and I had a suspicion that if anyone could pull it off it was Bahr. I didn't need an Einstein in the chair—television isn't designed for complex ideas. I needed someone who could talk, and there was no arguing that Bahr was a world-class mouth. I'd worry later about what came out of it.

With Bahr in the chair, we put the show into rehearsals for a week. The format would be technically complex but visually simple: Iso Bahr on a stool in his own studio would be recreated as a computer-generated Elvis on a screen about the size of a man in front of an audience in another studio. The on-screen Elvis would open the show with a few comments and then take a half hour of live audience questions. If we played it right, viewers at home wouldn't even notice that Elvis wasn't live in front of the audience.

On the day of the first taping, people started showing up in the Elvis studio—we'd renamed it Studio E—unusually early while technicians readied the set and Gelder fussed with his computers. I'd stayed away. I had a bad feeling about it. Nothing concrete, nothing even hard enough to be able to articulate. But I went through the morning worrying that something out there was ready to bite me. I had confidence in the technical setup: Gelder seemed to be on top of things, and the rehearsals, while not flawless, had actually gone pretty well. I guess I was worried about Bahr, whether he was up to it, what he might say. And, to be wholly truthful, I was worried about the show itself, whether anyone would watch it, whether there was a public out there that would actually give a damn. Though it was only public access TV—and in the middle of the night at that—I realized it would be a make or break for me with Leese. I'd thought it up, I'd pushed it, I'd sold it to Leese—and if it didn't work, my currency with him would be zero. A lot riding on a computer image.

Friday, 2:00 P.M. A hand-picked audience of about a hundred station employees and relatives fidgeted expectantly on folding chairs in the studio.

In the control room, Jolene keyed the mike on her headset. "Listen up everybody," she said, "this is for real. Edit one, edit two, roll record for air and let me know when you have speed."

On the set of Studio E, Iso Bahr sat up straight on the stool and picked at a piece of lint on his lapel. A few feet away, Gelder stood hunched over his computers.

Back in the control room, Jolene readjusted her headset. "Ready animation," she said, "ready cameras one through five, ready Elvis remote one. Let's make sure we get this right, everybody . . . and . . . three, two, one . . . take music, take animation . . ."

The sounds of "Heartbreak Hotel" filled the darkened control room as a montage of Elvis photos flooded across the screen.

". . . and fade music," said Jolene. "Cue announcer."

A man's deep voice: "From KVGO, it's Elvis Presley."

"And ready to cue Elvis." Jolene's voice was flat and unhurried. "And ready camera one, and take camera one."

In front of her, the living, breathing face of Elvis Presley filled the screen. "Hey there, folks," said Elvis. "It's real good to see you all again."

". . . and ready two," said the director, "and take two." Under her voice and so no one could hear her, Jolene looked at the screen and whispered, "Welcome back."

A dozen hours later and half a city away, Margaret Wares drew her bare legs under her and pulled her white robe closer up around her neck as she stared at the television.

". . . and then my dad and me drove into Memphis in that old Jeep we owned." Elvis's pouty mouth pinched into a grimace. "Man, I loved that car. More questions?"

The picture on Margaret Ware's TV changed to a wide shot of the audience. A couple of people had their hands up.

"There," said Elvis. "The lady in the front row. That beautiful lady in the blue. You have a question, ma'am?"

The camera cut to a tight shot. A middle-aged woman, blond hair, seventies-style granny glasses perched on her nose. Too much rouge. "I just wondered, Elvis, what your favorite food is?"

Presley grinned and looked off into space. The shot came in tight on him, his face filling the screen. "Linguine, ma'am. Lord-a-mighty I have missed linguine."

Another shouted question from the audience. "Where've you been?"

Back to his face tight. Presley rubbed his jaw with his hand and seemed to think about it. "That's a tough one," he said after pausing. "I mean, I don't really know. See, I don't have a memory of it. It's all blackness. But they say I've been on ice. I guess we'll have to leave it at that, huh? Let's just say I'm the Iceman."

Margaret Wares picked up the phone.

Across town, I was watching the show on the TV set in the bedroom and pouring Jolene a glass of champagne when the phone rang. "And so it begins." I picked up the receiver, grinning. "Upton here."

"I've been watching your show." A woman's voice, familiar.

"Uh-huh?" I shrugged and made a face to Jolene that I didn't recognize the caller. "And you like it?"

"Not particularly."

"Sorry, but who's this?"

"Margaret Wares."

Margaret Wares. The disastrous talk show. Department store mannequins and comic relief. Blue eyes and the quirky mouth. Big breasts. That Margaret Wares. "Good early morning to you," I managed, smiling into the phone. "So how's your book?"

"Better than your show."

"Pardon?"

"I stayed up all night to watch Elvis," she said, her voice pinched thin on the phone line. "I wish I hadn't wasted my time. I can't believe you'd put that kind of garbage on TV."

"Sorry?"

"Elvis driving a Jeep? Jesus, Upton. Elvis eating linguine? Elvis with his father? Get a grip. That isn't Elvis."

I covered the phone and mouthed Margaret Wares's name to Jolene. "Well, look, Ms. Wares," I said, uncovering the receiver. "I can appreciate your concern here but it's just a TV show."

"It's a piece of garbage," said Margaret. "It's all wrong. I don't know how you managed to do it, but you've got Elvis all wrong. He doesn't say things like that, and he doesn't move like that."

"Of course not. Elvis is dead. It's just a TV show."

"Barely," said Margaret. "Keep it up, you're going to have Elvis-lovers burning down your precious TV station." With that the line went dead.

"What was that?" said Jolene.

I put the phone down feeling like I'd just been sucker punched. "Our first viewer."

CHAPTER NINE

THE TAUT white sail bellied into a gust of wind and the deck tilted until the varnished teak rail was nearly in the water. I leaned back on the hard fiberglass bench and took a long sip of cold beer, feeling pretty much at ease with the world, and myself, as the big boat glided across the small waves.

At the back of the cockpit, a beefy man in a black tank top and a sunburned face held the stainless-steel wheel tightly in two thick fists. A wheat-colored late-day sun had reduced the western shore of the lake to a narrow black silhouette.

"I think I need to ease it up a bit," said the man, gesturing with his shoulders toward the top of the sail, which was beginning to wobble. "It's pinching a little." The owner of Texas Bob's Best Little Fordhouse brought the boat a few degrees off the wind and the sail smoothed out.

Across from me, Texas Bob's wife stared at the passing water with a blank look on her face. Thin blond hair bleeding toward gray, gentle eyes over a hard mouth set in the small tight wrinkles of a former smoker. A face that knew life could be bad—but eyes that expected it to be good. Though her baby-blue halter top had an embroidered anchor on it, she looked completely out of her element.

"Not having a good time?" I asked.

She turned to me with a self-conscious smile. "It's fine," she said. "I mean I love Bob's boats. It's the water. . . . I think Bob likes the water more than I do. Don't you, Bob?"

The big man at the wheel grinned large. "Love boats. Love water. Love it all. Shit."

The woman gave me a strangled look.

"I thought you liked motorboats, Bob?" I said. "I didn't even know you owned a sailboat."

"Love motorboats!" said the man. "Love sailboats. Love all kinds of boats. I don't own this. Chartered. Figured it'd be the last chance this fall before the weather starts turning. Get me and Carol out of town."

"Pinching again. I think you're too close to the wind."

The man moved the steering wheel slightly. "Better, huh Captain?" He snorted out a loud, rough laugh. "Sailboats are just a different kind of sailing, if you know what I mean, huh?"

At that instant, a stronger gust of wind caught the sail and the boat tipped hard to one side. The woman's eyes flashed a small edge of panic.

"Maybe we ought to bring it off a bit," I said, watching Bob fight with the wheel as the boat tried to nose into the wind. "Give Carol here a little bit gentler ride."

"Just getting to be fun," said the man, "but what the hell. Coming about!" With that he spun the wheel and the boat instantly came off the wind. I fed out line until the sail was almost at right angles to the boat and the deck had leveled out. "Want to take it for a while, Captain?" said the man.

"I get to steer when it's not so much fun?" I said, a teasing smile on my face as we exchanged places.

The big man returned the smile. "Anything for the god-damned client, right?" He popped open a can of beer and took a deep drink, then settled back against the rail. "Tell me, Captain: you actually like going out on my boats or are you doing it because you get paid to do it?"

"I like your boat, Bob. You buy ads from my TV station but you're still a friend. Good enough answer?"

"You seem to know what you're doing. You said you've sailed?"

"Mostly in LA. I like the quiet and the solitude."

"Get a lot of that on these things," said the man. "Maybe too much. So LA, huh?"

I nodded.

"You like it?"

"Has its points. Or had its points. I haven't lived there in a while."

"Why'd you leave?"

"A woman, what else?" I said it lightly, hoping he'd get the message that I didn't particularly want to talk about it and would rather move on to something else. It didn't work.

"She screwing around on you?"

I glanced at Carol but she was apparently used to that kind of talk from her husband: her expression said she was at least as interested as her husband in what I had to say. "No, it was something else."

Bob pressed the point—he was that kind of guy. "What kind of something else is there if it's not sex? She turn into a beaner?"

I gave him an uncertain look. "Beaner?"

"Beaner, as in les-beaner. Like my fat sister in Phoenix. Betty the Beaner, I call her. Married a woman, for Christsakes. Imagine that. Adopted a kid. Goddamned this world's screwed up. Poor little sonofabitch."

"It wasn't anything like that."

Bob backed off. "Sounds like that ground's still pretty wet."

"No, it's okay." Even as I said the words, though, a part of my brain was building a fire in the dry brush of the Hollywood Hills and a young woman with delighted eyes was laughing and climbing into a car with a cameraman and asking me where I was taking her to dinner that night. Our engagement dinner. She had the most extraordinarily beautiful mouth of any human I'd ever known. Her lips were moving: *Make reservations, dickhead.* If only I'd known. If life was just a few degrees fairer.

"You okay?" said Bob. He and his wife both were looking at me strangely and I wondered how long I'd been away.

"Fine." I smiled to show how fine I was. "I guess I nodded out there for a second. No. It wasn't sex or anything."

Bob seemed to chew the answer over for a few moments. "No kids, right?"

I shook my head. "No kids. We weren't married."

"Damned good thing. That sort of situation can be rough on kids. Carol and I are experts, aren't we, hon?"

The woman nodded and offered a tenuous smile.

"Five," said the man, holding up a large hand. "Five kids between us—three hers, two mine. Gonna be paying for college 'til I'm on a walker and a dribble bib." With that he laughed and drained off his beer. "So you sail and you run a TV station. What else?"

I glanced up. "Sorry?"

"What else in your life? No kids, no wife. What else?"

Oh Christ, I thought to myself—just exactly what I don't need—a day on the water and psychoanalysis of what's missing in my life. "I get around."

"I bet you do," said Bob, and I have to give him credit: he finally seemed to sense the shift in my mood and steered a new course. "So let's make this outing tax-deductible and talk a little business." In the man's north-Texas drawl, "business" came out "bidness." He opened another can of beer. "Carol here likes your show a lot, don't you, hon?"

The woman nodded vigorously.

"My show?"

"That Elvis thing," said the man.

Carol seemed to come to life. "I've watched all of them so far. I mean they're terrific."

"You actually like it?"

The woman nodded: "Well, I know he's dead and everything but it's Elvis sitting there. I mean I know it's Elvis. I don't know how y'all did it but it's awesome."

"And you get up at three in the morning to watch?"

The big man across from her spurted out a large laugh mixed with a fine spray of beer. "Get up? Jesus Christ! Her and her goddamned girlfriends are up all night, sittin' there drinking wine and sneakin' cigarettes like some high school pajama party, huh Carol?"

The woman seemed slightly embarrassed. "Well, my girlfriends love it, too. I mean it's all anybody's talking about. It's so—I don't know. . . . It's so real, I guess."

"Really?"

The woman was nodding intently. "Really. I think every woman in Dallas is watching it. Some won't admit it. I mean all women my age are secret Elvis lovers."

The big man broke in. "All women her age. Isn't that a tibrickler? So here's the thing, Nick. I think this sucker might make some money. You only been on like a month or something . . ."

". . . five shows."

". . . so five shows, and that's not much, but the thing is, it's getting some notice, people talking about it. You metered it yet to see what kind of numbers you're getting?"

Actually, we hadn't but that wasn't something I'd admit to a potential advertiser. "We've got some indications we're hitting a couple of thousand households, maybe more. It's mostly an experiment to see if we can do it. And it's public access so I can't advertise it."

"So, shit man, call it something else and sell it."

I nodded uncertainly.

"Trust me, Nick," said the man. "Texas Bob knows two things—Fords and advertising. And I know you got a little gem growin' out there. It's a word-of-mouth sort of thing and a lot of words are comin' out of a lotta mouths. So the thing is, how do I get a chunk of that?" The man peered at me and took a mighty drink of his beer, almost as if to underline the question.

I can't honestly say I was surprised. I'd had some hints people were watching: the mail was beginning to build and we were getting a few hits on the station's website from viewers asking for more. But I actually hadn't thought about trying to sell ad space around it. I'd conceived the show as a time eater, something to fill up a black hole, and didn't expect to make money. But that was before middle-aged women started staying up to watch it. Selling it would go a long way toward proving its worth to Clare Leese. "So you think a lot of people are watching?"

"I'd bet my showroom on it," said the man. Carol was nodding.

"Speaking of showrooms, how's the damage coming?"

"Goddamned tornadoes," said the man. "Almost rebuilt but them pointy-headed insurance salesmen are pushing my rates through the roof. Gotta do more bidness. Goddamned hand of god."

"FIVE SECONDS!" said the stage manager. "And four, three . . ." The audience quieted. The stage manager held up two fingers, then one, and dropped his arm. "Love Me Tender" welled from the speakers and the television monitors around the walls came to life with the now-familiar opening montage of Elvis stills. The voice of an unseen announcer came in fluidly over the music: "Ladies and Gentlemen, uncut and uncensored . . . tonight the Best Little Fordhouse in Texas, Texas Bob's Ford dealership, brings you . . . Elvis!"

A wave of applause from the audience as the picture on the monitor cut to the King.

In the next studio over—the Elvis studio—I was pacing back and forth nervously, just out of camera range, as Iso Bahr went into his routine. Duncan Gelder sat a few feet away watching his computers eat in the picture of Bahr and spit out the image of Elvis. Gelder seemed to be mouthing to himself almost every word that Elvis was saying.

". . . and it's purely a delight to be here tonight with a new sponsor," Iso Bahr was saying earnestly into the camera. "Texas Bob and I go way back." A short laugh. "It's hard to describe how close we've been over the years. Why, I consider Texas Bob to be almost like a relative. Little bit further than a brother, but a lot closer than a cousin . . ." Bahr was on a roll now—which meant Elvis was on a roll. The words were coming easily—and the patter was seamless. I had to hand it to the little weatherman: he was beginning to do a pretty good job.

". . . and I've told you about my love for Fords," Elvis was saying. "You're in the market for a car, you make your way to one of Texas Bob's five dealerships scattered around the Dallas–Fort Worth metroplex. Remember, when you think Elvis, think Ford. And when you think Ford, think Texas Bob. He's the car man. And you tell Bob, Elvis sent you. We're back in sixty seconds."

The picture on the monitor dissolved to a Ford commercial as a woman hurriedly dabbed a tissue at Iso Bahr's sweating upper lip. Even though we were taping it for broadcast overnight, we were still trying to do the whole thing real-time, and real-time in television means never enough time.

"Not bad," I said. "It's looking good. But let's ease off now a bit on Texas Bob."

Bahr nodded his head slightly, careful not to interfere with the makeup woman.

"You're doing the army today, right? You got that chapter okay?"

Another nod from Bahr. We were using an old Elvis history we'd found at a second-hand bookstore on Mockingbird Lane. Each chapter was one show. Bahr had turned out to be a pretty quick study.

The makeup woman finished and stepped out of the shot. Bahr gave me a sideways glance. "So it's okay?"

"It's terrific."

He smiled at that.

". . . and ten seconds," said Jolene's voice in a speaker.

I glanced over at Gelder.

"Routine," he shrugged.

Jolene's voice again: ". . . and five."

"Knock 'em dead," I said, stepping into the background.

Jolene's voice from the speaker: "Cue."

"So hi there," said Bahr in one monitor, Elvis in another. "I'm Elvis and I'm back. Thought I'd talk a bit today about the army. How I got in and how I came out and maybe a little bit about what I did when I was in there." A small laugh. "This won't be a war story, though, because I didn't actually kill anybody—unless my music killed them. . . ."

A quick camera change caught the audience smiling at the shallow humor.

CHAPTER TEN

ON A Monday morning a couple of weeks later, Texas Bob called to let me know I was, as he put it, a goddamned genius. And before I had a chance to take it too seriously, a good-looking redhead informed me I was one of the world's great morons.

I was in the morning editorial meeting when my secretary buzzed through with Texas Bob's call.

"Can you talk?" said Bob, the word "can" coming out closer to "ken." "Ken you talk?"

"In a meeting," I said, looking around at the dozen or so editors and reporters gathered at my conference table to figure out, more or less, what would be on that afternoon's news broadcast.

"Goddamn your meeting," said Bob. "You're a goddamned genius and we gotta talk Elvis."

"Elvis?"

"Elvis," said Bob.

I covered the receiver and looked around the table. "I need to take this."

The others rose and shuffled out. I suspected they were grateful for the interruption.

"Okay," I said, "your call, so talk."

"Goddamn, boy!" said Bob, his voice about an ounce shy of a shout. "You got yourself a winner, huh?"

I pulled the phone slightly away from my ear. "I got a what?"

"A goddamned winner, goddamn it."

"Slow down and tell me what you're trying to tell me."

"Shit. Okay, here's the deal, you canny sonofabitch. That

no-count kid of yours from Mississippi is selling cars. Even if those nosebleed overnights are still the time slot from hell."

"Come again?"

"Elvis, for Christsake. Something going on here, man, I shit you not."

"Sales are up?" I was grinning to myself even as I asked the question.

"Up? Jesus H. Christ! Up? You bet they're up." The man let off with a maniacal chuckle. "Nick, my friend, Texas Bob is selling a shitload of cars."

"You're sure it's Elvis?"

"It's gotta be. It ain't the weather, and it sure as shit ain't the economy, stupid. It's women buying Fords. I've been out there on the lots. I got women buying Fords like they was tampons. It's Elvis."

"Sonofabitch."

"Sonofabitch," echoed Bob. "We gotta move that boy to daytime."

"Excuse me?"

"Daytime," said the man, "the place the people are. Get him out of that crap hole you've got him in now. More viewers, more ads, more cars. Comprende, compadre? You with me on this? We gonna get your man out of that basement?"

I glanced up from the phone as a woman appeared in the doorway. Red hair. Blue eyes. "We'll talk, Bob," I said, dropping the receiver and getting to my feet. "Hello there."

"Hi," said Margaret Wares, self-consciously running a thumb through the hair over her ear. She was in blue jeans, boots and a white blouse and looked terrific.

In a quick half-second of silent appraisal, I kicked myself for forgetting about this striking woman. "Nice to see you. Interest you in a chair?"

Her lips drew into a shallow smile that was at once disarming and dangerous. "I don't think I'll be here that long."

"Then sit short," I said, taking her arm lightly and guiding her to the conference table. "Welcome back."

The woman looked around the office and seemed to gather her thoughts. "I know I said I'd never come back but I was in the neighborhood and all that . . ." She grinned to underline the obviousness of the small lie and paused briefly before plowing on. "I came down here because I have something important to say to you, something I need to say face-to-face."

"Something you maybe forgot to say in the column?" I offered the line with a friendly look.

"You saw that?"

"'Department store mannequins. Unintentional comic relief?' Yeah, I saw it. Maybe I should say that my boss read it to me."

"Ouch," said Margaret. "I guess I should be sorry about that—but I'm not particularly. I thought it was actually one of my better columns."

"Hate to see the others. So you happened to be in the neighborhood and happened to drop by?"

"To say something I needed to say in person, not in a column."

It sounded like an apology about to happen. "So say it."

It was no apology. "I think it's wrong what you're doing with Elvis."

"Here we go again."

"It just doesn't feel right. It's still like the first night, the night I called you."

I winced inwardly, remembering the glass of celebratory champagne in my hand and the angry voice of Margaret Wares on the line.

The dangerous smile again. "I'm over that. But I'm worried."

"Worried?"

"You've got him wrong," said Margaret. "I don't want to make a huge deal about this but you've dreamed up a guy who doesn't exist—who never existed. I mean, get a grip. Elvis wouldn't be caught dead doing most of the stupid things you've got him doing. You've got the wrong guy."

"It's TV," I said defensively. "We make this stuff up as we go along. It's not a history class, it's television."

Margaret nodded. "That's obviously part of the problem, Mr. Upton."

"Nick."

"It isn't a history class, but people see it as history, as what Elvis was really like," she said. "I mean, look at me."

"I am," I said, giving her what I considered one of my better smiles.

It didn't even slow her. "I studied this man for years and even I start slipping into believing it's him up there. But you're getting him wrong and when you do that you're hurting everybody—me, the viewers, the memory of Elvis. Good Lord. I mean, I have kids now coming up to me in class regurgitating the junk they're seeing on TV. I think you need to take the show off the air." The woman said the last part quickly, a challenging look in her eyes.

"Off the air? You're kidding, right?"

"Let him be dead."

"For crying out loud, he *is* dead. We're not pretending he isn't."

"He seems pretty alive up there on the screen."

"Okay, how about this? You take your book out of print, we'll take the show off the air. How's that?"

"It's not the same thing."

"They're both Elvis. One's your interpretation, one's ours."

"Mine's based on research, Mr. Upton. Yours is fantasy."

"Well, I don't think we're going to kill the show." I thought about the call from Bob. "There's even some talk about bringing it to afternoons, so more people can see it. We might be doing that." I didn't have a clue if we'd be doing that but it made it sound like I was on top of things, and that's where I wanted to be in this conversation.

"That'd be wrong," said Margaret, shaking her head to underline the point. "You have any idea the kind of power you're playing with?"

"It's just television. Nobody out there thinks Elvis is alive. It's entertainment."

"It's probably not something people like you hear too much, but you're wrong. Dead-headed, stupid wrong." She punctuated the words with a challenging look over a crooked, off-center smile. An odd, complex woman.

I threw up my hands in mock surrender. "Okay. I think you have a point."

The admission seemed to stop her. "A point?"

"I think we are getting a lot of it wrong. So why don't you help us make it right?"

"I'm not sure I understand."

"Help us get it right. Give us—or sell us—some of your expertise."

If she had an answer it was lost in the confusion as Felicity came bursting through the door. "We got a bad one, boss! Plane on final into Minneapolis. No gear, no controls!"

"Video?" I said, moving toward my desk.

"The Minneapolis affiliate's on the way."

"Network?"

"Not there yet."

"Anchors?"

"One's in."

"Fire up the set."

"Gotcha," said the woman, spinning out of the office and running across the newsroom shouting instructions.

"Sorry," I said quickly as I dialed the phone, "but it looks like it's going to get busy. You're welcome to watch." Into the phone: "It's Upton. Bulletin. Find Jolene and get across the net, we're lighting the set." I dropped the phone and glanced toward Margaret. "Come on. Maybe we'll see some real TV."

The control room was a scene of practiced chaos. Jolene was struggling into her headset and snapping out instructions and checklists to the mostly young men and women rushing in to join her at the main control console. Overhead, a large preview monitor showed the black male anchor already at the desk on the set, a makeup woman applying rouge in quick strokes to his cheeks while a technician was plugging a small plastic fitting into his ear and stringing the cord out of sight down the back of his jacket. On the other central monitor—the air monitor—a gray-haired man in bib overalls was stirring a large cooking pot on a set designed to look like a Southern kitchen.

I parked Margaret next to me at the rear console. "Anything from network?" I had to raise my voice slightly to make it heard above the other sounds.

"Nothing yet, boss," said Jolene without turning.

"How's the set?"

"Nearly there," she said. "Okay everybody, let's get organized. Edit one, edit two, get ready to roll record net. Effects give me lives, just-ins and a locator for Minneapolis. Let's ready animation. Do we have a map?"

"Building it," said someone.

"Okay," said the director, keying her mike. "How are we on the set? Floor manager, are you out there?"

A brief squeal of feedback. "Camera one here. No floor manager yet but we're good to go."

Jolene turned in her chair to look at me, pausing a beat as her eyes swept over Margaret Wares for the first time. It wasn't a friendly look. "Floor's good, control room's good. What do you think, boss?"

I keyed the intercom to the news desk. "This is Upton. What's the editorial?"

Felicity was out of breath. "Plane's five out. Still no gear, no controls."

"Net?"

"Not there yet."

"Fuck. Experts?"

"On the way in. And we've got a truck headed toward DFW for local react."

"Let me know when the truck's there." I switched out of the

intercom, my eyes on the line of monitors at the front of the control room. "Jolene, can we see the competition?"

She barked out a command and a new string of monitors came to life on the wall. "Shit," said Jolene in a low voice.

In the back of the room, Margaret Wares's intense eyes were taking it all in. "What's wrong?" she whispered.

I was watching the monitors. "The other networks have the picture up. Ours doesn't."

Margaret looked at the monitors uncertainly.

"See those four TVs," I said, pointing at the row of sets that had just been switched on. On two of the monitors, cameras were panning around an empty sky. A third was focused on a reporter standing in front of a steel hurricane fence, fire trucks behind him racing down an empty runway. All three had network IDs prominent in the picture. A fourth monitor sat in color bars. "The one with nothing on it is ours." I turned toward the front of the room. "Are we ready?" I asked, raising my voice to make it heard across the confusion.

"As ready as we'll get," said Jolene over her shoulder.

"Let's do it."

"You got it," said Jolene, keying her headset mike and spitting out instructions in a fast matter-of-fact voice. "Fifteen seconds, everyone. Camera one give me a medium wide. Camera two tight. Ready slate, ready announcer, ready effects, ready animation. Edits one and two give me a roll record and tell me speed."

Margaret Wares's eyes were still on the monitors. "But you don't have any pictures of the plane?" she whispered urgently.

"We're used to it," I said without turning. "Smoke and mirrors."

"Ten seconds," said a voice from the front of the control room. "Speed," said another. On the preview monitor, a woman dabbed a tissue across the anchorman's nose and retreated out of the picture. "And five," said the voice again.

"Stand by," said Jolene.

"Three, two . . ."

"Take slate," said Jolene, her words clipped, quick and forceful. "Roll animation. And . . . cue announcer."

On the air monitor, the gray-haired cook in the bib overalls disappeared, replaced by a stylized station ID with "Breaking News" rolling across the bottom of it. The deep voice of the announcer: "We interrupt this program to bring you a breaking-news event."

The shot changed to the black anchorman looking gravely concerned. "Good afternoon," he said. "A passenger jet on final approach to Minneapolis at this moment is in deep peril, its landing-gear broken, its control systems malfunctioning. We expect to bring you pictures from there shortly. In the meantime, we'll give you what we know about this. The jet, a MacDonald Douglas MD One-Eleven, was on an otherwise routine flight from Denver . . ."

"Take map," said Jolene and the picture of the anchorman changed to a colored map of the U.S. from the Rockies to Ohio with the route of the plane marked out in red.

"Cool," whispered Margaret.

"Smoke and mirrors," I whispered back.

"Ready camera two," said Jolene. "And—take two."

". . . at this hour are saying that the plane carries 243 passengers and a crew of ten. Again, we expect to see pictures shortly . . ."

"Fucking network," Jolene said. "Who has them?"

"I'm on," said a skinny man with a phone to his ear. "They say any minute."

"Any minute's too fucking late."

And suddenly, there it was: a small distant dot in an otherwise empty blue sky, small but visible on all the network monitors except ours. Heads craned to follow the picture, and even as I watched, the dot grew larger and I could make out the silver wings and could see that the jet was swinging back and forth as it lined up for its shot at the runway. Our own network was still in color bars. On the center screen, our black anchor was droning along.

"Put one of the other networks in preview," I ordered.

Jolene glanced back at me. "Boss?"

"In preview, Jolene. Cover the ID."

The director turned back toward the screens, her face set in a hard look. "Give me Remote three in cue. Effects, give me our station ID lower left. Make it big and thick. I don't want to see through it."

The picture in the preview monitor instantly changed to a wide shot of the plane coming in, the logo of a competing network prominent in the lower left. As we watched, the logo was buried by a bright red box with "KVGO" on it.

"Sure about this?" said the director. "It's not our picture."

"Choices?" I shot back.

"Limited."

"What's happening?" whispered Margaret.

"We're stealing the picture."

"Boss?" said Jolene.

"Give it a second."

". . . can see it coming in now," the anchor was saying, looking down at a TV set recessed into the top of his desk.

"What do I do?" said Jolene, her voice tight.

"Take it."

"Take Rem three!" Jolene shouted and the central monitor switched instantly from the face of the anchor to the picture of the plane slewing wing-down in its final turn. "Cue the set! Talk!"

The anchorman's voice came up under the picture. ". . . see it now. Flight 193 from Denver to Minneapolis. Two hundred fifty-three souls on board. All controls out. Coming in now for an emergency landing. You can guess there are many prayers on that plane right now. This, coming to you live from . . ."

Margaret Wares sat there in growing dread and horror as

the big plane became real in front of her eyes. Her hands were clenched into fists in her lap and her stomach was knotting and beginning to cramp. It was almost unbearable to watch, yet she couldn't pull her eyes from the screen, imagining in flashes of vivid terror what must be happening on the plane.

"Crispy fucking critters," said a voice in the control room.

"Lose it," said Jolene, quietly.

The plane came on like some giant doom, a mechanical nightmare dropping slowly, inevitably into fatal reality from the empty blue sky. Suddenly it seemed to crab to its right for an instant and then straighten up, its nose still high, its tail low.

"Our network's up!" shouted Jolene. "Take net! Take net!"

A sudden jiggle on the screen and the shot changed slightly.

"Give me audio!" yelled the director.

". . . oh boy, oh boy," a reporter at the scene was saying, "the people. Here it comes. Here it comes. Oh my . . ."

The plane's tail struck the runway in a blast of smoke and sparks and seemed to hang there for an instant before the wide aluminum fuselage smashed down onto the concrete in a gush of flames and a roar of twisting screaming metal. The big plane veered to the side and did a half cartwheel into the air, then came back down onto the concrete with another jarring, grisly smash and hurtled in convulsive, disintegrating fire and smoke and debris down the runway. It seemed forever before it finally came to a stop, a giant bonfire now of gray metal, red flames, orange fire trucks with arching streams of white foam, and tiny people running jaggedly out of clouds of black smoke and collapsing on the ground.

". . . it's down, it's down"—the reporter was almost sobbing—"and there are survivors, there are survivors, we can see them running across the grass. . . ."

"Boss?" said Jolene, glancing back.

"Stay with him."

". . . the fire trucks are there now, directing foam onto the flames. The plane's burning, but I say again there are survivors. . . ." Even as he said it, though, the camera was pushing in on a dark lump on the runway. It was a slow push and it was five, almost six seconds before Margaret Wares realized she was looking at a human head.

"I NEED another one," said Margaret, pushing the wineglass clumsily into the center of the table and searching across the packed lunch-time crowd for a waitress. Her eyes were a few degrees off-center and her mouth had developed a hardness I hadn't seen before.

"Talk to me," I said gently.

Margaret squeezed out a thin humorless laugh. "About what? The Rose Bowl parade maybe? The Dallas school board? Or how 'bout my class schedule?" She was staring at her fingers. "My hands are shaking."

I didn't know what to say. After an hour in the control room, I'd realized I had to get her away. As the feeds had begun to come in, we'd gotten an enormous number of pictures from the crash site. Most of them we put on TV. But some of them were too graphic for television, too gruesome to be transmitted. Margaret Wares had seen them all.

I suppose that somewhere deep, somewhere I couldn't quite reach, the pictures had an effect on me as well. They were bad pictures—scenes of unbelievable carnage and almost pornographic violence. Pictures like that affect people. But over the years I'd grown more and more immune to those sorts of images—or made my peace with them.

It was odd how TV could twist things around. One dead child in the bottom of a swimming pool is a shocking tragedy. Eighteen thousand dead in a Turkish earthquake is a curiosity. For me, a plane wreck lived somewhere in between. Interesting—but not shocking. Maybe there'd been too many plane wrecks, too many severed heads sitting on runways. I'd realized too late, though, that for the woman sitting across from me, the pictures were real; they still had meaning and content, and still had the power to overwhelm.

"Some people lived through it," I said. "You need to keep that in mind. We saw people coming out."

Margaret looked up, her blue eyes haunted. "Most didn't. What do you do now? You're a man with easy answers. What do you do? Go on about life like you haven't just watched two hundred people burn to death? How do you do that?"

The waitress brought new drinks and Margaret took a long pull, draining off almost half the glass. She set it back clumsily on the table and used the napkin to dab at her eyes. "Sorry," she said, "but I'm feeling . . . I don't know what I'm feeling."

The two of us dropped into an uncomfortable silence. "The first one I ever covered was in Chicago," I said after a while. "It was a bad one, too. Two hundred seventy people. Lost an engine on takeoff, rolled and plowed into the ground about half a mile from the runway. I got there pretty fast. Too fast." I took a sip of my drink, the images of that day welling up behind my eyes. That was early on, when the images still had the power to numb.

I skipped over the part about how the plane had come down in a dog kennel and how the remains of humans and dogs were blown toward a tall steel fence that caught the flesh like a lint filter. "I walked through the crash and forgot why I was there. I just plain forgot. I wasn't a reporter anymore, I wasn't anything. I guess it was so overwhelming that the reasoning part of my mind shut down. I've thought about it a lot since and I can't tell you to this day how long I was closed down. Maybe it was forty-five minutes, an hour, something like that."

Margaret took a drink and remained silent.

"I'm wandering around out there and I guess I start realizing I have to do a report on this. I'm a radio reporter and so I need a phone. No cell phones back then. So I make my way to this house on the edge of the wreck." I remember the house. It was more a shack than a regular house back off the road a hundred yards or so under two large cottonwood trees. Its windows had been painted black.

"So I'm pounding on the door and this guy appears, lets me in and guides me down a hallway to a desk with a phone. I'm calling the station and starting to do this live report and my eyes sort of focus and right next to the phone is a giant box of rubbers. Trojan rubbers. It's the strangest thing. I swear to God my mind splits in two: half of it is talking on the radio about the plane wreck and the other half is looking around this strange place and slowly realizing I'm in the middle of a whorehouse."

Margaret is watching me now as I speak. Her eyes are cautious.

"And sure enough, I'm not even halfway through my report when the girls start showing up. Three or four of them, I think, all in this sort of cheap lingerie, breasts sticking out, heavy makeup, all of them watching me do this radio report. Figure that one out: 270 people have just died across the street from them, and what they're really interested in is some kid doing a radio report. They applauded when I finished."

Margaret shrugged but remained silent.

"I guess stupid things happen if you live long enough." I smiled to punctuate the comment. "It was even stranger after that. It's like I turned into a sex fiend in the days after the crash. I was pretty motivated in that department anyway, but after the crash it was like an obsession. I found out later it's normal— that nurses, cops, people like that who deal with violent death all the time experience the same thing. A shrink friend of mine told me it's like a denial, or refutation, of the death we've seen."

There was silence at the table for a time, the woman tracing her finger over the bead of water on her glass.

"I'm sorry you saw the pictures," I said finally. "You have somebody at home? Somebody maybe you could stay with?"

"Why didn't you put the pictures on the air?" She asked the question quietly, her eyes averted.

I was momentarily lost: we had put the pictures on the air. "The pictures?"

Margaret said it again. "Why didn't you put the pictures on the air?"

"We did."

"I'm talking about all of the pictures," she said, an edge of challenge creeping back into her voice. "There were a lot you didn't show anybody."

"Right. And give people nightmares? You saw the pictures. You want all of those on TV?"

"But you're not being honest, are you? I mean, you just show the mild stuff. That's not honest. There was really awful stuff out there on the runway, but you didn't put it on. Why not show it?"

"We filter it. For kids, for the squeamish, for the people who can't take it. That's our job."

"I thought your job was to tell the truth?"

I took a long time answering. "There's some truth the public can't handle."

"You guys are having a lot of problems with the truth these days, aren't you?" The woman finished her wine and set the glass carefully back on the table. "Thanks for an unusual morning, but let's not do this again ever, huh?" She gathered her things together and rose from the table, shooting me an odd, crooked smile before making her way uncertainly across the restaurant and out the door.

CHAPTER ELEVEN

IT WAS an invitation-only party and Clare Leese had done it up well. The ornate ballroom of a downtown hotel, strolling violins from Southern Methodist University's music department, champagne and tuxedoed waiters, an ice sculpture of a guitar and discreet video monitors here and there along the walls playing scenes from the station's Elvis show. All of it overly expensive and overstated. Leese, Iso Bahr and a few other station employees were the hosts and the scenery. Duncan Gelder was there, too, in a new tux selected by Leese's assistant. No sign of Leese's man from Cleveland, Alan Haldeman.

The guests were a handpicked list of the big advertisers of Dallas plus, of course, their wives or mistresses—dealer's choice on that issue. Texas Bob and a half dozen of his car-selling competitors had turned out along with the head of a carpet warehouse chain, the regional vice president of a national grocery store, a dot com idea man who'd recently gone bankrupt and was moving through the crowd like a hungry shark and a whole tier of lesser mortals whose advertising dollars made the local television market a legalized form of money printing. My plan was to put the big bucks and the product together and see if they clicked. If they did, Elvis would be headed for a better time slot.

I got there late. The ice sculpture was melting down to the shape of a fattened penis and most of the good old boys in the room had already endured their couple of polite glasses of champagne and switched to the hard stuff. The place was getting noisy and smokey.

Texas Bob had cornered the rug merchant and was talking about horizontal and vertical integration. Gelder had stationed himself next to a table of food, chewing and listening as the dot com fellow talked earnestly into his face. Leese and Iso Bahr were holding forth for a small knot of the heavier spenders. Leese caught my eye and excused himself from the group, making his way slowly through the throng.

"Good crowd," he said, smoothing the lapels on his tux, a small look of irritation crossing his face. "Everybody's here. Where have you been?"

I started to give a smart-ass reply—I'd been running Leese's station—but he didn't offer the chance. "I think Westin's hot," he said, forcing a neutral look to his face as he glanced toward a dark man talking to a half circle of other businessmen. "Texas Bob, too, maybe a couple of the grocery store boys. I'm not getting much in the way of vibes out of the computer boy. Think maybe he's broker than he's letting on."

We shifted our gaze causally toward the man talking to Gelder, a man known around town as Dot Harley, the "dot" part coming from his internet-advertising business. He was young—no more than late twenties—and casual, the kind of casual you had to work hard at to make it seem convincing. Tonight he'd chosen a gray suit over a black T-shirt.

"I've called him a couple of times," said Leese, "but never got much in the way of interest. Actually didn't think he'd show up tonight. Now he's stuck with that weird guy of yours . . ."

"Gelder."

"Whatever. Let's get this ball rolling, huh?"

The presentation was much like the first one when we'd unveiled Elvis to the station: Elvis in his white sequined outfit on a huge wide-screen television monitor at the front of the ballroom—his image cloned through the room on the smaller screens—talking about his childhood, about his disappearance, and now his reemergence. We'd taped the presentation, making sure Bahr-as-Elvis mentioned by name some of the guests we knew would be in the room. It added to the drama of the moment.

". . . in front of such a group as this," Elvis was saying. "Dallas's finest. Whooee!" With that he laughed and ran his hand through the unruly lock of hair hanging in his eye. Elvis looked directly into the lens of the camera—and the effect was that everyone in the ballroom believed he was looking straight at them. "There's Texas Bob out there. How ya doin', Bob?" The car salesman smiled and bowed. Next to him his wife, Carol, smiled and colored slightly. At one side of the room, Iso Bahr was looking on with a small paternal smile on his face as he watched his own taped performance roll on the screen.

"And there's Joshua Westin," said Elvis. "Love your carpets. We can do some truly good things with Westin's Carpet Ware-houses, huh, Josh?"

With that the shot pulled back. Elvis climbed onto a stool and cleared his throat. "So my good friends, ladies and gen-tlemen, I want to thank you all personally for coming out tonight, and I want to get down to business. That's why we're all here, right? Business?" Light laughter spilled across the room. "So business it is then. Let's talk about the amazing American dollar. When I first came back a couple of months ago, we did television for free. I went up here on TV every Saturday morning and did my thing, and we did it all for free, thanks to the kind-hearted folks from KVGO—how are you tonight, Mr. Bahr, Mr. Leese? Good to see you, good to see you. Then we found out people were beginning to watch. Real people in real numbers started showing up. Just word-of-mouth, things heard on the street. But the message started getting out that Elvis was back and KVGO had 'im." Elvis laughed out loud. "It's amazing the way people are. Here I've been dead for years, but people haven't forgotten. So they started watching. Now, you're going to have to talk to Mr.

Leese there and to Texas Bob to get the exact numbers—but when we started advertising, it really took off. I mean took off like a moon rocket. Bob, your sales are up, what? Ten percent, something like that?"

Texas Bob took a small step forward. "Eleven point three percent last week, Elvis," he said, and stepped back. I silently wondered if the man understood that the Elvis he was talking to up on that screen wasn't real.

"That's what I mean," said Elvis, looking down at the crowd from the screen. "Real numbers. People are watching. And those real numbers are coming at one of the worst times of the day—three-thirty in the morning. Three-thirty in the morning? Phew!" Elvis pursed his lips and wrinkled his nose as though he'd just tasted something bad. "I didn't even get up that early when I lived on the farm. I'm usually going to bed about then. But people are getting up, or at least setting their VCRs, because people are watching. The numbers from Texas Bob's Best Little Fordhouse are not lies. They're real numbers."

Elvis rose from the stool and began to pace. "So the good men and women at KVGO have been thinking: these sort of numbers at three-thirty of a Saturday morning, what happens if it's five on a Monday afternoon, huh? Picture it. Oprah Winfrey on one station, a couple of other professional talk-show talkers on the others. And Elvis on KVGO. Who do you think's gonna win? I'll tell you." Elvis laughed out loud. "No, I don't think I will tell you. You men and women I'm talking to tonight haven't gotten to where you are by being stupid—and you folks can figure out who's gonna win that race."

With that, Elvis reached down below the sight of the camera and came up with a guitar. He picked at it a couple of times searching for a chord. Then, fastening his eyes on the camera, he strummed it and began to sing "Love Me Tender."

The screen faded to black and the crowd broke into an uneasy applause. Leese stepped in front of the monitor and put up his hands to quiet things. "Ladies and gentlemen," he said, "ladies and gentlemen. Good, good. Well. So that's just a taste of what lies in store for us here at KVGO. I hope you liked it?" A brief scattering of applause and Leese bowed slightly. "You're all here tonight because you're our friends, because we think this is really going to take off, and because we want you along with us when it does. I think the product pretty much speaks for itself: it's Elvis Presley, it's real and it's here now—and we think it has the potential to be an enormous money machine." A couple of people clapped.

"As most of you know," said Leese, "I'm new to the TV business. But I'm not new at being able to recognize a good business opportunity when it comes along." Quiet chuckles at that: there was no one in the room who wasn't aware of the legend of Clare Leese, how he'd washed up in Dallas with little more than a hundred dollars in his pocket and ten years later was one of the wealthiest men in the state. "And I for one think this is a good business opportunity. Now, here's where it's going to get just a touch technical. So I've written it down." With that, Leese reached into his jacket pocket and pulled out the card I'd written for him that morning. "We think we can bring Elvis in as a significant day-part to our programming," said Leese, looking from the card to the crowd and back again. "Five days a week, Monday through Friday. We're still looking at the slots available but we're leaning more and more toward five o'clock. If the numbers are as good as we think, it's a golden lead-in to the first cycle of news."

The carpets man, Westin, spoke up from the crowd. "What sort of numbers?"

"As good as Oprah," said Leese without missing a beat, "maybe better. The sampling we've done over the last couple of weeks indicates the audience is out there. I'm serious—it's out there. We know it's large, it may be huge. People are hungry for this sort of TV. . . . it's homey, folksy, it's a little jazzy at the same time, and it's Elvis, don't forget. That's the draw and it's been a big one."

Westin again: "And you can sustain it?"

Leese nodded. "We can sustain it. Our plan is to throw whatever resources we have to at the show. We have the people and the technology to do it up very proud."

Texas Bob raised his hand. "Live or tape?"

"Live at this point," said Leese.

Westin again: "How soon?"

"That, I think, will depend on all of you."

Texas Bob stepped forward and shook Leese's hand. "Clare, you are one canny sonofabitch. Put me down as joining the founder's club right here, right now." The other men in the room edged up closer and soon there was a circle of tuxes five deep around the station owner. Lots of hands being shaken, smiles, fresh cigars.

I stayed back from the group, cadging shrimp and cashews and watching with admiration as Leese worked the crowd. So my little brainstorm was going uptown to weekday afternoons. Damn, that felt good. I'd worked hard for this moment, and it was paying off. At the same time, though, it felt almost—daunting. As though to underscore the notion, Leese gave me a hooded look from the crowd that I didn't need any help translating: my ass was on the line big time now.

DAWN HAS *finally arrived here but it's gray, cold, wet—and profoundly melancholy. Gusts from the North Sea carry the memory of sea ice and dead fish and swirl in eddying confusion across the brown water of the Thames. On the path below me, a man trudges toward some morning errand bundled against the chill in a shapeless black coat. His hunched walk, the way his shaven head is tucked down into his collar, everything about his form says he is an unhappy man on an unhappy journey.*

Nowhere, I realize, is it clearer that weather is the engine of national character. It is ten months gray and bitter here—much like the people. Only a couple of months each year does the sun touch the soul and spawn the smile. Or perhaps it's me. The shaking, creeping dread that is the casting couch of my nightmares infects even the daylight now so that the benign form and substance of everyday routine takes on a melancholy and menace.

It was sunnier in America, at least in a metaphorical sense— and at least until recently. An optimistic smile seemed to be the national default setting, a central feature of the national character. But bad things began happening, and the smile began to change, to twitch around the edges as though it was forced and unnatural. From there you could almost trace the disappearance of hope as the smile turned into a grimace of pain.

The television is black and inert this morning. I don't need it anymore: the images are imprinted permanently in my mind. The terrified, bewildered people in the snow, the soldiers with their rifles, the bonfires. It is all so out of place, so alien. In my America, bonfires were torches of celebration and rite, of Halloweens and homecomings, of happiness. In Nebraska, those bonfires are bea-

cons of despair. I wondered if they were burning in Dallas as well.

Dallas. Appropriate, in a warped sort of way, that the city that shot JR and JFK would be the one to bring Elvis Presley back to life. A city with a proven record of creating myths and martyrs and an astonishing inability to care about the difference between right and wrong. Perhaps the two go together. Whatever the reason, it is undeniable that the resurrection of Elvis was popular. It grew, in fact, into the biggest thing to hit the city since the Texas School Book Depository.

Elvis Live at Five. *Other stations in the town could just as well stop broadcasting during that hour each day: everyone was watching Elvis. His homespun wisdom and fifties morality knocked the afternoon shock-merchants into obscurity.*

Lines formed outside the bunkerlike concrete station walls well before dawn each day as anxious locals showed up hoping to score a coveted ticket. Jostling and fistfights weren't unheard of, and the station had to hire guards to keep things under control.

And the money poured in. How the money poured in. Barrels and barrels of money—mountains of money—the likes of which local television in Dallas had never seen. ·

Advertising rates for the Elvis show soon climbed to the highest in the U.S. for a locally originated broadcast. The carryover of viewers from Elvis to other shows on the station drove those rates up as well. The six-o'clock news that immediately followed Elvis became the highest-rated local news in Texas. In a city of 2 million people, almost a million watched KVGO from five to six each day. It was the video motherlode. And I was one of the miners.

CHAPTER TWELVE

"Please sit," said Clare Leese, gesturing to one of the leather-covered chairs at the coffee table. Outside, the rain was falling in buckets across the Dallas skyline and streaming in rivulets down the broad glass windows of O'Dell's former office.

The abrupt summons from the boss had come without explanation, and I'd immediately worried—again—that I was being fired. I was tense and frightened.

Leese sat down across from me and smoothed his gray hair. "I'll get to the point quickly," he said in his familiar clipped delivery. "It's a new year and a new start. The station is doing adequately. In the months since the restructuring we've grown the profit margin significantly. I won't bore you with details. The trend is upward. I'm pleased with that. But there's so much more that has to be done." He rose abruptly from the table and approached a glass-covered pedestal that stood near the desk. "You ever see this?" he asked over his shoulder.

"Sorry?" I said, lost by the direction Leese had taken. Maybe I wasn't being fired.

"This, Mr. Upton. I ever show this to you?"

I got up and approached the pedestal. Inside the glass box, a small antique revolver lay on a blue-satin pillow. "No sir, I don't believe so."

"A work of God," said Leese, running his hands lovingly across the glass. "Know what it is?"

"A gun?"

Leese shot me a smile that wasn't in the least friendly. The corners of the small man's mouth actually seemed to drag down at the sides to produce an effect that was as much a snarl as a smile. "Not just 'a gun,' as you put it, Mr. Upton." He ran his hands along the top of the case again. "It's a Colt repeater. Six shots, cylinder action, made in Oberlin, Ohio, in October 1893. Issued to the U.S. Army in May of the following year, 1894."

Leese moved around the pedestal until the two of us were facing each other across it. "Now, this 'gun' is actually the revolver that Teddy Roosevelt carried on the ride up San Juan Hill. The Rough Riders, Mr. Upton, remember?"

I did, vaguely, in a high school sort of way. Spanish-American War. Cuba. Teddy Roosevelt and the Big Stick. I nodded tentatively. This was sounding less and less like a prelude to a firing.

"I came across it at an auction some time ago," said Leese. "Pricey, but worth it. A lot of history wrapped up in that small weapon. Here, help me with this." Leese unhooked a latch at the base of the chamber and tilted the glass box back on its hinges. "You hold that for me."

I steadied the box as Leese carefully removed the pistol and then stepped back as the man swung his arm out full length toward the window. Leese sighted down the blued barrel, pulled the hammer back with a deliberate motion and squeezed the trigger. A loud metallic snap as the hammer fell home on the empty cylinder.

"That's good, isn't it?" said Leese, lowering his arm without taking his eyes off the pistol. "Good action. I can see why Teddy loved this weapon. Handsome tool, handsome tool. Here, let's put it back." Leese set it carefully on the satin pillow and I helped him close the case.

"I like to collect things with meaning," he said, gesturing around the office. "Over there, that's a remnant of the unit flag from George Custer's marching column. The actual flag. I bought it from a Sioux Indian in Montana. Next to it, that's an original sextant from the *Titanic*. They brought it up a year ago. And it's mine. The only one there is in the world. In the world."

With that Leese walked up to the windows and surveyed

the skyline, his back to the room, his hands clasped at his back. "But the pistol is the thing we must study on, Mr. Upton. It's both historical and modern, in the sense of what it has to share with us today." The small man looked back over his shoulder. "You any idea what that link might be, Mr. Upton?" I was lost and it was obvious.

"History, Mr. Upton. The past is but prelude, as they say. Study the past well and a smart fellow can discern the shape of the future. Take that pistol, for instance. The man who used it drove this nation out of isolationism. Opened borders and markets. Created the possibility of the greatness that the twentieth century gave us. Oh, I'll admit, it also gave us some hard times. But think what else it did. The markets that Teddy Roosevelt opened up created a prosperity that the world has never known, never even imagined could exist. This pistol, Mr. Upton, was one of his small tools. Following me so far?"

I managed to nod, though I had little notion of where the conversation might be leading. I'd decided I probably wasn't being fired. Beyond that, though, I had no idea where things were.

"Try to stay with me," said Leese. "This is fundamental to what we're doing here, to what I want us to be doing here. The Spanish-American War. You know how that little spat got started?"

I shook my head.

"A battleship, Mr. Upton. Remember the *Maine*? Blown up in Havana harbor? Hundreds of American sailors maimed, killed? The *Maine,* Mr. Upton, surely you remember the *Maine*?"

"I do."

"Excellent. Now, do you know how it got blown up?"

"Cubans, sir?"

Leese cackled with delight. "Hardly, Mr. Upton, hardly. William Randolph Hearst. His newspapers, Mr. Upton, weren't doing well. So he started a little war to increase revenues." Leese was actually smiling at that, not the snarl I was used to, but something very close to a human smile of pleasure. "Can you imagine?" he said. "Start a war to sell newspapers? Crude, but brilliant. And, of course, it worked. Hearst's papers had the scoop. Of course they had the scoop. They blew up the battleship. That's brilliance."

"Murderous brilliance," I said.

Leese shot me a stern glance. "Let's be careful here, Mr. Upton. Let's make sure we don't let confusion and misplaced morality cloud our thinking. War was coming anyway. Hearst hurried it along a little. As a matter of fact, he gave those brave men something real to fight for. And, in the long run, that war was good for America. Most historians will tell you that war made America into a superpower. And being a superpower has had an extraordinary effect on the Average Joe American's standard of living. I grant you, Mr. Upton, that a few hundred people died. But the act itself created better lives for literally hundreds of millions of others. You tell me if the sacrifice was worth it? No, Mr. Upton, that was a stroke of brilliance. If it's good for the economy, it's good for America. And if it's good for America, it's good for me. Remember those words, Mr. Upton—*it's good for me.* Let's sit back down, shall we?"

With that, Leese dropped into one of the chairs and seemed to sigh. "So Mr. Upton—Nick, I think it's going to be from now on. So Nick. I'm parched. Pour us some of that apple juice there."

I filled two cut-crystal glasses. Leese took a long pull and smacked his lips. "Apple juice from Texas Hill Country. Best thing there is for what ails you. Now, to business. I'm not talking about this station blowing up battleships." A wan smile. "There aren't any battleships around to blow up anyway. But I think we do have a unique opportunity with your man Elvis. He's a strong property, and I think two pretty good minds here could find a way to grow that franchise, to leverage it, the way Hearst leveraged his newspapers. Know what I'm talking about?"

I nodded, guardedly. I'd actually been thinking about that quite a bit as the show's ratings swelled.

"The important thing about Hearst," Leese continued, "was he had papers all across America so he could absolutely command the big advertisers. Now we've taken Elvis just about as far as we can in this pissant little market. We raise those rates any more they're going to charge us with armed robbery." A small chuckle from the little man. "So the question is, how do we grow it? Ideas?"

I pretended to reflect on the question for a few moments. Every number I'd done, every survey I'd looked at, told me that moving Elvis beyond Dallas was the next step. If anything about television could be said to be logical, this was. "I think we should take him national," I said.

Leese turned his head so he was looking me directly in the right eye. "I've been thinking the same thing. We can do that?"

"Seems to me the logical next step," I said. "They did it with Oprah and with Jerry Springer and dozens of others. All of those people started out as local TV shows and went national. I don't see a reason why we couldn't."

"And how do we do it?" said Leese, his eyes intense, his words quick.

"I've been doing some research. There are companies that broker it, distribute it. We put a price tag on it and any station that wants to buy it, we satellite it out to them."

"And we advertise it," said Leese, "and keep the profits?"

"More or less."

"You've obviously been doing your homework," said Leese, "and I like that. I've been doing some, too. Get a good property, you can see returns sixty to sixty-five times investment. Now that's money. I like that. Do you like that, Nick?"

"It does have possibilities."

Leese stood and moved back to the windows. "Are you a wealthy man, Nick?" he asked over his shoulder without turning to look.

I smiled inwardly, picturing the rented apartment I lived in, the clapped-out car. When I'd moved from LA—run from LA—all that I owned had fit in the trunk and backseat. I hadn't added much to that list in the couple of years since. "No, not wealthy, Mr. Leese."

"Would you like to be?"

It's not a question I'd ever had to consider but the answer was easy. "Sure."

Leese turned from the window, his face serious, his gray eyes intense. "Here's the problem I face, Nick. I understand money. I understand investment. Maybe you've heard of the man they call, behind his back, the Blender King?" A tight smile as he said the words. "I do have some fundamental understanding of human nature. But I do not understand television, at least not in-depth. I believe you do. So I make you a simple proposition, Nick. You give me an Elvis that owns the world, I'll make you a wealthy man. What do you think?"

I began to answer but Leese silenced me with a motion of his hand.

"Let me refine this notion, Nick. That woman on television, what's her name?" He didn't let me answer. "She mentions a book on her show, it's an instant best-seller. She says she doesn't eat beef, cattle prices plunge. Now that's power. And power translates into wealth. Nick, I think we have a better product than those other folks, if we do it right. It's different. And it's something we have and they can't get. So my intentions are to do this properly, to grow our product into the most powerful figure in television. Are you the man for it?"

I didn't even pause to think about it. "I am, sir."

"Excellent," said Leese, rubbing his hands together. "You'll have whatever help you need. Lawyers, accountants, whatever it is. I own some of the finest sharks in the world. You tell me what you need and you'll have it. I'll ask Mr. Haldeman to take over the news department so you can devote your energies full time to Elvis. I want this to succeed."

Leese sat down behind his broad desk and pulled a small

book from a drawer. "By way of getting you focused, I'm writing you a check for seventy-five thousand dollars. Let's call it a preproduction bonus. This works, you're in for ten percent of profits."

Leese ripped the check from the book and handed it to me. "Guard it well, Nick."

I took the slip of paper and glanced at it furtively. It was the largest chunk of money I'd ever seen anywhere in one place at one time in my life—the kind of money I thought I'd cut myself out of when I slammed the trunk of the car and pulled onto the freeway headed out of LA. Maybe life wasn't all downhill. "Thank you, sir."

Leese rose from his desk and walked me toward the door. "Something I want you to keep in mind, Nick. We can get everybody to tune in once. But we have to keep them watching and that's not guaranteed, even if he is Elvis Presley. You dwell on that."

"I will, sir."

"And Nick, one more thing to dwell on. Those four little words I mentioned. 'It's good for me.'"

I walked from the office holding my breath. When the door closed behind me, I unfolded the check and gazed at it for a few long moments, then gave a silent whoop of joy, pumping my fist into the air and doing a small off-balance jig down the carpeted hallway. Nick, baby, you've graduated to the big time. No more little tornadoes—no more fires, I thought in a flash of delight—and now my little Elvis is going big. Damn right. With Leese's bucks and my savvy, there was—as they say—no where to go but up. I went out that afternoon to Texas Bob's and got a great deal on a new car and stuck the rest in a savings account. I literally laughed all the way to the bank.

Chapter Thirteen

Elvis went national less than three months later. It was an intense, manic time for me—like nothing I'd ever experienced before—as I commuted almost weekly to New York and Los Angeles to put the deal in place. Life speeded into fast forward, and I had neither the space nor the desire to look back.

Beyond buying the car on that first day, I hardly had time to spend the money Leese had given me. I also hardly had time for Jolene, and the relationship hit the rocks. Not that it bothered me that much: I didn't care about anything that wasn't connected with putting Elvis into every house, every trailer, every tent in America.

For the first time ever, I was living life large and almost instantly developed a taste for it: first-class tickets, airport executive lounges, hotel suites, limos with leather seats and uniformed drivers—people showing me a deference I'd never known but which now seemed a natural part of the association with Leese and the Elvis project. It was as though I had somehow magically stepped through a plywood door into a world of burnished steel and lacquered rosewood.

I'd also stepped into a world that pandered in more ways than one to the senses. The big-money deals, I came to discover, weren't done in boardrooms or paneled offices but over the white linen of extraordinarily overpriced restaurants. Dining was so much part of the business culture that after the first time or two, I thought nothing of five-hundred-dollar lunches and thousand-dollar dinners.

One of the best was in LA when a Hollywood company

mad to get its hands around Elvis invited me out for an afternoon at one of the city's hottest restaurants. The company trotted out its senior management and a handful of spectacular-looking women described as account reps. A few actual Hollywood stars even managed to drop by the table. Waiters in tuxedos and sneakers poured the first champagne aperitifs at one. By the time they were handing around the last snifters of cognac at nearly five, things had gotten more than chummy and I'd decided an "account rep" with catwalk legs and a cover-girl face was about the sexiest woman I'd ever met in my life.

Funny coincidence, that, but an hour later I came out of an uneasy alcohol-driven nap to find the woman knocking on my hotel-room door. She had a bouquet of roses in her hands.

"Hi there," she said, moving smartly past me into the room and setting the roses on the bureau. "The flowers are thanks for a lovely lunch."

I smoothed my hair and tried rubbing the alcohol haze from my eyes. "Roses, huh?" I managed to say. "That's nice."

"We take care of our friends," she said, and kissed me lightly on the lips. I can't actually pretend I was surprised when the woman cupped my groin in her hand.

"It was a nice lunch," I said, feeling myself instantly harden.

"But I think you missed a course," said the woman. "Relax and let me take care of dessert." She gave me a gentle push backward onto the bed. As I lay there, the woman slid out of her blouse and unhooked her bra, rubbing her breasts with her fingers. She reached behind and unzipped her short beige skirt and wiggled it off. She was naked underneath.

"Lovely."

"Thank you," the woman said as she pulled my trousers off and unbuttoned my shirt, managing to brush my cheek several times with her nipple. When I was completely naked and perfectly erect, the woman rolled on a condom and took me into her mouth. The whole thing was over in less time than a muffler commercial.

Between trips to the coasts, I took an option on the old Texas Theater in Dallas and began around-the-clock renovations to make it the new home of Elvis. It was the same movie house where Lee Harvey Oswald was arrested trying to hide out after he gunned down John Kennedy. The city had tried making it a tourist site but it never caught on, and it was moldering toward ruin when Elvis came along. In its excitement over the project, the city of Dallas gave Clare Leese so many tax breaks that the building was almost free.

As winter grudgingly made way for spring, the old movie house in its quaintly ornate Art Deco neon was being transformed into one of the most sophisticated video-production centers in the country. In one wing we installed a suite of offices to house the nearly one hundred people we were hiring to book guests and run operations. For the rest of the renovation, Gelder made up the lists and Clare Leese wrote out the checks for video and computer equipment so advanced that some of it was still experimental. The center's silicon brain, once in place, could do a hundred Elvis's or even a thousand, and satellite those images out to hundreds of television stations simultaneously.

Leese had renamed the place the Theater of the United States. I thought it pretentious but kept my mouth shut and said nothing. I would realize only later how much I had underestimated the depth of Clare Leese's ambition.

I pulled up to the theater one warm mid-March afternoon to find Leese's red Dodge pickup parked out front. The building was still covered in scaffolding and plywood. In the lobby, workmen were painting new plaster walls and laying red carpeting.

Leese was sitting alone in the middle of the main theater looking up at the stage. I squeezed sideways down the row of new seats and sat down beside him. Leese glanced around and nodded and looked back at the stage. "Almost there," he said quietly.

"Yes, sir," I said, following his gaze. The set was simply decorated with a sofa and a couple of chairs. Next to them, a large video screen about the height of a grown man commanded the center of the stage.

"Odd," said Leese without turning.

"Sir?"

"Odd that it's this close."

He was right: we were close. I'd returned from LA the night before with a signed contract for distribution. In two weeks time, the face of Elvis Presley generated by computers in the next room would satellite out to fifty-three television stations. Some of the stations were big—Chicago, Los Angeles, New York—and some weren't—Grand Forks, Missoula, Bangor, Baton Rouge. Together, they would hit a potential viewing audience of almost 100 million people. Not everyone in that audience, of course, would be watching. But it was still huge. As Clare Leese had pointed out, it was a market William Randolph Hearst could only dream about.

"You ready for all this?" said Leese without turning.

"I think so."

"It's going to get strange, you know."

"I know."

"People are unpredictable," said Leese. "Some will like it. Some will hate it. We'll be vilified in some quarters. Hailed as geniuses and pioneers in others. You need to be prepared for that."

"I think I am."

"I have some concerns about the others." Leese's eyes were still on the stage. "Bahr in particular. He's getting pushy."

"I'll talk to him."

"Wants this, wants that. Called me yesterday to talk about a limousine with a driver."

"I'll talk to him."

"Perhaps you might remind him how imminently replaceable he is."

I nodded. I'd known for some time that the diminutive weatherman was due for deflation.

"I'm also a shade troubled by Mr. Gelder," said Leese. "He seems, well, almost detached."

"I think he's okay. Last I checked he was about the happiest guy on the face of the earth. But I'll talk to him."

Leese got up and made his way to the stage where he stood silently in front of the monitor for fully a minute, maybe more. At length he turned and looked out over the rows of seats, his gaze finally falling on me. "I'm worried, Nick," he said, his nasal voice echoing through the empty theater. "I'm worried about Elvis."

"How so?"

"Is it enough?"

"Enough for what?"

"Enough to sustain?"

"I'm not sure I follow."

"So we're going to put this guy up here and people will tune in for gee whiz. Once, maybe twice. What brings them back fifty times?"

I didn't answer.

"That's what worries me, my friend. That's what we must dwell on. *It's good for me.* But how's it good for me. I suspect there's a core audience out there that loves this guy enough they'll watch come hell or high water. But what about the rest, what about the people who aren't Elvis lovers? There's a lot of people out there who are going to watch us a couple of times to see what's going on. But after that, unless it's good for them, they're not going to come back. How do we make it good for them? That's where we're going to live or die. That is what we must dwell on."

With that Leese took a long look around the theater, turned and walked across the stage and disappeared into the wings.

CHAPTER FOURTEEN

A FINE April afternoon and the Theater of the United States was glowing in its new white paint and plaster, dozens of small American flags on its facade snapping to a warm north Texas breeze. The audience line stretched down the street and out of sight around the corner.

Liveried parking attendants were waiting for the special guests and pages in new blue uniforms escorted them inside to a private room where Clare Leese offered them canapes and champagne. The mayor and most of the city council had turned out, along with a good selection of the city's monied class and a sprinkling of television and sports celebrities. The first broadcast of *Elvis Live at Five* would be a study in control and class.

Backstage things were a mess.

"What the fuck is it?" I said for a third time, raising my voice above the general din of the dozen or so people working in the studio where in just a few short minutes we would put Bahr on a stool and transform him into Elvis Presley.

Duncan Gelder shrugged. "I don't know."

"Try again," I snapped. My eyes were on the row of monitors behind Gelder's computer keyboard.

Gelder hit some buttons and the show's opening montage of Elvis video jumped to life on the screens. It ran for five or six seconds but then abruptly switched to a grainy black-and-white movie clip of Roy Rogers standing next to his horse Trigger. Roy smiled at the camera and waved his white hat. Gelder hit a button and the cowboy's face froze in digital paralysis.

"Fuck me," I said, feeling an edge of panic creeping into my brain. "Where's it coming from? Somebody been fucking with this? You realize we're on in less than an hour?"

Gelder glanced at me from the corner of his eye. His busy mouth seemed to be working for several seconds before the words actually formed up and made their way out. "It's somewhere in the software. I need a little time."

"We don't have a little time," I snapped. Next to me a technician scooped up a ringing phone, listened for a minute and handed it over without a word.

"Upton," I barked into the receiver. A pause of a few seconds. Then: "You tell that dwarf fuck to be here now! Okay, whoa, wait." I covered the phone, looked around the studio. Jolene had come up beside me. I took a couple of deep breaths and uncovered the receiver. "Okay," I said, forcing my voice to an unnatural calm. "Tell Mr. Bahr for me that the limousine remains an item of discussion, but not for today, okay? Tell him, please, that we're on in forty-five minutes and he needs to be here. Got that? Good. Thanks." I handed the phone to Jolene. "He doesn't show, I will rip off his head and piss in his neck. How are we?"

"Exactly what 'we' did you have in mind?" she said, giving me a sharp look.

"Jolene, goddamnit. I don't have time for this."

"Just kidding," she said. "I think we're okay—if we can get rid of Trigger." She punctuated the comment with a giggle and I realized she was a lot better at taking the pressure than I. "We can always lay in the opening montage later for the other time zones. Everything else seems to be working." Jolene rapped her knuckles for luck on a metal counter and scooped up the ringing phone again. "Trouble on the floor," she said without even looking my way.

I found the floor manager in a side room off the main theater locked in a shouting match with the dozen or so actors and actresses we'd hired to "salt" the audience, as they called it in the industry. Unknown to most of the public, many of the big shows are elaborate deceptions. While it all looks spontaneous, most audiences are heavily rehearsed to provide, on cue, the requisite anguish, rapture or outrage the host's comments call for. Hired professionals are sprinkled—salted—throughout the crowd, primed with well-rehearsed questions to move the show along. In some shows, professionals make up the whole audience. For Elvis, we figured a dozen would be about right.

I grabbed the floor manager by the arm. "What's the problem?" The clock was ticking and we needed to get this thing moving.

"He's being a cunt," said a thin fellow with short red hair and a matching goatee. A couple of people next to him nodded their agreement.

"Jim?" I said, turning back to the floor manager.

"It's a union thing," he said. "They say they're covered by AFTRA and that AFTRA rules give them a dinner break right in the middle of the show. I've pointed out that Texas doesn't have unions."

"You're a cunt," the ginger-haired man hissed. "We miss dinner, you pay."

"How much?" I said.

"They're not covered by a fucking union," said the floor manager.

"Thirty-five dollars," said the ginger-haired man. "Each."

"Pay them," I said. "Anything else?"

The ginger-haired man was smirking.

"What's your name?" I asked him.

"John Streets," he answered.

"Let's do a little business here, Mr. Streets." I pulled a wad of bills from my pocket and peeled off a couple of tens. The man's smile grew wider. I handed the money to him. "Here's dinner, asshole. I don't like getting mugged. Now get the fuck out of this theater and don't ever let me see you back here again, or I'll knock that fucking smirk all the way to your asshole."

The man's freckled face flushed with blood. He started to say something but thought better of it, turned and stomped away.

I glanced around at the others. "Any more issues?"

The group seemed to be studying the floor.

"Good. Now let's get this circus moving."

Back in the control room, Jolene was bringing the operation on-line. "And steady up everyone," she said into the small lip-mike suspended in front of her mouth.

I slipped into my chair at the back of the room and surveyed the monitors. In one, Iso Bahr was fidgeting on his stool. So he finally showed up. Deal with that later. In the monitor next to Bahr's, Elvis Presley was making the exact identical movements. Though I'd seen it now a thousand times at least, I still found myself marveling at how realistic the image was. On the monitor next to Elvis, a theater camera was panning across the mildly expectant faces of almost five hundred people.

Jolene keyed her intercom to Gelder. "Computers?" she said. No answer.

She hit the switch again. "Mr. Gelder?"

Gelder's voice came on. "Sorry, but just a second." Overhead on the monitor, we watched as the tape of the opening montage started to play, paused and went into rewind.

"How are we?" Jolene asked, her voice taking on an edge of impatience. "We need to start making some television here."

As she spoke, Clare Leese slipped in and took a chair next to me.

Silence from the intercom box.

"Talk to me, Duncan," said Jolene. "How's the Elvis shot?"

"Elvis is fine. It's the montage. Man, I don't know. This Roy Rogers thing is weird. Maybe a virus but if it is I can't find it."

"Fixed?"

"Maybe," said Gelder, but his voice sounded uncertain. "If it's bad, I can go in and fix the video later."

That seemed to satisfy Jolene who swung around on her

chair and faced me and Leese. "It looks like we're ready to do Elvis. When you are."

Leese scanned the room, his eyes lingering on the shot of Elvis. He turned to me and I nodded. "Let's do it," he said softly.

Jolene spun back in her chair and eyed the big lighted clock at the center of the control-room wall. "Ready all," she said firmly. "Edits one and two roll for record. Ready Elvis remotes, ready studio cameras. How are we on the floor, Jim?"

The floor manager's voice came up on the control-room speaker. "Good to go on the floor."

"Stand by," said Jolene. "Ready animation, ready announcer." She was watching the clock as its second hand swept toward the top of the hour. At ten seconds to go, she started the countdown. "And ten, nine. Ready animation, ready announcer. Look lively, cameras. This is it. And three, two . . . and take animation. We've got air."

In the main theater, the monitors along the walls and the giant screen in the middle of the stage burst into life with a video of Elvis Presley in a shiny dark suit and white turtleneck singing "Love Me Tender." The picture rolled for a few seconds and the music faded as an announcer's voice came up: "Ladies and gentlemen. From the Theater of the United States, and from the deepest memories of all of us, please welcome back Elvis Presley!"

"And take two," Jolene ordered as the applause signs switched on and the audience began clapping.

"Applause could be better," I said to no one in particular. "Need to sweeten that later."

"Gotcha," said Jolene without turning. "Let's give this thing a little class. Camera three, show me the quarterback."

Next to Jolene an assistant thumbed quickly down the seating chart and keyed her mike to the cameraman. "Fifth row, right side, six seats in. Big white guy, blond crewcut."

The picture on one of the small cuing monitors followed

the movement as camera three tracked across the sea of faces and stopped, pushing tight almost into the nose of a crewcut blond man. The camera focused and pulled back.

"Good work," said Jolene. "Ready three. Take three." The man's face filled the screen. "Camera two stay wide. Coming back to you next. Floor, we're five seconds to Elvis."

"Five seconds, got it," snapped a voice from the speakers.

"And ready two wide. And—take two."

The shot changed back to a wide view of the audience as the applause began to die.

"And ready Elvis," said Jolene.

I felt my stomach clenching.

"And—take Elvis."

The signs around the theater flashed on and off and the audience broke into a swelling roar of applause. In front of them in the main-stage monitor, the shot of Elvis singing melted into a shot of the real thing, or at least so it appeared: Elvis Presley in his white sequined outfit, his dark hair rakishly in his eyes, a guitar hanging from his shoulder. Elvis Presley looking out at the audience with a nervous, expectant grin. Elvis Presley, for all intents and purposes alive and breathing there before them on the screen. The applause deepened. The paid actors stood up cheering and the rest of the audience joined them.

"Camera two stay wide," snapped Jolene. "And camera three, let's find our girl."

"Second row, first seat left on the center aisle," said the assistant without looking at her seating chart.

"Got it," said the disembodied voice of the camera operator as he zoomed in on the ecstatic tear-streamed face of a forty-something woman.

"And—take three," said Jolene.

"One of ours?" said Leese quietly next to me.

I nodded.

"Lovely."

"A little wider," said Jolene and the camera pulled out as the woman started jumping up and down and screaming. The hidden mike we'd wired on the woman before the show picked up and amplified her frenzy and seemed to spread it like a contagion to the people around her.

"Camera three, give me a slow pull," said Jolene coolly. "Let's see who's doing the screaming."

The camera shot widened out to reveal most of the audience jumping up and down, shouting and cheering as they applauded the image on the screen in front of them.

"Okay," said Jolene. "Let's give 'em some Elvis. Cue the King."

Ed Skowski watched the first Elvis show from behind a barber chair in his shop on Ridge Road on the north side of Chicago, a perch from which Ed had been watching the world go to hell for forty-two years.

". . . excited to be here," Elvis was saying, his face almost filling the barbershop's television screen. Ed Skowski paused in mid-snip to watch. "I mean, you can't really imagine the feeling," said Elvis. "To be back after all these years, and to find out there's so much love out there. It is a joy, a true joy."

The shot changed abruptly to show Elvis on a large video monitor being watched by a huge studio audience. "But I'm back now and you've got me. So here we are. I thought today for this first show I'd open things up to questions. If you've got something on your mind, I'd like to hear about it. We'll keep this kind of informal. What do you think, huh?"

The shot held as a man in the audience stood and an usher hurried down the aisle and held a microphone out to him. "Elvis," said the man, "I first off want to thank you for coming back"—scattered applause from the crowd—"and tell you what an honor it is to actually be able to address you." More applause.

"We're proud to be here, sir," said Elvis, his face serious. "You have a question for us today?"

The man cleared his throat nervously. "Well, weight loss, Mr. Presley. I'm not quite sure how to put this, but do you ever use drugs to take the weight off?"

"Good question," said Ed Skowski, and the head he was barbering nodded in silent agreement.

"Drugs?" said Elvis, his voice raised slightly in a tone of disbelief. "Let me be clear, sir. Drugs are a tool of Satan"—a swell of applause rippled across the audience—"a giant step on the road to perdition."

"You got that right," said Skowski to the television screen.

"It's a long step on the short march to Hell. Let me tell you about drugs and people who sell them. Drugs are a sinner's paradise, an ignorant man's Eden. They're bad, they're addictive"—the shot changed to show Elvis full face in the television screen—"they're deadly, they're dangerous. They kill our dear mommas and they kill our innocent babies. They're a poison in the veins of our country."

"I thought Elvis was dead," said the man in Ed's barber chair to no one in particular.

"And if you want to do this country a favor," said Elvis, "get rid of the pushers." The crowd burst into a roar of applause. The picture changed to show Elvis peering down from the screen as the audience clapped, a hollow, haunted look on his face. "We thank you," he was saying, "we thank you, ladies and gentlemen. Time now for one of those commercial things. But stay right here, we're back in sixty seconds."

"Just goes to show you," said the man in the barber chair as Ed Skowski brushed talc across his neck.

In the small studio in the theater in Dallas, a makeup woman was trying to swab up the sweat running in rivulets down Iso Bahr's cheeks. In the rear of the room, Duncan Gelder was peering back and forth into his bank of computer screens.

"Fuck," Bahr was saying. "This is tough."

"I know," I said. I was hurriedly paging through a stack of

notes on a clipboard. "I know it's tough, but it feels like it's working."

"Thirty seconds," shouted a voice off the set.

"Fuck," said Bahr and the word reverberated back from wall speakers in Elvis's voice.

"Careful," I said. "Okay, second section. Five minutes. Let's get off the drug thing."

"I can't fucking talk for five minutes."

"You have to. Let's do music this time."

"Fifteen seconds."

"Music?" said Bahr, a pained look on his face. "I don't know shit about music."

"And five, four . . ."

"Rock and roll," I said backing out of the shot.

At the Cattle King Grill in Billings, Montana, Karen Tarrant was drowning her fifty-sixth birthday in a fourth margarita when Elvis started singing on the television set over the bar. "I love him," she said.

"Who?" said Karen Potts, her coworker and girlfriend of too many years to count. People called them Karen One and Karen Two. "Who do you love?"

"Him," said Karen One, gesturing with a sweeping arm toward the television and managing to knock over an almost empty margarita glass. "Shit. Dead soldier."

Karen Two giggled loudly and covered her mouth in mock embarrassment. "We have to get back to work."

"Frig work," said Karen One. "I want to listen to Elvis. He's always been my favorite. Where's that stupid tarbender. I need another dink."

Karen Two giggled again.

On the screen, Elvis put down the guitar. "Music's always been the balm for my soul. It's what I did when the world got too close." The shot widened to show the audience, with Elvis on the video screen in front of them. "Any of you have more questions?"

"I have one," said Karen One in a loud stage whisper. "How big's your dick?"

Karen Two choked out an enormous laugh, spraying the table with a mouthful of margarita.

"You got stuff on me!" said Karen One.

"How big's your dick?" said Karen Two. "That's what you want to know? Elvis is back and that's all you want to know? How big's your dick?"

"The way he moves his hips," said the other Karen with a wide leer, "that's gotta be more than a Twinkie in there."

Another eruption of laughter from Karen Two and a couple of faces turned to see what the commotion was.

". . . inspired you to mix soul and rhythm and blues?" a dark-haired man on the television was saying. The shot changed to Elvis, full face. "Well sir, I think it was a couple of things. . . .

"I wonder where he is," said Karen One.

"Where who is?" said Karen Two, looking around the restaurant.

"Elvis, stupid."

Karen Two focused on the screen. "On the TV, stupid."

"I know that. I mean, I wonder where he is is."

"Nashville, maybe?"

Karen One nodded wistfully. "Wouldn't that be neat? To have all those years to live over? Damn, I wish he'd never died." A waitress set two new margaritas before them and they both took a long drink. "I always wanted to see him," said Karen One, dabbing at a smudge of salt on her lip.

"Me, too."

"He was playing in Vegas once but the dirtball wouldn't take me."

"He's the father of your child."

"Still a dirtball."

Karen Two closed her eyes and shook her head. "That's bad luck. You shouldn't say that."

"What? Calling dirtball a dirtball?"

"Ooh," said Karen Two. "Don't do that."

Elvis had picked up his guitar again and was strumming it softly.

"I sure love him," said Karen One from behind watery eyes.

"Me, too," said the other Karen.

CHAPTER FIFTEEN

I DON'T like looking stupid!" Leese said, smacking his fist into his hand and turning to fix the rest of us with a stare that had little in the way of friendliness in it. Leese's anger had driven his voice higher and deepened the east Texas twang. "We can't afford—afford—to look stupid. Like a bunch of bush-league amateurs. That's right. You saw that, maybe? That's what the *New York Post* called us. 'Bush-league amateurs.' Did you happen upon that, Mr. Upton, in your voluminous readings—or was your eye drawn to the racing page instead?" Leese almost spit the words and I sat stock-still in my chair. Behind me, Duncan Gelder rubbed at an imaginary spot on a computer screen while Jolene pretended she wasn't in the room. Iso Bahr sat off to one side looking like he was deep in thought. Midmorning Friday after our second full week and we were all tired.

I cleared my throat tentatively. "I saw the review."

"And . . . ?" said Leese, his voice acid.

"And they didn't like us much."

"Astute, Mr. Upton, very astute." Leese waved a newspaper in the air. "No, they didn't like us much, did they? The *Chicago Sun-Times* didn't like us much. The *Portland Oregonian* didn't like us much. The *San Diego Union-Trib*. The *Detroit Free Press*. The *Miami Herald*. A lot of people didn't like us much, did they?" Leese threw the paper disgustedly on the floor and paced back and forth in front of us a few times, his hands clenched behind his back, his eyes cast downward. At length he turned and faced us again.

"Look around you," he said. "I built this. One of the best

theaters in America, probably the world. Why? To do Elvis. To bring people an Elvis they haven't known in a lifetime. To re-create something great. I built this." He turned and paced again a couple of times. "We have the tools for greatness here. We have the potential. But we're not realizing that potential." The small man held up his right hand and peered at it intently. "It is slipping through our fingers. We have to study on that. We have to analyze that. Mr. Upton, you're astute this morning. What's happening?"

I started to answer but Leese broke in before I could speak.

"Let me ratchet this all back a little," he said, his voice taking on a more reasonable tone. "I don't want this to be an Inquisition. We're all in it together, and we need to think our way out of it together." The small man dragged a studio chair up and straddled it backward, like he was getting on a horse, propping his chin on his cupped fist. "Friends. We're all friends here. Now, Mr. Upton? Thoughts?"

"Well, it's only two weeks of shows and there were some good comments, too. They liked the technology."

"Due in great part to Mr. Gelder here," said Leese. "Credit where credit's due." The others looked around at Gelder and nodded. Gelder turned pink.

I continued. "A couple papers, Memphis and Detroit mostly, had a lot of criticism for the character himself. They said we weren't getting him right." I glanced at Bahr as I said it but he was looking off toward the other side of the room.

"Our research has to be better," said Leese. "Mr. Bahr, this is no offense to you. We just need to be smarter."

"And we had his age wrong when he went in the army."

"Research again," said Leese.

"I do know an Elvis expert," I said, recalling the scene with Bahr the first time I'd laid eyes on Margaret Wares, "but she hates us."

"Hire her," snapped Leese.

"I don't think she's interested."

"Make her the right offer. We have to get this fixed."

"I'll try but she was damned stubborn the last time I brought it up." I paused for a second to collect my thoughts. "Some of the big papers had problems with just the fact that we exist. The *LA Times*, for instance. They had some nice things to say about our technical ability, leading edge and all that, but in almost the same breath they questioned whether America needed another afternoon talk show. We got that from all sides. Too many trashy talk shows out there now, the trivialization of afternoon TV, blah blah blah and why should America make room for yet another afternoon big mouth, even if he is Elvis."

"That's a problem," said Leese at length. "Our numbers were strong for the first week. People were watching it. But it began to slip. It's what we feared early on. Remember, Mr. Upton? Once we get past the novelty of what we're doing—once we get past the technology—we're just another afternoon talk show. Why watch that? What's the draw? It's just another afternoon loudmouth."

Silence around the room.

"Radio?" said Duncan Gelder. The word came out quiet, almost tentative, and all eyes turned toward the odd man at the console.

"Radio?" said Leese.

"Yes, sir," said Gelder, his mouth working as he looked shyly toward the boss.

"Go on."

"It's just an idea I've been playing with."

"So tell us your idea."

"It may not be very good."

"Tell us anyway."

"Well, I read the reviews, too. And, you know, I was thinking about television. How some people say it's just sort of radio with pictures, that sort of thing. Not that it is or anything. But it got me thinking about radio. They've got talk shows and everything just like us. They're all pretty bad but there are a couple that are pretty good. I'm thinking of a couple of the New York shows that have syndicated nationally." Gelder paused and looked around uncertainly, as though unsure whether he should continue.

"Go ahead," said Leese.

"Well, they do things a little differently—and maybe it's something we can learn from. They're a different medium and all that so I guess they have to. But they're doing things a little bit better."

"How so?" said Leese.

"Well, there are two real good ones right now. I mean good, if you like that sort of thing. But I listen to them quite a lot. You can get them on the net so I've got them on quite a bit. Both of them do guests and things like that, just like we do. But both of them also do news. That's what's different." Gelder leaned back in his chair and looked around the room like his argument was complete.

"News?" said Leese.

"News," said Gelder, nodding.

"So?"

Gelder started, apparently realizing he hadn't made his argument as completely as he thought. "Well, sir, what I mean is I think the news is the thing. They both have sidekicks who read the news first and that way they have something to talk about. I mean, it makes it current. When you're listening to them you know that mostly they're talking about things that are actually happening." Gelder looked around the room uncertainly, took a breath and plunged on. "I mean, we have Elvis sitting here talking about things that for most people are ancient history. The army, his music, things like that. That's stale. I mean that's the other-side-of-the-moon ancient history. And even when we try, it's not current current, if you see what I mean. It's sort of a topic that's out there, but it's not that day's news. That's what radio can do. It can do what's happening right now, right that day. I think that's why people are interested. I mean . . ." Gelder looked down at his hands and lapsed into silence. It was the longest speech anybody could remember coming from him.

Leese thought about it for a time, then swung off his chair, a smile growing on his face. "I like it, Mr. Gelder. I think I like. You might have just answered some fundamental questions here. And it's something we can do now. Mr. Upton, it's Friday morning right now. Let's shoot for tomorrow morning here. Let's bring in the anchors from the station, see if we can't get something flying by the next taping. That gives us two days." Leese caught Bahr's eye. "Are you up for it, Mr. Bahr? It may mean missing a day or two of golf. Think you can stand that?"

Bahr played golf before work five days a week and was on the course all day on the weekends at a country club up north. To say it was a religion for him was to understate the passion. He nodded to Leese, but it wasn't a happy nod.

Leese smiled at that and did a sudden pivot so he was almost nose-to-nose with Duncan Gelder. "And you," he said, "you keep those good ideas coming, you hear?" Gelder nodded, his eyes almost crossing as he tried to focus on Leese's face.

FRIDAY'S OPTIMISM collided head on with Saturday's reality. Without the words there before them on a teleprompter, the two television anchors seemed almost incapable of thought.

Of the two, the thirty-something white woman was by far the worst. Her initial reluctance at working a Saturday hardened progressively through the morning as we had her read wire copy and try to ad-lib comments about what she was reading. It didn't work. Her delivery was flat and listless and the ability to talk intelligently about the news just wasn't anywhere present in her genetic envelope. I sent her home at noon with a tight-lipped thanks that barely concealed my irritation at her planklike thickness.

The fifty-something black anchor was better. He read the

news with animation and apparent interest—a trick of age and experience—and actually seemed to enjoy the process. I thought it was just about what we were looking for, but Leese seemed to have reservations. We ran through the show two times, and then Leese ordered a third. At the end of it, Leese sent him home.

"Sometimes a great notion," said Leese, dropping dejectedly into a chair at the rear console in the control room.

"Yeah," I agreed, sitting down beside him. The room felt empty without Jolene in her usual spot up front. "I actually thought he did a pretty good job. Better than the blond."

"I get so tired," said Leese to no one in particular as he rubbed his knees.

"Me, too. My dad always told me to get an education so I'd have a nice indoor job. I didn't think it'd be this much work."

"Good Lord that woman was stupid," said Leese. "Beautiful, but so stupid. Tell me where the justice is in that, huh?"

"That's a problem with some TV people," I said. "You get these pretty ones you put on the air for their looks. And some of them are too dumb to know how dumb they are and start thinking they're smart because they're on TV. Creates some real monsters. Both men and women. Didn't used to be that way. Now it's everywhere."

"Too bad," said Leese. "Too bad about that fellow's skin, too."

I glanced at Leese, surprised. "His skin?"

"Too dark," said Leese.

"Well, he's an African American. What'd you expect?"

"More African than American, by the looks of things. Too African for the show."

I started to argue the point but was cut off by a squeal of feedback as Gelder's voice came over the speakers. "Mr. Leese, Mr. Upton, you in there?"

Leese looked around the room and glanced at me helplessly.

I hit a toggle switch on the console. "We're here, Duncan. What's up?"

"Something you might want to see. I've got it cued on edit one."

"Up there," I said, gesturing to a small monitor on the wall. Into the mike: "We're watching."

A colored countdown spun backward from ten on the monitor and a man's face came on. His lips were moving as though he was speaking but there was no audio. It was the face of a white man: serious-looking, squared-off jaw, intense dark eyes, maybe early fifties. His black hair was streaked in gray over the ears and his cheeks showed a hint of five-o'clock shadow. It was a very masculine face, a face that exuded a sense of quiet confidence and lead-dog authority.

Watching the image play from the darkened wall, I had the strangest sensation: it was like I knew the man, that somehow we were old friends, but my brain was having trouble making the connection and bringing up the name. The sense of familiarity grew as the image played on. I glanced furtively at Leese who was staring raptly at the image.

After a minute or so the screen went to black.

Leese turned in his chair, a look of confusion on his face. "We know him, don't we? Who was that?"

I shrugged and keyed the mike. "Duncan, who was that?"

A momentary pause, then Gelder's voice. "I call him Bob. Maybe you want to meet him?"

"I started playing with it yesterday, after the meeting," Gelder said as Leese and I walked into the studio. Above him, the image we'd just seen was paused in a freeze-frame in a string of monitors. "It's still sort of rough. I mean it's not where I want it to be yet, but I think maybe it has some promise. You want me to play it again? I don't think you had audio."

Gelder reracked the tape and hit the play button. Above him the numbers spun down and the man's face popped up again. This time there was sound.

"Good afternoon and here are the headlines," said the man in a deep but pleasant voice. "More market uncertainty as China moved for the first time to devalue its currency. Latin

American markets were off substantially. In the Midwest, floodwaters are beginning to recede along the Mississippi, where three weeks of torrential spring rains forced the big river and its many tributaries from their banks. Federal officials put the loss at more than a billion dollars."

As I watched the tape, I had the same feeling again. My brain knew the face but couldn't find the name.

"And finally today," the man was saying, "the mayor of New York announced his third successive get-tough policy on crime. More police on the streets, more cells for prisoners. Zero tolerance, says the mayor, for anyone doing anything at any time. More news later." The man offered a soft smile as the screen faded into black.

"Do I know him?" said Leese as Gelder stopped the tape.

Gelder turned with an almost guilty smile on his face. "Sort of," he said, and let off with a low chuckle.

"And . . . ?" said Leese. I could read growing impatience under Leese's question and worried that Gelder wasn't picking up on it.

"Who was it, Duncan?" I said.

"Wrong question," answered Gelder, his voice cascading over a low series of giggles.

"Duncan . . ."

"Okay, okay," said Gelder. "It's not who was it, it's who were they."

"Excuse me?"

Gelder turned to the console and fiddled with some buttons. I realized for the first time it was a defense mechanism in the man, that when his voice and his face were beginning to run out of control, he always turned back to his machines. The act seemed to restore his emotional balance.

Gelder hit a switch and the man's face came up again on the monitors, frozen openmouthed in midsentence. "It's kind of the same thing as Elvis," said Gelder, "only a little different. With Elvis we're taking one human form and projecting it onto another. This thing's a composite."

Leese: "That's a computer image?"

Gelder nodded. "A composite built by the computer."

"A composite of what?" said Leese.

"Well, basically, of newsmen."

"Newsmen?"

Gelder busied himself with buttons as he spoke. "Newsmen," he said. "I went in and scooped up images of all the great ones. Murrow, Rather, Cronkite. It was weird but most of them have been CBS—and then threw in Huntley and Brinkley just to get a little more variety. Put them all together and this is the guy you get." Gelder hit a button and the picture came to life.

"Good afternoon and here are the headlines," said the face on the wall. "More market uncertainty as China moved for the first time to devalue its currency."

I took a step back and watched the picture roll. Now I understood the odd feeling I'd had when I saw it the first time. Familiar in an eerie sort of way, like I knew the face but couldn't put a name to it. There was no single identifiable feature that brought to mind the individual faces of the men combined in that picture. It was a sort of moving Rorschach creating a series of feelings and memories. The face gave off a distinct impression of confidence, maybe trust. I couldn't exactly identify it or give it a single name, but it came to me as I stood there watching that whatever it was, the face made me feel pretty good.

Leese must have been experiencing the same feelings. "I like that," he said. "And let me get this straight: that's the computer's idea of what a guy would look like if you put all those faces together?"

Gelder nodded without turning. "An average, sir, that's right."

"And it's like Elvis?" said Leese. "I mean, that's a real human under there and you're projecting the form on top of that."

Gelder nodded to his console again. "That's actually me under there."

"And what exactly do you do with him?"

Gelder seemed flustered by the question. "Well, it's like the radio thing I was talking about. I mean, I was thinking we use this guy to start the show."

"Not bad," said Leese softly. "Not bad. Might cut down on the overhead. And the complaining."

"Weird," I said.

"I like it," said Leese. "That's a good face. What'd you call him again?"

"Bob," said Gelder quietly.

"Bob?"

"I call him Bob," said Gelder.

"Let's get this on the air," said Leese. "I want rehearsals noon tomorrow. Can you do that?"

Gelder nodded.

Leese stepped up close to the monitor. "So what's new, Bob?"

CHAPTER SIXTEEN

I SET out early Sunday morning before the rehearsal with our new electronic anchor to find Margaret Wares. Actually tracking the woman down proved tougher than I expected: I finally discovered her address with help from a friend on the city desk at the newspaper and then spent the better part of an hour wandering through the northern suburbs of Dallas looking for a street that wasn't on the maps. I suppose I could have called, but I don't like asking directions.

The reason for my difficulties was apparent when I arrived: the street was little more than an unmarked dirt lane, and the structure that sat at the end of it in a forest of pecan trees was hardly a house. By the looks of it, the place had begun life as a shed or barn and had grown as though by whim: a kitchen tacked on here, a bedroom framed out there, a patio added in the middle almost as an afterthought. The work appeared sound enough, but it had that not-quite-completed look of do-it-yourself stores and handyman projects.

No answer at the front door. Through the window, I could make out a small kitchen with a single chair at a formica and chrome table. Beyond that, a larger room with an overstuffed sofa and walls of bookshelves.

A power saw whined to life from somewhere in back. I followed the sound around the patio and along a small garden to the rear of the place. Margaret Wares in paint-smeared jeans and a blue denim work shirt was guiding a circular saw down the center of a long piece of plywood. She straightened when she noticed me and brought the saw out of the wood. Its blade coasted to a stop.

"Morning," I said. I was struck again by the woman's uncommon beauty, which even the work clothes did little to dampen. "So a carpenter, huh? You're full of surprises."

"Morning," said Margaret, wiping a smudge of sawdust from her face and tucking back an errant strand of red hair. Her expression was friendly, but her blue eyes were question marks.

"In the neighborhood and thought I'd drop by," I said, repeating the words she'd used the day she came to the station. Had that been six months ago?

"Right."

"Plywood?"

"Flooring for a new greenhouse," she said. "In the neighborhood?" The words came with the same odd, challenging smile I'd remembered from before.

"Something like that," I said. "Have time to talk for a minute?"

Margaret laid the saw gently on the sheet of wood. "Sure. Let me buy you a glass of tea." With that she led me back around to the patio and disappeared inside for a minute before reappearing with two large plastic glasses of iced tea.

"So you were in the neighborhood?" she said, taking a long drink and placing the glass back carefully on a rough wooden crate that served as a table. I remembered how she'd clumsily put the wineglass in the center of the table last time we were together—after the plane crash. "Let's see," she said, "Sunday morning. Maybe you were on your way to church?" The words came out around a smile.

"Church," I said, nodding. "I was on my way to church and decided to drop by."

"How very Christian of you. I'm surprised you found me."

"Not easy."

"I like it that way."

"Nice place. You live here alone?"

"I like it that way," she said again. "So on your way to church and you decided to drop by?" The crooked smile.

"You do the work on this place yourself?"

"Most of it," said the woman. "Do you ever get to the point?"

"I'm working on it," I said, grinning. "Actually, I wanted to talk to you about our project at the station. The Elvis thing."

Margaret wrinkled her nose. "The Elvis thing."

"I know, I know. You think we're morons. Or Frankensteins. I know where you are on this. Actually, I'm headed to rehearsals at the theater now but wanted to see you first."

"Rehearsals on a Sunday?"

"Thing's turned into a seven-day-a-week job. We've got a new twist to things and wanted to see how it would work. So Sunday, yeah. Anyway, truth is I dropped by because we need some help."

"What kind of help?"

"Thinking help."

The woman looked at me, an open question in her eyes.

I took a long drink of tea. "All right. The truth of the matter is, we just don't know a hell of a lot about Elvis. I mean we know enough to get him on the air and make it seem pretty genuine. And that was enough when the whole thing was sort of a lark. Now it's serious but when we get into the minutia of his everyday life, things begin to fall apart on us."

"I've noticed."

"You've watched?"

"Hard to miss."

"And what do you think?" I said it with a teasing grin on my face, a grin that I hoped would hide from her the importance I put to her answer. I hadn't cared in the past. But for some reason now, it mattered to me what this woman thought about what I was doing.

"You really want to know what I think?"

"Yeah, I do. All the teasing aside, I'd like to know."

The woman took a small sip of her tea. "One of the biggest questions I hear out there on campuses is what's real. I mean, kids these days are asking that: what's real? Television, movies, the Web—everything today is chipping away at reality." She paused with her eyebrows arched, as if asking me silently if she should continue.

I nodded her on.

"It's everywhere," she said. "Think about the movies. There's one where people's entire existence has been faked by a machine. Or another where humans are just one of the drives in a cosmic computer. And it's all over television: morphing, electronic billboarding, digital masking, things I don't even know about. You can't tell what's real anymore and kids are confused." She paused to reemphasize the point.

"So we're confusing kids?" I said. "That's the problem?"

"And so—you're adding to people's confusion. Not just kids', but everyone's. Nobody knows which way's up anymore. You asked so I'll answer you. We're getting to the point now where we can't trust any of it. Remember the plane pictures? Same thing there—you didn't show them all. We can't trust any of it anymore. So what do we do then, huh? What do we do when there's nothing out there we can trust?"

"I think you're exaggerating."

"You're not on the campuses, Nick."

"Maybe. But TV is TV. It's what it's always been."

"You're wrong. Can't you see that it's twisting everything— it's distorting reality. Look at it, Nick: seeing's no longer believing. I'd say it's scaring a lot of people but that would be wrong. People don't even know it's happening to them."

"So working with us is out of the question?"

Margaret smiled gently. "You, Nick, are out of your mind. Do you like my flowers?"

The change in conversational direction threw me briefly.

"Weather's turning," she said, "so they're not all out yet but it's about to be glorious. When it gets a little hotter, this place will blaze with color."

"I bet," I said, trying to sound interested.

"But you don't care about that much, do you?"

I shrugged. "I don't know much about plants. Maybe you could teach me?"

"That monster on the trellis is wisteria. When I got him he was just a little twig. I wasn't sure he'd make it in the heat. I use Miracle-Gro. And no I can't be bought and no I won't help you with this thing." She took a drink of tea and rearranged herself on the metal chair, tucking her legs up under her and bringing her hands together. "So, Mr. Upton? What else would you like to talk about on this fine Sunday morning as you're headed off to church?"

"No Elvis, huh?"

Margaret shook her head. "I guess we can't talk flowers, huh? We could talk carpentry. My dad carpentered in his spare time—when he wasn't selling cars. Taught his only daughter. It's a good hobby. Keeps me out of the pool halls. You want more tea? No, I guess you've still got quite a bit don't you. So I like to build things. This place was tiny when I got it years ago. I added on that kitchen. Nice kitchen, huh?"

I nodded.

"And I put up the spare room and then carved out this space for the patio. And so you've stopped talking to me?"

I remained silent.

"Great," said the woman with an inflated sigh of exasperation. "Now I'm sitting here on a lovely Sunday morning with a nice-looking man having a conversation with myself. What is it about this life that makes it so tough?"

A nice-looking man, huh? I remained silent.

"Look, Nick, I'll get serious for a minute. I see your problem. I'm sorry for you. But I won't help you on this. As you can see, I have some ethical problems with it. I think you're engaged in mass manipulation of the lowest sort. You're playing to people's fears and fantasies just to make a buck and I've got problems with that. You're also screwing around with reality, and there's enough of that out there already. It's a free country, more or less, and I can't make you stop. I gave up on that. But I am telling you I don't want anything to do with it. Go out and hire a good researcher. This isn't something I want to be involved in."

She rose and took the glass from my hands. "Now why don't you go on to church, or wherever it is you were headed when you happened to be in the neighborhood, and let's close the morning as friends. Okay?"

"Fair enough," I said, rising reluctantly from the table. "No more Elvis. How 'bout dinner this week?" I was surprised at my own question.

The woman seemed equally surprised, but at least didn't dismiss it out of hand. "Dinner?"

I smiled. "Dinner. Me, you, man, woman, eat. Dinner. Yeah?"

"What about Elvis?"

"Elvis who?"

"Good answer."

"Tuesday?" I said.

"How about if you give me a call?"

"I'll call you, then."

"You have my number?" Her eyes were sparkling.

"I'll get it."

"No Elvis."

"No Elvis," I agreed, shaking my head.

Her mouth was working into a mischievous grin. "Now go to church."

I drove away watching her in the rearview mirror. I'd tried, and I could tell Leese I'd tried. But she wouldn't budge. Dinner, though. That had possibilities. It had to be someplace nice but not too nice. Understated but classy—I had the money for it. The kind of place that showed her sophistication but hinted at wildness. And the conversation had to be right. No mention at all of Elvis. No issue that could cause any sort of disagreement. This one I had to get right.

Chapter Seventeen

I ARRIVED at the rehearsal to find Leese and Iso Bahr leafing through a stack of news stories. A couple of camera operators were dollying their big machines around the studio setting focus and angles while assistants arranged and rearranged piles of snaking cable. Gelder was at his console, his busy mouth working furiously on a wad of gum, his eyes about half-hooded in a dreamy way.

"Late," said Leese curtly as I walked in. Leese, as ever, was in a gray suit with a dark tie.

"Trying to hire the Elvis expert."

"How'd it go."

"It didn't."

"Damn."

"Told me to go out and hire a professional researcher."

"So do it," said Leese.

"I'll take care of it in the morning." I looked over Bahr's shoulder at the news stories. "Just the headlines," I said. "We don't want to get too heavy into news."

"I'm with you on that," said Bahr. The small man was in his Sunday golfing casual: custard-colored nylon slacks and a bright-red cotton shirt. "We've put together three or four stories here. Figure we'll give them twenty, thirty seconds each and move on."

"What are we keying on?"

"Gun control. Playing off a school shooting in Utah last week. Funerals today."

Inside the control room, Jolene and about a half dozen others were going through checklists and getting the equipment readied. She threw me a frosty look and I gave her a brief nod. "So how are we this fine Sunday morning?"

"Go fuck yourself," she said.

A couple of people turned away to hide their grins, and I wondered briefly if Jolene had somehow caught on to my morning's visit with Margaret. It surprised me to realize I didn't care. "So how's it looking?" I said, stripping the friendliness out of my voice.

"Like shit," said Jolene. "This thing's complicated."

"It's just TV."

"Just fucking tough TV," said Jolene, turning her back on me. "We're not only doing two characters now, but we're adding more video. It's complex. We worked on this stuff most of the night." She leaned across the console and pushed a button on the intercom. "How's it coming?"

Gelder's voice came up on a speaker. "Waiting on you."

Jolene looked around the control room. "Okay. This is a rehearsal. Everybody set?"

Leese ducked into the darkened room and took a seat next to me. "I had some of our people do some work on a new name for the anchor," he said in a loud whisper. " 'Bob' doesn't work. Too light, too trivial. Not trustworthy. So it's going to be John. John Sinclair. Sounds sincere, doesn't it? Sinclair. Sincere. I like that. What do you think?"

Before I could answer, Jolene barked out a series of commands and the central monitor came to life in a rolling countdown. At two, the screen went to black. Then, welling orchestral music underlaid with an urgent mechanical drum beat filled the room. It actually sounded remarkably like the opening theme of a network news show. The first pictures: a brief montage of news shots done in ochre and shades of gray: a tank firing, a tall building burning, a tornado on the horizon. The deep voice of an announcer: "And now, from the Leese Broadcasting Network, John Sinclair with the news you need to know."

With that the montage faded to reveal our new computer-generated anchorman in a dark-blue suit at a mahogany desk looking down as though scanning a sheet of paper. Behind him, a softly focused image of a busy newsroom. In a box over his left shoulder, a network logo: the letters *LBN* in deep blue with a stylized red lightning bolt running through them.

The man looked up—the same intense face from the day before, the dark hair, the masculine jaw line. "Good afternoon. I'm John Sinclair. The first elements of the UN intervention force—led by the brave men and women of America's own Eighty-second Airborne—began arriving at their staging point in central Africa today . . ."

As the man spoke, the screen changed to a shot of a giant military cargo plane touching down on an asphalt runway. A quick cut to the vacant stare of a teenaged African soldier with an automatic rifle casually draped across his shoulders. Another cut to heavily armed American soldiers lining up in formation on the runway as helicopters hovered in the distance throwing up clouds of brown dust amid groves of palm trees.

As I sat there in the control room, I found myself marveling again at the technical magic Gelder was managing to wring from his boxes. I knew I was actually watching a short and not particularly bright weatherman named Iso Bahr making those sounds, reading the news. But for all the world, it was someone else. It was a trusted, experienced journalist who'd been everywhere and seen everything and was now distilling that lifetime for the audience in nuances of expression and tone. It was a face we could all recognize—but couldn't quite place.

". . . first indications of what scientists fear may be a major eruption." The shot changed to show a stream of bright orange and red lava coursing down a rocky mountainside. "Seismologists worry that an increasing number of small tremors around Mount Rainier in the last few days may be a precursor to the big one and are drawing up emergency evacuation plans."

The camera came back to the anchor: "And finally, news of a different sort today from Washington"—the shot changed to a picture of the Capitol dome and tilted down to a group of dark-suited Congressmen gathered on the steps as though for a group photo—"as the Senate leadership moved toward approval of a ban on semiautomatic assault weapons." The picture changed to a shot of a man wearing ear protectors firing an automatic rifle at a paper target on a shooting range. Another shot change tight to the face of a thick-lipped woman wiping tears from her eyes, then a longer sequence of a flower-draped casket being carried by four sober-looking young men in dark suits. "This, as residents of the small Mormon town of Salt Rock, Utah, buried two students killed last week in a hail of gunfire at Salt Rock High. Even long-time gun-ownership advocates are beginning to admit defeat as the shootings in colleges, high schools and primary schools all around the nation continue without any apparent end."

The shot changed back to the anchorman, the LBN logo again over his shoulder. "And that's the news you need to know. I'm John Sinclair. Stay tuned now for *Elvis—Live at Five*."

Jolene called out instructions and the screen went to black.

"Not bad," said Leese, his eyes on the darkened screen.

"Not bad at all," I echoed, watching Leese watch the screen. "Commercials in here, right?"

"Two minutes," said Jolene over her shoulder. "We've cut that down for the rehearsal."

Another stream of instructions from the director and the screen came back to life, this time with the opening sequence to the Elvis show. Again, the announcer's voice: "Ladies and gentlemen, from the Theater of the United States, the Leese Broadcasting Network is pleased and proud to present . . . *Elvis Live at Five!*

"Applause goes in here," said Jolene.

Elvis gestured with his arm to settle down the imaginary crowd. "Hello out there, ladies and gentlemen. It's a pleasure to see you all here again, you good folks here in the studio audience, and you millions and millions of others gathered around the video fireplace in your homes this day. We've got some guests coming on later I think you'll like and appreciate. We've got a few special surprises in the show for you. And we're going to take on a tough subject. You may have heard John Sinclair talking about the Senate, which is ready to put a ban on semiautomatic assault weapons. Well, we're going to talk a lot about that. And we're going to hear from the actual people involved in what can only be called a twenty-first–century tragedy. Our subject today—you just saw it on the news—Salt Rock, Utah, that little Mormon town where those poor kids got killed and where they're being buried today. So stay with us. . . .

"Let's fade to black," said Jolene. The image on the central monitor dropped into darkness and the control room quieted. She swiveled in her chair. "Gentlemen?"

Leese was looking around the room, his eyes doing a quick survey from one face to another. They finally came back to rest on the blackened screen. "I like it," he said quietly. "Gives us currency, topicality." A short pause: "How'd you do all the pictures?"

"The same way we do Elvis," said Jolene. "We added in the other video the same way we'd put it into a newscast at the station. That part's pretty routine."

"The newsroom shot behind the anchor?" said Leese.

"Virtual reality," said Jolene. "The computer builds it."

"The soldiers in Africa?"

"From our library. Tape from a different war in a different place but it worked just fine I think."

"The lava? I didn't know Mount Rainier was erupting?"

"Gelder built that video. We were going to build a tornado, but it's the wrong season."

Build a tornado? I started to ask about that but Leese interrupted me.

"How'd you get the fat woman crying?"

"From network," said Jolene. "The funerals happened today."
Leese rose from his seat, straightening his tie and smoothing his jacket. "How soon can we do this for real?"

"We're ready now."

Leese surveyed the faces in the room again and brought his gaze to rest directly on me. His voice was so low I had to strain to hear it. "Remember the pistol, Mr. Upton? Teddy Roosevelt's pistol?" Leese's tone seemed almost haunted. "I think we have our small tool. Let us put it to work. Now. I want to see our new Mr. Sinclair on the air tomorrow. And let's hit this school-shooting thing so hard that the country can't help but notice. Use our tools." With that he turned his back and walked silently from the room.

I waited until the door had closed and keyed the intercom to Gelder. "You got a minute?"

"Sure."

Gelder was gazing at a computer screen and looked up as I walked in. In the background, Bahr was unhooking himself from the mike and the cameramen were stowing their gear.

"So, nice job, Duncan."

He grinned shyly.

"Let me ask you this. That volcano stuff. Library pictures, something like that?"

"Some stuff I grabbed from a *National Geographic* documentary," he said. "I think it might have been Hawaii."

"Jolene mentioned tornadoes. Said you were going to build one but it was the wrong season."

Gelder nodded helpfully.

"Let me ask you this," I said. "When we first worked together—remember back during the Marilyn days?"

Gelder was still nodding.

"We had that bad tornado? Where'd you get that video?"

Gelder gave me a short glance and looked away. "It's a long time ago. I remember the story but I don't remember the sourcing that well. I think it might have been weather service stuff, something like that."

"You didn't shoot it?"

"Nobody could shoot that. That storm was a killer. I think it was handout stuff from that tornado place in Oklahoma. The Severe Storms Center, I think."

My mind was tumbling with what I was hearing. "Duncan, look at me. You didn't climb up on the water tower and shoot the storm?"

He remained silent.

I glared at him. "But you told me you got those shots."

"I didn't say that. You said that. You made such a big deal out of it that I was embarrassed to say anything."

So I'd been right to suspect it back then. It was fake. But the station had won an Emmy for those pictures. I'd won an Emmy for those pictures. How do you give back an Emmy? Simple answer: you don't. "So you built that video?"

Gelder gave me an uncertain look. "There's some pretty good stuff out there if you know where to look."

I sat back and rubbed my eyes, the face of Margaret Wares washing into my mind. Maybe she knew something I was too dim to see. Whatever he had done, though, it was too late now to fix it. Water under the bridge. Or was it lava under the bridge? Six months before when I suspected there was a problem, I should have fixed it—but I did not. I took the easy path. I should have felt outrage—but I did not. Another easy path taken. Now there was just numbness.

CHAPTER EIGHTEEN

GOOD DAY. I'm John Sinclair. Bad news today from the Pentagon." Sinclair's face was replaced by a shot of soldiers in green camouflage loading a black plastic body bag onto a helicopter. "Three soldiers of the Eighty-second Airborne are dead, killed overnight in the first reported skirmish between UN peacekeeping forces and the insurgent Congolese Democratic Front. No word on enemy casualties." A shot change to the exterior of the White House. "The president and his National Security staff are meeting to formulate their official answer to congressional demands that American troops be pulled out of that zone of conflict."

Inside the Theater of the United States, the audience watched as the shot on the big screen changed to show the inside of a church, the camera tilting down from sunlight streaming through a stained-glass window to a pew of black-clad mourners weeping, then a quick image of a pair of caskets. Sinclair: "Anguish, anger and despair linger in another American town after another school shooting. The place this time, Salt Rock, Utah. Two young people buried over the weekend and finally the government looks set to enact the first real limits on gun ownership." A shot change to the Capitol dome. "The Senate has been in session all day and sources tell LBN News there could be some form of agreement as early as tomorrow outlawing the ownership of semiautomatic weapons."

Back to the anchor's face which was serious, and a little sad. "And that's the news you need to know. I'm John Sinclair. *Elvis Live at Five* is up next. Good day."

A few coughs from the audience as the screen dropped to black but otherwise the room was silent.

In the studio next door, Bahr was almost shouting with adrenaline and excitement. "Hot dog, let's MOVE this thing!" he yelled as technicians picked up the desk he was sitting at when he was John Sinclair and literally hauled it off the set so he could become Elvis. The three cameras around him readjusted their shots.

"Doing great," I said, helping Bahr with the wire leading to his lapel mike. "One segment at a time."

"One minute," said Jolene's cool voice through a speaker.

"Doing great? I am fucking great," said Bahr. "Bring 'em on, bring 'em on."

"One segment at a time, Iso. Salt Rock, Utah. Gun control. Senate taking up a law to ban semiautomatic assault weapons. We think we like this law but we're still not too sure. You okay with that?"

Bahr nodded his head, a manic look in his eyes.

Jolene's clipped command from the speaker: "Forty-five seconds."

"Forty-five seconds," said Bahr. "Yeah!"

I tried steadying him. "Two things to keep in mind. On one side, the right to own and bear arms. Second Amendment. We like it a lot."

Bahr managed to hold still as the makeup woman swabbed sweat from his forehead and upper lip.

"The other side is kids and guns. We don't like dead kids, okay?"

Bahr shook his head. "Like the Second Amendment but don't like dead kids. Got it."

"Thirty seconds."

"Keep it short," I said. "Introduce Salt Rock. Then intro the parents. We've got some good video to lay over that. Gelder fixed up a still of the dead kid so he's playing baseball. We'll cue you in your ear when the video's running. Remember baseball, the kid loved it. Talk about the Senate. Doing the

Lord's work there. Tough issue, gun ownership versus the bad things kids with guns are doing. Got your notes on the parents?"

Bahr nodded.

"And remember that video. There's good stills of the kid on a pony, the kid with a fish. The best stuff's the baseball video."

Bahr nodded again. "Let's do it!"

"Fifteen," said a voice from the loudspeaker.

"I'll be on the cans from the control room," I said, backing out of the shot. "Knock 'em dead."

"And ten, nine . . ."

The sounds of the opening animation rolled as I stepped out of the studio. By the time I'd ducked into the control room, Bahr as Elvis was well into his opening monologue. Clare Leese was already there, his eyes on the monitor, and said nothing as I slipped into my usual seat.

". . . tragedy for a town like this," Elvis was saying. "I know small towns; I grew up in a town so small there wasn't even room for a traffic light. And I know what death can do to a small American town. Kids die in a place like New York or LA, it doesn't make the papers. Kids die in a place like Salt Rock, it touches every single life in that town. We're going to talk about that today. And we're going talk about guns. I imagine that's going to make some of you out there twitch, but it's something we can't ignore anymore. So stay tuned. We're back in a flash."

"Fade it black," said Jolene, "and . . . take commercial." The shot changed smoothly and Jolene eased back in her chair. "Good work everyone. So far." She looked around the room, catching my eye briefly with a glance that was openly questioning. I thought about Margaret Wares and the dinner promise. I needed to make that call.

An associate director read out a time check: forty-five seconds to the end of commercial.

I cued my intercom to Bahr. "You're doing great." On one of the monitors, Bahr glanced briefly into the camera and back down to a sheet of notes. On a monitor next to it, Elvis Presley did exactly the same thing. "So we're going to go about five minutes in this segment," I said. "Let's introduce the parents right at the beginning and let them tell their story. Let it run if you can." Iso-Elvis nodded without looking up.

"Fifteen seconds," said Jolene. "Give 'em the signs."

Over the stage in the theater, applause signs started pulsing on and off and the professionals salted through the audience began clapping and chanting for Elvis. Quickly the whole crowd joined in. Jolene opened the second segment with a medley of shots panning rapidly across the roaring crowd. The roar grew even louder as Elvis appeared on the central monitor.

"My oh my oh my," he was saying, his mouth arching into a large grin and his eyes wide with surprise. "You are a good group of people today." At that the audience seemed to explode, and Jolene brought the cameras back onto the faces, lingering briefly on one particularly good shot of a youngish woman with a baby in her arms weeping in exaltation. She was one of ours. Jolene took the shot wide to show the whole audience. The room was beginning to feel like a church revival meeting, and Jolene let the cameras play for a few more seconds before she brought the shot back to Elvis.

". . . okay, okay," he was saying, his hands out flat in front of him as he worked to bring the crowd under control. "Oh, you are a good audience, but we have to get on with things." Slowly the clapping subsided. "So I need your help today. We need to get serious here for a few minutes. There are some things out there stalking the land that we have to stop. And I'm going to need your help."

"You got it, Elvis!" someone yelled, and Jolene called a quick shot change to catch a middle-aged man in a brown sports coat standing and waving. He was also one of ours.

"Thank you, thank you," said Elvis. "And I surely appreciate that. You've all heard about the tragic school shooting in that little town of Utah. John Sinclair just had it on the news didn't he? Those sad pictures of the people in that church? Those small coffins? Purely an American tragedy." A shot change to show the audience watching and listening intently, and back to Elvis. "Our hearts go out to those folks. I wish I could be there myself in this hour of need. But I can't. So I've done the next best thing. I've brought them here. Ladies and gentlemen, I'd like you to meet face to face and in person as only we can do here on this broadcast where life doesn't get any more genuine, I'd like you to meet the parents of one of those little kids so brutally shot down last week. Ladies and gentlemen, a big Elvis welcome for Jane and Collin Dufour, all the way here from Salt Rock, Utah."

With that the audience erupted in emotional applause, standing almost as one as a man and woman were led onto the stage by a striking brunette in a black gown. The couple slowed briefly to take the applause, and the woman led them to a sofa arranged so it faced both the audience and the central screen.

"Jane and Collin," said Elvis as the applause died down and the audience took their seats again. "Jane and Collin. I am so proud to have you here."

Jolene called a shot change and the screen filled with the face of the man—he had the lined leathery skin of someone who worked outdoors, gray hollow eyes, a slight quiver to a weak chin. Another change and the face of the woman appeared—plain, a little overweight, thin brown hair, the same hollowness around the eyes. Both faces were turned slightly up toward the monitor to watch Elvis, creating almost incidentally a feeling of supplication.

"Jane and Collin. We flew you here today so we could help, so we could find out personally from you what we could do to ease the pain." Elvis turned to the audience. "Their son Charlie was twelve years old"—the screen abruptly changed to a still photo of a young boy in a straw cowboy hat sitting on a brown pony—"he loved his little horse, Oscar"—another picture, this time of the boy in blue jeans and a T-shirt grinning broadly as he held a fish up in his hand—"he loved to go fishing with his dad"—a shot change to the home video Gelder created—"Geldered," we were calling it—from a still photo. The boy standing at home plate, the baseball comes in from the right and he hits it and runs toward first base, the camera following him as he tags the base and jumps into the air with his hands out in triumph, and the camera swings around to see his mother jumping in the air as well—"young Charlie loved to play baseball, he was darned good." The screen changed back to Elvis. "And Charlie was shot to death last Wednesday as he sat in a school lunch room with his friends eating a baloney sandwich his mother had made him that morning. Ladies and gentlemen, please, a moment of silence as we think about this tragedy and bring it into our hearts."

Elvis looked down as though in prayer. The cameras panned across the audience, locking onto one well-dressed woman who actually was in prayer, her head bowed and her hands folded.

"Nice," said Leese. "Ours?"

"Not one of ours," said Jolene without turning.

"Okay," said Elvis, looking back up to the camera and, in effect, back to the audience. "Jane and Collin. Jane and Collin." His voice was low, his gestures subdued. "I said earlier we brought you here to see what we could do to help you through the pain. That's our job here today. That's why you're here. Jane, let's start with you. First off, a question we have to ask. You've lost a son in a brutal and violent way. How does it feel?"

One of the stage cameras had moved in close to the couple. Its shot framed the woman from just below her mouth to the top of her eyebrows. The audience had fallen profoundly quiet, some watching the stage, others watching the small monitors along the side of the hall that showed what the camera was seeing.

The woman seemed to be trying to collect herself. She took a couple of long, measured breaths and squared her shoulders. "My husband and me are both honored you'd have us here, Mr. Presley," she said in a voice that was unexpectedly high and nasal. Elvis nodded from his screen and the woman continued. "The past week's been a blur, I guess you could say. The shooting, the call from the police"—the emphasis hit the first syllable, so the word came out POlice—"then the TV people started coming. My God, there was a lot of TV people. We had 'em all over the front yard, and that's not a very big place." She looked around at the audience and back at Elvis. "I don't know. I mean, I guess . . ." She faltered but Elvis stayed quiet. After a moment she started in again. "I guess it's the emptiness that's the worst thing. His little spot at the dinner table. The other kids have been good about it, but I know it's rough on them."

"How many kids do you have?"

"Three kids, Elvis."

Next to her, her husband silently held up two fingers.

The woman looked at his hand and stifled a sob. "Two, we have two children now."

Elvis let the silence play for an extra beat. "Two children—now," he said, repeating the obvious for the audience. "A week ago, Jane and Collin set three places around their dinner table for their three little kids. Tonight they're setting two, and there'll never be a third for the rest of their lives." Elvis swung his gaze back down to his left, as though looking back at the couple. "Collin, tell us about you. What kind of work do you do?"

The tight shot again, trembling chin to hollow gray eyes. The man ran his tongue around the inside of his lips and swallowed. "Mostly an auto mechanic, but times ain't really been great lately."

"You're out of work?"

The man nodded. "For about a year now."

"Your wife works?" A camera change to the woman from the chest up.

"Yes, sir. Down at Rose Buds."

"Rose Buds?" said Elvis.

The camera came back to the man. "Yes, sir. It's a flower shop in town."

"So you're raising a family—kids in school—on what your wife makes down at the flower shop?"

The man nodded. "That, and what the church helps out with."

"The church helps?"

"Food and clothes. Help like that. And there was some employment insurance from the state but that's petered out."

"And two little mouths to feed?"

The man nodded silently, his head bowed toward his knitted hands.

Elvis turned to the audience. "We're back in sixty with Jane and Collin. Don't move."

I was watching Bahr in the cuing monitor and hit the intercom as soon as the commercial rolled. "It's good, it's real good. Now let's get on to the gun control thing." He is good, I thought silently to myself. Who'd have thought it?

"Which direction?" said Bahr. "We for it or against it?"

Leese looked at me and glanced uncertainly at the intercom. "May I?"

"Of course. Hit this button and you're talking to Bahr."

Leese hit the switch. "Iso, can you hear me? It's Clare Leese. Can you hear me?"

Bahr glanced up at the camera. "I hear you, Mr. Leese,"

"Son, you're doing a great job in there. A great job."

"Thirty seconds," said Jolene from the front of the room.

"I think we should stay off gun control," said Leese. "I think you've hit a gold mine here on the money thing. Out of work. Wife working in a flower shop. Hungry kids. Church helping. That's very good."

"Fifteen seconds."

"So here's what you do. Get them to talk about how hard life is and start an appeal. Call it the Charlie Dufour Memorial Fund or something like that, care of this network. Let's see who's watching out there."

". . . and three, two, one."

Applause up and down. The crowd now heavily with Elvis. The couple a little more relaxed. Bahr-Elvis quickly to the point.

"I guess before this show we knew you were in tough times. But until now we didn't know just how tough times could be. Now we do. Out of work, living on charity from the church and what Jane there can make working in a flower shop. Four mouths to feed and a twelve-year-old son brutally shot down by a madman. Can the Lord be more testing?" Elvis paused to let the question sink in.

"So before we get too far gone here—and the clock is running down on us—we think maybe we can help. But we need to know a bit more so we can figure out just how much we need to help. Jane, you work at the Rose Bud flower shop in Salt Rock. This is a personal question but I need to ask it. How much money do you make?"

The woman looked at the image of Elvis on the screen, then glanced uncertainly toward her husband. He shrugged, as though to say answering it was her choice. She looked back at the screen. "Well, Elvis, I make about a hundred and twenty a week."

"A hundred and twenty a week? Dollars? A hundred and twenty dollars a week?"

The woman nodded.

"So it's part-time work?"

The woman looked uncertainly at the screen and shook her head. "No, Elvis, that's five days a week. And sometimes I help out on Saturday as well. That's their busy day. People off work and everything and getting ready for Sunday and all."

Elvis looked down at his own hands. "I need to do some figuring here. You work six days a week and make a hundred and twenty dollars. That tells me you're making twenty dollars a day. That sound about right?"

The woman nodded helpfully.

"So you're getting paid about two and a half dollars an hour."

Another encouraging nod.

"But that's not even half the minimum wage," said Elvis. "What they're paying you isn't legal."

"Well, that's all right," said the woman, her voice uncertain and a little worried. "They told me when they hired me it was the best they could do. It's a small shop and such and they just can't pay any more."

"But they're breaking the law."

"Please, Elvis. I need the work."

"I understand," said Elvis in a voice that said he understood far too well that the poor woman was being badly used. "So tell us about your expenses. You're making about a hundred twenty a week. That would be four hundred and eighty a month. From that, you pay what? Rent, food, clothing?"

The woman nodding again. "There's the rent. That's the biggest slice. Then food. We get quite a few clothes from the church. There's nothing left at the end but we're getting through."

In the control room, Jolene cued up the Geldered video of the slain boy.

Back on the set, Elvis was looking at the couple. "You add that all up, it's a tough life. Collin is out of work. The shop where Jane works is engaging in illegal slave labor—there's no other word for it—and they're trying to feed and clothe a family of five—well, a family of four now. And they're trying in all this to come to terms with the brutal murder of their little boy."

I hit the intercom to Bahr. "Video of the kid."

Elvis turned from the couple to look head on into the camera. The shot faded from his face to the video of the boy—Charlie in slow motion this time hitting the baseball and running for his life toward first base. Under the pictures, Elvis's voice was low and troubled.

"I need to talk directly to you good people here in the studio audience, and to the millions watching at home this afternoon. This is an American tragedy. If you have any doubt about that, just let your minds play over what these people have gone through, what they're going through. Their boy Charlie dead in a public school that was supposed to be a place of study and joy, and sanctuary. Shot down by a madman, the blood of his little heart pumping onto the cold gray cement of a school cafeteria floor. And this good family struggling not only with their grief—and it's a grief I don't think either you or I have any way of comprehending—struggling not only with their grief, but with the everyday struggle of keeping themselves fed and under a roof."

The video ended and Elvis peered intently out from the screen. "One reason this country is a great country is we don't sit idly by and watch. We do things for people. People are down, we give them a hand up. People are hurt, we bandage them up. People are hungry, we feed them. Jane and Collin Dufour and their two surviving children are down, hurt and hungry. So starting today, I'm announcing the Charlie Dufour Memorial Fund and kicking it off with a ten-thousand-dollar check from my own account. You want to help—you want to be a true American—you contribute to that fund. This isn't fancy. It's not a come-on for something else. It's to help the Dufour family of Salt Rock, Utah. You got fifty cents, send it along. I don't care what it is, but let's help this family. You call in here to this program with whatever it is you can spare, and I guarantee every cent of it will go to Jane and Collin Dufour and their two surviving children."

Elvis turned his gaze back down to his left. "Jane, Collin, bless you. Bless you for having the courage to come here and share your tragic tale with us. Bless you for your bravery and your honesty. Bless you in your grief. And if the Lord's willing, better times are coming."

The camera switched to a tight shot of the woman's face. Below eyes streaming with tears, her trembling lips mouthed the words, "Bless you, Elvis."

Chapter Nineteen

As I looked around the conference room, it was obvious it was far too early for business, and everybody was dead tired. Jolene in baggy sweats had pulled her hair into a tight pony-tail. Eight in the morning indoors in a windowless room and she was hiding behind sunglasses and mainlining black coffee from a Styrofoam cup.

Gelder sat as though in a daze, his arms akimbo on his belly, his legs splayed beneath the table and his eyes locked on a wall monitor that was soundlessly playing a morning car-toon show. Only Iso Bahr seemed lively. He'd dressed carefully in a dark wool suit with an expensive yellow tie that made him look like a cross between a politician and a salesman.

The door opened and Clare Leese in his ever-present gray suit walked briskly in and took the chair at the head of the table where he opened a thin briefcase and pulled out a sheet of paper. His manner was that of a college professor getting ready for a lecture class.

"My apologies for the early call," he said, with no hint of apology in his voice. "I thought we should meet early to go over a few things." He paused to scan the paper. "Our people on the coast did the overnight numbers on the new format." He pushed the paper into the center of the table. "Good. Not great. But good. A six share. Respectable."

Leese pulled another piece of paper from his briefcase. "I called the switchboard early. I imagine you know this, but after the dead-kid show ran yesterday, we had to bring in more staff to answer the phones. Are you ready for some numbers?" Leese looked around the table with a slight, almost pixie grin twisting his lips. "By sixty-thirty this morning we'd gotten"—he looked down at the paper—"nine thousand three hundred and ninety-three phone calls." He looked back up. "Nine thousand three hundred and ninety-three phone calls. Imagine it. All for a dead kid." Leese was actually smiling. "And pledges of more than four hundred thousand dollars." Leese's words started coming even faster than usual. "Nearly ten thousand phone calls, nearly a half-million dollars. From one show." His voice was rising. "From one television show. A show with a pallid six share. Ten thousand phone calls from a six share. A half-million dollars. Ladies and gentlemen, I think our new format has given us a place to stand."

Silence dropped over the room as Leese retrieved the papers from the center of the table and returned them carefully to his briefcase. Adjusting his tie, he cleared his throat in a solemn way. "We're getting there. Not to sound too cynical, but we need more dead kids. You know what I mean by that. I don't wish ill on anyone in the world. But we need the compelling issue, the story that tears at people's hearts. We're perfectly placed for that sort of television. Give me a grieving mother and I'll give you another share rating. Give me the stuff of human life—tragedies, hate, love—and I can give this country television people will watch."

Another long silence as Leese looked from person to person around the room, as though to emphasize and underline the words he'd spoken.

Finally, he seemed to loosen a little. "I realize it's early. Everyone's been working hard. But it's paying off. Any questions before we move on?"

A quick darting of looks around the table and it was Bahr who spoke up. "A question about revenues?"

Leese nodded him on.

"Well, I guess we're all curious to know how the show's doing with advertising. We've been on for a while now, and we figured maybe you'd have an idea now that the organization and overhead's in place."

Leese cleared his throat again. "To be honest with you, it's not been great yet. We're above the break-even point but barely. I've been supporting it out of my own pocket." He paused and looked around the room from tired face to tired face. "I appreciate how hard we've been riding this horse." A thin smile. "And I don't want it to fall down. So check out your pay packets this week. I think you'll be pleased. I'm the kind of man who rewards hard work." Faces brightened quickly at that and at least some of the fatigue was forgotten. "More questions?"

Silence this time around the table.

"Fair enough. So, Mr. Upton. What do we have for the rest of the week?"

"Dead Boy day two today. We have his teacher and his baseball coach. Duncan's been Geldering more home video."

Leese was nodding. "Excellent."

"And we have a satellite link to the NRA convention in Las Vegas where one of their flacks is going to defend gun sales."

Leese pursed his lips. "Let's go easy on that. We need to be careful not to anger either side in the gun-control debate. Show us the blood and the tears and leave the opinions to others."

"It's a strong point of view," I said defensively.

"The wrong point of view," Bahr interjected from across the table then quickly looked to Leese for approval.

"Mr. Bahr's right," said Leese. "With a six share, we can't afford to alienate anyone. Give me a twenty share and we can start getting people angry."

"I think you're right," said Jolene, the first words she'd spoken. "A satellite head doesn't give us much. We need people on the stage, in front of the audience. And we need good pictures. Tell a good story well and use great pictures."

"Lose the NRA," said Leese.

"Fine," I said, privately furious that Bahr had jumped in with an opinion expressly designed to suck up to Leese—and that Jolene had taken Bahr's side.

"The rest of the week?" said Leese.

"Not there yet," I said. "We were looking at a cult story but I think it's going away."

"Cult story?"

I shrugged. "Bickens, Brickens, someplace like that. I think it's Nebraska. Looked pretty good at first. Dead kid. Young—ten, eleven, something like that. Looked like a cult did it. Now the police say suicide."

"Too bad," said Leese. "Nothing else there?"

"Not much. Cult seems pretty harmless—meditation, gurus, things like that."

"And no link between the kid and the cult?"

"Nothing."

"Find something better," said Leese, shooting up his cuff to check his watch. "I have another meeting but before I go, there's something I want to say." With that, Leese stood and briefly turned his back on the room. When he swiveled around to face us again, the expression on his face had hardened. "Those early reviews were right," he said. "Who needs another afternoon talk show? Who, indeed? So we have to be different." Leese approached the table and placed his hands on it, palms downward, fingers splayed out. "A quick analysis, if you don't mind—what they have and what we have. They have a famous host who gets up in front of an audience and talks about issues, interviews stars, talks to the common man. As Mr. Gelder pointed out a few days ago, their issues are general. Another way of saying that is they're stale. Now we have essentially the same kind of show. A famous host, an audience, famous people to interview. Now, though, we have currency. John Sinclair is a stroke of brilliance. Today's issues today. That sets us apart. Makes us different. I want to hit that hard. Questions?"

He looked around the room. We were all silent.

"We also have the technology," said Leese, "to be even more current. Let's make the technology work for us. The way we did with the dead kid and the baseball game. That was genius. That baseball game didn't exist before Mr. Gelder here got his hands on it—before he Geldered it." Leese smiled thinly at the word. "I like that expression. Geldered it. I like that very much. I want more of that. And I tell you, we can focus this country. If Sinclair says it's news, it's news. When Elvis says it's important, it's important—and we give them the pictures to show them why." Leese paused and looked from face to face around the table. "From now on, we don't follow someone else's agenda, we set our own."

But there was no agenda midafternoon when all hell broke loose.

We were well into the show, with Elvis interviewing a thirty-something man with a blond crewcut who had coached the young Charlie Dufour in Utah.

From the rear of the control room, I was studying faces in the audience, trying to figure out why some could show so much emotion while others were blank slates. It was a good crowd, not as good as the day before when something like a tent-revival mood had swept over them, but still a good crowd. And now they were very much with Elvis as the coach talked about the little boy.

The monitors around the room were repeating over and over the one good Gelder-manufactured string of video of the boy hitting the baseball and running to first, his mother jumping to her feet. Gelder had improved on his own work by amplifying the roar of the crowd and adding a good loud smack when the boy hit the ball.

At first I thought the popping noise was Gelder's sound effects and I didn't pay attention. But it came again, and again. It was no baseball game.

"Somebody's shooting!" said Jolene coming out of her chair.

I jumped to my feet, peering frantically at the monitors.

"All cameras! All cameras!"—Jolene's voice was loud but commanding, under control—"find the shooter, find the shooter!" A flurry of camera moves, then Jolene's voice again. "Rear hall, to the left."

On the monitors, people were screaming and diving into the aisles, some clambering up and over seats as they dodged the gunfire. On the set, the baseball coach had jumped over the back of the couch. Elvis was looking out from the big screen confused. In the background, a couple of pops from the gun and more screams. Almost at the same time, one camera found him, and then two more cameras came in on him—a dark-haired man in glasses, his arm stretched out toward the front of the theater, in his hand a small black pistol. Even as the first camera zoomed in, the man calmly squeezed off a shot and the glass across the Elvis monitor shattered and cascaded onto the stage.

"Camera one, stay tight on that man," ordered Jolene. "Camera two go wide. Three give me a shot of the stage. Now!"

I glanced at the three camera monitors as I bolted toward the theater.

I had to fight my way through a stream of pushing and elbowing hysteria to get through the main doors. Inside, what was left of the audience was lying flat below seat level. The screaming had stopped, replaced by low sobbing. The only figures visible were the three cameramen and the lone shooter. I was peripherally aware of one of the cameras swinging onto me as I made my way into the room. The shooter followed the motion and turned toward me, the pistol almost casually coming around to point in my direction.

I felt my head grow light and wondered blankly if I was about to die. I instantly regretted everything—the show, Elvis, my career, television, the man with gun, and more than all of that, my own stupidity at barging into the theater as though I might be able to do something about a maniac with a gun. I flicked a glance toward the first row of seats, one part of my mind calculating the odds of successfully diving for cover, the other part trying to think of something, anything, to do next.

"Put down the gun." I heard myself say it and wondered where the words had come from. "Put it down now."

The man looked at me for a long instant, then let the gun twirl on his fingers and drop to the floor. A dull thud reverberated through the studio as the steel hit the concrete. "It's empty," said the man mildly as he put his hands into the air in surrender.

A swarm of uniformed security guards flooded into the theater and roughly grabbed the man and bent him over, handcuffing his arms behind him. Even as people started rising cautiously from behind the seats, a pair of technicians was wheeling a new monitor onto the stage.

The guards hustled the man up the center aisle toward the exit. As he passed, he nodded and gave me a shallow smile. A few minutes later, the new monitor in the center of the stage came to life with the form of Elvis.

"It's all right, it's all right," he was saying soothingly. "Is anyone out there hurt?"

Cameras panned back and forth across the audience. Many people had a dazed look on their faces. Some were still sobbing. A couple in the center of the theater close to where the gunman had been were holding each other in a tight embrace.

"Police are on the way," Elvis was saying. "Everything's fine. If you'll just stay where you are, we have first aid on the way. Is anyone out there hurt?"

I turned from the theater and made my way slowly back toward the control room. The first cops to arrive were pushing through the lobby, guns drawn. Behind them I could hear the wail of an ambulance siren.

Inside the control room, Jolene was still calling camera shots.

I cued the intercom to Bahr. "Wrap it," I said quietly.

On the central screen, Elvis was speaking calmly and soothingly to the audience. On my words, he paused for a second, and took the camera in with a long, intense look. "So ladies and gentlemen, another day on the front lines of America. A man with a gun. Shots fired. How many times have we heard that? Too many, I'm afraid. But we're okay here. As far as I can tell, no one was hurt. Scared, yes, but no one hurt. The fellow with the gun is under arrest. And . . . well, I guess . . . what can I say. We'll see you here tomorrow, same time, same place. I'm Elvis Presley. So long."

"Roll it," snapped Jolene and the closing sequence of Elvis stills came on over the sounds of "Heartbreak Hotel." "And—credits."

I sat back in my chair, feeling the adrenaline beginning to ebb from my bloodstream. My legs felt like rubber bands and my hands were shaking badly.

Jolene was counting down from ten. "And—fade to black." She watched the monitor drop into black and, like me, leaned back in her chair. She took her headset off and wiped her forehead with the palm of her hand. "Tough show," she said quietly. "Fuck me but that was a tough show."

CHAPTER TWENTY

I THINK if anyone is a hero of this story today, it's Mr. Upton here." Leese turned toward me. "Maybe you have a few words to say?"

I cleared my throat and looked at the sea of lenses pressed like a football scrum into one of the theater's VIP guest rooms—and now all pointing toward me. It seemed like every camera in Dallas had been called out to the news conference. Our own station had three and was covering it live. I'd spotted crews from all the networks and an unfamiliar satellite truck that I suspected was feeding the event live into a national cable-news broadcast. Big time. Bigger time than I'd ever experienced.

I cleared my throat again nervously—I'd never been on this side of the camera. "I guess I just did what I had to," I heard myself saying. "I didn't really think about it. It just sort of happened. And it turned out the pistol was empty so it wasn't actually that big a deal." I didn't tell them I'd almost messed my pants when the gunman turned toward me in the theater. I didn't tell them that I had spent most of my time trying to find a place to hide, even when my mouth was telling the man to put the gun down. I didn't tell them how much I regretted pretty much everything in the world as that small pistol took a bead on my head. So much not to talk about.

A surge of shouted questions, some repeated twice, as reporters tried verbally to shove their competitors aside. Leese took control. "The young lady there," he said, pointing. "Yes, you."

"Has the gunman been identified?"

"You'll have to talk to the police on that."

More shouts, but the woman got another question out, this one about motive.

"Motive?" said Leese, gesturing to quiet the crowd. "I don't know if madmen have motives. He hated Elvis, that's pretty apparent. The police said he was talking about some sort of vengeance, but I don't know what he was avenging." I gave Leese a hooded sideways look: I hadn't heard anything about that.

The comment drew an excited surge from the herd and they charged in the new direction. Leese quieted them again. "I don't know what he was talking about. I just don't know. Something that happened to him in Missouri or Montana or someplace like that—you'll have to figure that out on your own. I don't think he said much more about it, and it's not clear to me at all what the connection is. You'll need to talk to the police about that."

"Security?" yelled a reporter.

"Obviously not good enough," said Leese. "We'll be changing that and implementing new security measures with tomorrow's show. I would like to go on record right now guaranteeing the security, absolutely guaranteeing the security of all guests to the Elvis show. This will not happen again, you have Clare Leese's word on it and you can take that to the bank. Now I think that's enough for today. It's been a full day and we have a lot of work to do. I promise I'll keep you informed. And either I or Mr. Upton here will be available whenever and wherever you need us if there are more developments on this."

"Can we talk to Elvis?" shouted a reporter.

Leese turned back toward the cameras. "This has been tough on him. We'll talk to him and let you know. Now that's it for today." With that he waved at the cameras and the two of us walked from the room amid a barrage of shouted questions and jostling cameras. Outside the door, Leese whispered: "My house. I'll send a car for you. Seven o'clock."

I stopped and watched Leese disappear down the hall, a

retinue of reporters dogging his heels. I realized dinner with Margaret would have to wait. It was the first time I'd ever been summoned to Leese's actual home, and it was an invitation I couldn't ignore.

"POUR YOU an apple juice?" Leese said as he escorted me into the large living room. A servant heard the comment and disappeared into another part of the sprawling house.

"Arrange yourself however," ordered the small man as he took a seat in a rocking chair at a large limestone-fronted fireplace.

Where Leese's office at the theater was filled with all sorts of art and curiosities, this room was austerely barren. Unadorned gray-white walls, a marble floor with a few Oriental rugs and a scattering of expensive but simple furniture. The only item that showed a human touch was a red-sandstone Indian peace pipe about two feet long on the fireplace mantel highlighted by small spotlights recessed into the ceiling. Otherwise the room seemed as lifeless as a hotel lobby. Beyond the floor-to-ceiling windows, an acre or more of carefully tended lawn and gardens was beginning to slip into darkness with the approaching evening.

Leese leaned back in the rocker and cupped his head in his webbed hands, watching the fire for a moment before turning in my direction. "What'd you think of today's show?"

The question took me by surprise. With everything that had happened, I'd hardly considered it a show at all. More like an on-air disaster, like a *Titanic* sinking or a shuttle exploding with cameras rolling. I said as much to Leese.

The small man smiled largely at that and gave off a sound from his throat that was very close to a chuckle. "Oh, but it was a show," said Leese. "Probably the best we've done yet. I want to run it again tomorrow."

"Again?" It was the last thing I had expected.

"We'll run it again," said Leese. "I want you to get in there and Gelder the bejesus out of it and do a minute-by-minute analysis of what happened. That girl director is pretty damned good. She got the whole thing on tape. The whole thing."

The servant entered silently and put down two frosted glasses of apple juice. Leese nodded him away and took a small sip and set the glass back down.

"So we run it again," said Leese. "Not the whole thing, of course, but the good parts. Start off with John Sinclair doing a news piece on it. Then show the man shooting, the audience scrambling down on their bellies, the shot where he takes out the Elvis screen. You walking into the room like the Lone Ranger. Him dropping the gun to the floor and putting his arms up. That's good television. You can do that?"

I nodded. We'd have to work most of the night, but we could do that.

"Some good things have happened," said Leese, his voice taking on a more contemplative air. "The news conference today. It ran live on two national cable-news outlets. I watched NBC and ABC tonight. Both did stories on it. Used some of the actual footage. CBS mentioned it but it wasn't a piece. It was shorter."

"A VO," I said. "Voice-over."

"Right, a VO. But we were there, on the big three. You can't buy that kind of advertising. And tomorrow I'm on all three morning shows. Early—six o'clock. But we're on all three big ones. That, my young friend, is exposure. I'll bet you this time next week our numbers are doubled." Leese took another sip of his apple juice and seemed to savor the taste. "So there's something I wanted to talk to you about. Privately. I realized that when I mentioned motive at the news conference. You looked startled."

"I hadn't heard anything about that."

"I'm sure you hadn't." Leese's voice had dropped to a whisper and I found myself craning toward him to hear. "One other person knows this," he said and then paused and looked away, apparently lost in thought. Finally he brought his gaze back around to me. "We've worked together what? Six, eight months?"

"About ten, actually."

"And it's been a good ten months, right? I mean, you've made some money. I recall that first bonus check I gave you. I trust you've spent it well?" Leese smiled at his own question and continued. "Mr. Bahr asked this morning about the revenues. I'm afraid I misled him. He's too greedy for his own good. The fact is very large amounts of money are now beginning to roll with this show. By next week they'll be huge. You're still interested in money, I trust?"

I nodded, but warily. Leese was up to something and I had no idea what.

"That's good. Because I think in the coming days and weeks we'll all be earning it. Today, for instance. Today was an expensive day."

"I'm sure it was."

"My young friend, I'm afraid you don't know the half of it. I need to ask you right now for your word. I need your word that what is said in this room will never leave it. Do I have that?"

Promises are easy. I nodded.

Leese shook his head. "No, I'm afraid I can't allow it to be that casual. Where I come from, you're either with me or against me. Before this conversation continues, I need to know which it is. If you're with me, I have your sacred word, and some challenging new horizons will begin to open for you. If you're against me, we shake hands like a couple of businessmen and you go down the road and don't look back at either me, or LBN or Elvis—or those new horizons. I'm afraid this is a powerfully real moment."

Though I didn't know where he might be leading, there wasn't actually much to weigh. Clare Leese had been good for my career—and my bank account. Very good. I was well on the way to being wealthy. The thousand-dollar dinners, the first-class treatment. Life lived large. I'd acquired the taste. And it wasn't like I had a whole theaterful of options screaming at me to go somewhere else and make a similar wad of money. I looked across at Leese and held his gaze. "I'm with you."

"Excellent," said Leese. "Today's event wasn't accidental."

It's funny how you can hear a stream of words, hear them as a sentence, and each individual word seems logical, but the sentence itself doesn't add up, doesn't produce any meaning, almost as though it is gibberish. That was my first reaction. Gibberish. Then my mind played the words back again and the brain brought them into a sequence, and it was suddenly as if the room I was sitting in had leaned to the left. Wasn't accidental. Accidental what?

A half-smile had formed on Leese's mouth. "The fellow's an oil worker from east Texas. Our families go way back. He's one of my trusted people."

"One of yours?" I said, dully, the full weight of Leese's words beginning to register.

"One of mine. The gun is untraceable, as is the man. Notice no one was injured. I made sure of that. We won't press charges and he'll be out in a week or so. I have good friends at the police station and in the courts. Very good friends. Marital problems, his wife ran away—which happens to be true. Snapped under the pressure. What do you think?"

What do I think? I didn't know what to think. "You staged the shooting?"

Leese looked pleased with himself. "A shooting that pushed this little show into the headlines. Everybody in America's talking about us. We'll be able to ride this like a strong horse for days and days. What do you think?"

I sat there staring at my small host—my host and boss, the man who signed my paychecks, who controlled a large chunk of my life. What did I think? That faking something like that ran counter to everything I'd ever been taught—everything that I'd come to stand for along the way. What did I think?

That a lie is a lie and sooner or later the truth will come out. It always does. And when that happened the liars would be discredited. Maybe I'd gotten it wrong when I thought the man with the gun was the maniac. What did I think? Before I could speak, Leese answered for me.

"It's almost as though the words are floating out over your head. I can read it in your eyes, in the stiffness of your body, the tightness of your mouth. You don't like it. It's not honest, not real. That's what you're thinking, isn't it? You're wondering about me, aren't you?" He took another delicate drink of his apple juice. "And I've offended your precious sensibilities, haven't I? Your newsman's sensibilities?"

I didn't say anything.

"I suspected as much. Well Dorothy, this isn't Kansas, and Mr. Upton, this isn't the news business." He paused to make room for a response but I didn't say anything.

"Let me ask you something," he said. "You didn't seem particularly upset with the dead kid when we took a photograph and brought it to life. In fact, I think it was your idea. But now you're upset with this when all we did was bring an idea to life. What's the difference?"

I was silent for a few moments, my eyes on the red peace pipe, my mind whirling through the day's events as I put my answer together. "There's a fundamental difference," I said at length, choosing my words carefully. "We were just sweetening the kid. He loved baseball—we all knew that—and we improved the pictures to illustrate that, to make the point. We took what was real and made it easier to see. We didn't change the reality. You can't change reality."

Leese smiled. "You make me laugh, Mr. Upton, you honestly make me laugh. Reminds me of Churchill's old joke about the man offering money to a woman if she'll go to bed with him. You've heard it? She won't do it for a hundred, won't do it for a thousand but warms up to the idea when he gets to a million. The fellow says now that we've established you're a whore, let's get down to bargaining. That's you, I'm afraid."

"It's apples and oranges."

"It's not," said Leese, the humor draining from his eyes. "We Geldered the dead-kid tape to prove a point—that he loved baseball. We brought on a guy with a gun to prove a point—that there are a lot of guys with guns. It's the same thing—we elbowed the truth around a little to prove a higher truth.

"I'll tell you the kind of business you're now in, Nick. You need to know this if we're to continue working together—and I want that very much. It's called show business. Our job is to package the emotions of human existence and sell it. That's what we do. And you know why I chose you? Why you're good at it? I'll tell you. It's because it's the same thing you've been doing all your life. Oh, I see you're surprised at that—you think I'm wrong. I'm not. You've been in the same business all your life. You happen to call it news, but it's almost the same thing. We're just taking it a little bit further, that's all. We're not pretending it's anything more than what it is—it's show biz. That there might be some manipulation involved doesn't hurt anybody—it's harmless, and it's entertaining. And entertainment sells. It really sells. The phones are melting this afternoon. Seems like everybody wants a chunk of us now. Everybody. People who wouldn't be bothered to answer our calls yesterday are today our new best friends. We're hot. What do you think about that?"

That question again. The first thing I thought was I wished he would stop asking me what I thought. I didn't know what I thought. A large part of me was repelled by the idea of staging the shooting. It was a sick trick. And he was right: it ran counter to everything I'd learned, everything I'd come to stand for. My line of work had been to report reality. To package it, yes—but it was still reality, it was still the truth. At the same time, though, another part of me was fascinated by the genius of what Leese had done. In one brilliantly conceived maneuver, Leese had put Elvis on the national map. It was almost unbelievable in its sheer audacity—if no one found out. And if I thought on it hard, I'd have to admit that the step from my previous life to this wasn't a big one. It was all a matter of degree.

As I sat there with the apple juice warming in the reflection of the fireplace, it occurred to me that Leese had brought me to a fork in the road where I had to make a fundamental decision. One path led back the way I had come: newsrooms, anemic paychecks, tedium, wrong choices, pallbearers. Pallbearers. Was what I had been doing all that noble? People had gotten hurt. People had died. Because of me and my grand pursuit of the truth. I looked into the fireplace and a wall of flames was climbing up a dry canyon, and a young woman with a beautiful mouth was laughing and calling me a dickhead.

I pulled my gaze away and looked at Leese. The other path was uncertain. I didn't know what lay along that road—and I decided sitting there that I didn't care. As long as I knew what it was, knew what to call it, I could do it. I couldn't stand to go back the way I'd come. "We'll do a good show," I said quietly.

Leese's face was serious. "I hoped you might say that." He pulled a slip of paper from his inside breast pocket and held it out. "For services rendered, for services to come."

I looked at the paper. A check, with my name on it, for $150,000. This time, I wasn't surprised, nor did I do a clumsy jig or pump my fist in the air. I simply folded the check in half and tucked it into my pocket. "Thank you."

"And thank you, Mr. Upton. Consider that a down payment for great ideas. I need you with me to make this work. Let's do this right tomorrow. I think it can be very good."

And the show the next afternoon was very good. We worked through the night, isolating on the tape the second-by-second movements of the man with the gun, Geldering it into a seamless video choreography of terror. The first screams of the audience, confused and frightened eyes, the off-camera pops, the cameras swinging wildly through the chaos and locking on to the shooter. One camera going close in on his face. Another staying wide showing his whole body, his arm out, the pistol doing a slow circuit of the room. A tight closeup of the gun firing—we didn't have that from the original shooting but Gelder found a scene from a television cop show that worked seamlessly. We laid in a medium-wide angle of the Elvis monitor as it shattered to the floor. Back to the shooter's face as he smiled with the shot. Me standing in the doorway. *Put the gun down.* My voice steady. My eyes locked on the shooter. *Put it down.* In tight on the gunman as the gun slowly swirled on his finger and dropped. The loud metallic thunk as it hit the floor. Tight again as his arms came into the air. *It's empty.*

We went back into the tape again and again, sweetening the sounds, slowing the movement, freezing the best moments, Geldering in extra video wherever we could find it until we had an eight-minute-and-thirty-second run of powerful television. The event itself had lasted fewer than two minutes. I wrote a news story for John Sinclair—and a narration for Bahr to read in Elvis's voice over the tape. By dawn we had most of it in the can and left for a couple hours of sleep.

Newspapers across the country that next morning headlined the shooting with still photos lifted from the tape Jolene had so coolly recorded. Leese was on the morning television shows and the tape was played again and again. By the time the Elvis show ran that afternoon, there were very few Americans who hadn't heard the story. I put Leese's check in the bank.

The Elvis show that day had the highest ratings ever recorded for a daytime-television talk show. That night, Leese threw a champagne dinner for the staff. The next day, we scrapped the planned schedule and did the show again, this time with an expert on self-defense and a woman who had lost her husband and daughter in a Texas department-store shooting a year before. We Geldered tape of a different shooting—from three years before in Los Angeles—and ran those pictures as the woman talked about her terror and her grief. It was a very good show.

*T*HE TIDE *is fully out and the Thames has shrunk to a narrow muddy stream under a thin blue sun. A great heron is working the garbage-strewn bank and gulls wheel and argue in the sharp air.*

Upstream a couple of hundred yards, a hunched figure rowing a long narrow boat appears from under the bridge. After a couple of strokes, he locks the oars, stands and pees over the side. I turn away from the window, but there's the TV screen again. Still black, still inert—and still somehow charged with menace and mute accusation.

I must have slept sometime because I have an image in my head that could have come only from a dream. It's a confused sepia memory of a man with a wrinkled traveler's check. It's in British pounds. A fifty, I think, and he's trying to hand it to me. He wants me to buy a briefcase but I don't know if the case is for me or for him. And then somehow I'm in a bed in a room as dark and airless as a sealed tomb. There's a woman lying next to me. She's a stranger. Maybe she's Marilyn Monroe. She has her hand on my thigh and I'm getting hard, but there's something about her fingers that frightens me, and the sepia image fades and I come to in a clammy sweat.

Back out on the river, the man in the boat has drifted downstream and out of sight. Two crows are heckling the heron.

The touch of the woman's fingers still lingers on my thigh. It's difficult to concentrate, to get the thoughts to come out in a linear form. Dallas. The televisions. The show.

I keep thinking about that old saying that success breeds success. It is so right that it almost had to come down from a god somewhere, or from centuries of hungry people watching the fat get fat-

ter and coming to their own conclusions about how the universe works. For the Elvis venture, success bred success. What began as a quirky hobby in a converted garage became a national hysteria affecting tens of millions of otherwise sober-minded people who knew on one level that Elvis was quite dead, and who on another level opened their homes and their imaginations to him every afternoon five days a week and listened to what he was saying as though he actually had something important to tell them.

It would be easy here for me to throw up my hands and say I can't explain it, that people are funny, go figure. Television offers that kind of deniability. After all, you're just pumping out picture and what people make of it has nothing to do with you. That's the defense. But it's not honest.

In a nation of strangers and corporate gypsies who move every three and a half years, television is the pub, the park, the café where villagers gather to gossip, to brag, to condemn, to pass judgment and pass time. It's where people go to reaffirm their place in the village, to prove to themselves that they belong. I think that at some fundamental level, Clare Leese understood that more profoundly than anyone else. He realized that the benches and shade trees might be gone, but that the deep hunger for them remained. And he figured out a powerful substitute. In Elvis, he created a national village where people could feel like they were part of the gossip, where they could listen in on the things everybody was talking about—the sex, the violence, the politics, the money. Elvis got to the root of our national conversations—not just the little boy shot in a school or a gunman in a theater, but the people who were powerful, the people who were stupid, the pretty ones, the talented ones, the calf born with five legs, the train conductor whose drunkenness killed a dozen people, the politician who couldn't keep his hands off other men's wives, the baby who fell down a well, the woman who was a hundred and ten. And the technology that gave us Elvis also gave us the pictures that made the stories whole.

The power structure hated it, dismissing it as a mindless fraud, a circus freak show, an electronic stunt that pandered to the lowest and basest instincts among us. The hatred from the chattering *classes of the East Coast seemed to grow in parallel with the show's popularity—and I wondered if there might not be some connection, that the great unwashed outside the subscription lists of the* New York Times *and the* Washington Post *took a perverse delight in rallying behind a program that was so extraordinarily anti-intellectual and so politically incorrect. The people couldn't get enough.*

The problem was that Clare Leese couldn't get enough either—and it wasn't an issue of money. As a merchant of gossip, Elvis began making so much money for Clare Leese that it was difficult to keep track of it. And Leese wasn't stingy with it: we all shared to one degree or another in the show's rabid success.

No, it wasn't an issue of money. I look at the lifeless television screen sitting here in front of me and wish it had been the money. Things would have been so much simpler. For Clare Leese, the money was only a marker, a symbol, to let him know how he was doing in his true passion.

Success breeds success. I remember another television talk show. It's long gone now, killed off by the Elvis phenomenon. But at the height of its popularity, it was an awesome example of power. The woman who ran it, though, was careful not to abuse the power, careful about what she said and did. I think she realized how potent it was.

Clare Leese realized it, too. And unlike her, he reveled in it. For a long time, I didn't see it, didn't appreciate what was happening. I thought the whole thing was about Elvis and show business and about making money. I wish I'd been smarter. What I didn't understand, what I missed completely, was that for Clare Leese, the only issue that mattered was the power.

Chapter Twenty-one

When I finally got to the theater, the last fire crew was rolling up its hoses. A knot of police officers was standing around looking at the ugly black smudge where the homemade bomb had hit the stone facade. The plastic marquee above it had melted at one end and a couple of the red letters that spelled out Theater of the United States had fallen off. Otherwise, the place was mostly untouched. I found Leese in his office on the phone. He waved me into a chair.

"We might have it on tape," he was saying into the receiver. "We're checking that now." He listened for a minute, then: "Well, I do understand what you're saying, governor, and I thank you for that. But it seems to me we have one of two things going on here. Either it's kids or it's something more ominous, like an organized attack from people who knew what they were doing. Either one's a danger. You know and I know, governor, that the streets aren't safe anymore from these juveniles running out of control. And if it's something worse than that, we've all got a bigger problem. I think you have to agree with that."

As Leese paused to listen, he gestured with his eyes at the phone and made an exaggerated face as though the voice on the other end of the line was a nuisance or a fool.

"Governor, governor, I'm sorry to break in here but let's cut to the chase now, shall we? Somebody tried blowing up my theater. You deal with that pronto, huh? I'll be back in my office at five fifteen. You call me. And give my regards to Helen." Leese hung up the phone and turned to me. "Man's a fool but he's the only fool we've got at the moment. He'll set this right or he'll wish he hadn't ever seen a polling booth. So where have you been?"

"Sorry," I said, wondering silently to myself if the bombing was real or another Leese stage show.

Leese nodded. "Got the call a little after four this morning. I got here quick but it was already over. Jolene's checking on the security cameras. We should have it from at least two angles. The thing is, I need some help on another project. It's something that's just come up today and I think it might be tough. Can you help?"

"Happy to."

"Don't be too quick to jump. This one's serious as cancer." Leese was playing absently with a newspaper clipping on his desk. "You ever hear of a man named Gordon Karas?"

"As in Senator Gordon Karas?"

Leese nodded. "One and the same." He pushed the clipping toward me. "This little gem was in a New York paper yesterday. Research pulled it off the Internet."

Under the headline "Senator Urges Talk Probe," the story detailed how the head of a Senate committee with oversight on television licensing was calling for hearings into what the Senator called the "excesses" of talk-show television. It was written in the peculiar polite code that politicians and journalists use to say things without actually saying them, but the message was clear: a senator was going after Elvis. I handed the paper back to Leese.

He crumpled it and threw it toward a wastebasket but missed. "This one's odd, Nick. There isn't one thing this man can do to our show. First Amendment takes care of that. Might try to get the station license revoked, but that would take years, and we can do Elvis without the station. No, it's something else and I don't think it's Elvis. This Karas fellow is sinister, and he's been after me for years. I think this is a smoke screen. My accountants tell me we've been summoned in for a tax audit. So it looks like this guy's coming after me on all fronts. Put simply, I'd like to stop him in his tracks."

"Bad blood?"

Leese nodded. "Goes way back. Before I got to Dallas. Let's say Mr. Karas and I don't exchange Christmas cards."

"What do you need?"

"I'd like you to send me Mr. Gelder," said Leese. "I have a little project for him."

Five days later, a young man named John G. Karas was on the Leese Broadcasting Network. The G in the young man's name was for his father Gordon—as in Senator Gordon Karas.

Clare Leese had gotten word to the senator to be sure to watch television that afternoon. And it was very good television, although the tape of John G. Karas was a little blurry and its movements frequently jagged and abrupt and the lighting was poor because it was shot in a men's toilet. It was only seen once: John Sinclair played it in his news segment and it did not run in the main Elvis show. And the tape was short: it was used as a lead-in to a discussion of the growing problem of homosexual encounters in public restrooms after a young movie star was caught literally with his pants down in a Los Angeles park. And John G. as in Gordon did not get a credit by name. That's because it was a warning to his father only and no one else.

In his sixteen seconds of infamy, the unnamed young man is first seen washing his hands carefully at a sink, his face occasionally obscured by an electronically generated blur that moved as he did but, conveniently, did not always keep up. In the second shot, he's leaning casually against the open doorway of a toilet stall, rubbing the crotch of his jeans. In the third and final scene, the young man unzips his jeans and exposes himself. His erection is tastefully concealed by a small moving blur on the videotape. The Karas name is never used.

In fact, the Karas boy was never there at all. Gelder had worked for a week to find exactly the right sort of police undercover video, to find a still photo of the young man himself, to reanimate it, and then to Gelder that animated head onto the grainy video.

Before the show was over, Leese took a private call in his

office and emerged to say that the unfortunate misunderstanding with the senate committee had been resolved.

That was the same week the problems with Bahr came to a head. Leese dealt with them just as ruthlessly.

I'd met people like Bahr before in the business—it seemed to attract the type: people who were so fragile they spent a lifetime wrapping themselves up in layers and layers of ego. After a while, the layers got so thick there was little sign left of the original human being. Bahr was a lot like that. He'd become very nearly a caricature of himself; a pompous little man who was smart enough to fool some of the people—and not smart enough to realize that others saw right through him, and laughed behind his back. The Elvis role made it all worse as his twisted personality started taking on some of the more base characteristics of the man he played on television.

Bahr's sexual misadventures had been a problem long before the Elvis role came along. They had been a standing joke in the newsroom, but in that odd, deformed world of newsroom sexism, word of them seldom made its way to his wife and four kids in the big house on the north side. In the parlance of the newsroom, what went on the road stayed on the road. With the arrival of Elvis, though, it blew up into monstrous proportions. Even Bahr couldn't keep a lid on it as he set about bedding every woman he could get his chubby little hands on.

It came home to me the day after the show with the senator's son when Barbara Bahr—everybody called her BB— showed up at the theater without warning, stopped me as I was walking down a hallway and calmly announced that if we didn't put a leash on her husband's pecker, she would take the matter public, and when she got through, there wouldn't be an Elvis show.

"Nice to see you, too," I said, easing back against the wall and hoping the comment might take some of the sting out of the encounter.

BB frowned, the act forming pronounced dimples in the

ample flesh of her cheeks. "Nick, I don't think you're hearing me very well. You have to make that man put his pecker back in his pants." Bahr's wife was trying to whisper but she was a large woman—probably a full head taller than her diminutive husband and at least half again as heavy—and the whisper sounded like a shout in the narrow hall. Over BB's broad shoulder, I saw a young female intern do a double take and reverse directions back the way she'd come. "Here's the deal, Nick. Either he buttons up, or I go public. This country is crazed to know the secrets behind Elvis—and I have them."

"Let's take this to my office," I said quietly.

Inside, BB arranged herself in a padded leather chair and reached into her purse for a tissue, as though she'd already gone through the lines that were about to come and knew they'd produce tears. "This can't go on, Nick."

I nodded blankly and didn't point out that this sort of thing had been going on for years without her doing anything to stop it—and I believed she had to have known. I wondered silently to myself what had changed this time around. Maybe it was the sheer numbers that had finally gotten to her.

"So what do we do, huh?" She said it lightly, almost kiddingly: she knew exactly what we were to do and was here to tell me. "There I am being little molly homemaker, and there's Iso being little monster home wrecker all over town." She formed a question in her eyes. "I'm sure you've heard?"

"There's been some talk," I said blandly.

"Oh, there's actually been quite a bit of talk. Let's see now. There's been talk about a cute little blond cashier at the bank. She's quite a little number. There's the waitress at that Mexican place. I think she's a brunette." She ran a hand through her own thin blond hair. "That's not like him." She looked around the office for a moment before continuing. "And now there's this very young thing where he gets his hair cut. She's a manicurist." A blank, almost baffled look around the office. "A manicurist. Can you imagine that? My husband is fucking a manicurist?" The word "fucking" seemed foreign to her mouth and she said it awkwardly. She paused and looked at me as though waiting for some sort of response.

"I'm sorry," I said at length.

"I was a schoolteacher when we met. Did you know that?"

I shook my head but she didn't seem to notice.

"Master's degree," she said. "I had a career. I had a good, decent career. My mom and dad paid for our wedding. My dad was so proud. I don't think Dad liked him very much. But he was proud of me. Did you know we were farmers? Dairy farmers. I thought I'd married up." She paused as though waiting for a response.

"I'm sorry," I said again but I needn't have bothered—she wasn't listening.

"Boy, was I wrong about that," she said. "I think my father knew. I think that's why he didn't like him. The wedding bed hadn't even cooled when I started popping babies. Charlie was born and I thought I could get back to work, but Melissa came along and then Margo and then Brooke and there I was, I'd been out of work five years by then and I wanted to get on with my career but four little kids at home so it was another five years and he started playing around and I started getting bigger."

She paused and seemed to focus on her surroundings. "Quite a mess, isn't it?" She looked me hard in the eyes and I saw the first signs of moisture in hers. "Sad for the kids. They're young. Pretty shitty answer when they ask what daddy does. Well, he's on TV and he fucks strange women. Lots of strange women. Quite a legacy to pass along to his children, huh?"

I remained silent.

She rearranged her skirt and in the process seemed to collect herself: I could almost see her placid body hardening up. "So," she said, "we know what he's doing. Now we need to figure out what we're going to do about it. I've finally reached a point where I can't allow this to continue. Here's the deal. You either stop him fooling around—immediately—or I go public. I think you can guess how much the networks would like to have Elvis's wife on their morning shows. I have their phone numbers. I also have the phone number for *People* magazine and *60 Minutes*."

She gave me a hard look in the eyes. "Just imagine what happens to your show when the country learns that the exalted Elvis is actually a grasping little man with a penis the size of a wad of bubblegum out sleeping with manicurists while his good and decent wife sits at home trying to raise his four children." She dropped into silence and waited for me to respond.

I admit I was at a loss. Telling Iso Bahr to stop screwing around was like trying to tell a bird to stop flying or a tree to stop sprouting leaves. On the other hand, allowing her to go public would be to allow a national scandal that very easily could destroy everything we'd built over the last year. A rock and a hard place. "That's a tough one," I said.

She nodded. "I know it."

"I don't know if anybody can make him stop."

"I know that, too."

"It could just drive it underground."

"It has to be a full stop."

"Castration?"

She smiled at that, but only thinly, and rose from the chair. "Sorry to lay this on you, Nick. You've been decent to me in the past. But you've also been one of the guys." She let her gaze linger on me to make sure the words had registered. "I'll call you this time tomorrow. Depending on what I hear you say, I have a whole long list of phone numbers. And I'll use them."

As the door closed behind her, I picked up the phone and dialed Clare Leese's extension. When he finally picked up, his voice was muffled and hard to hear.

"Where are you?" I said loudly.

"Houston," said Leese. "What's the matter?"

"Problems with Bahr."

"Big?"

"Huge."

"Is he dead?"

"I wish."

"I'll call when I land."

LEESE PACED in front of his desk, his hands clenched behind his back, the oyster-gray look on his face matching exactly the gray of his suit. He'd chosen a plain black tie, as though in mourning.

Bahr was sitting at the conference table, his face equally grim, his body rigid. I was across and down the table from him, working on the dozenth cup of coffee of the morning and glancing frequently at my watch as BB Bahr's deadline ticked inexorably nearer. After phone calls lasting well into the night, Leese had told me to be in his office at eleven A.M. I, like Bahr, had no idea what was coming.

At last the door opened and a train of three men and a woman entered, nodded to Leese and took their places at the table. The men were all in black suits and I caught a glimpse of expensive watches on their wrists. The woman—late thirties probably—was in a black skirt and blazer with a man's tie around her collar. Attractive, in a button-down mannish sort of way. I'd never seen any of them before.

Leese didn't bother with introductions. Turning abruptly, he held Bahr with a prolonged, ugly stare of contempt. "Mr. Bahr, you've brought discredit on this enterprise. We're here to do something about it."

A look of uncertainty and fear washed over Bahr's face and he started to say something but Leese silenced him with a gesture of his hand. "Show him the pictures."

With that, one of the black-suited men opened a file and pushed a stack of large photos across the table, fanning them out as a dealer would fan a deck of cards. As Bahr's eyes focused on them, his cheeks turned crimson.

I think mine may have colored as well: the photos were extraordinarily explicit. I felt a small shock at the intrusiveness of it all and wondered with a dull chill in my spine whether Leese had the same kind of photos of me.

"I believe," said Leese, "that you'll find the young woman is not giving you a manicure in that first one there. That's oral sex, Mr. Bahr, and that's you. You're free to look through that file. I think you'll come upon at least four of your other little friends." Leese paused for a moment. "You looked startled, Mr. Bahr. Do you think I'd make an investment like this without protecting myself. We know what you do and we know who you do it to."

Bahr's eyes were swinging from the photos to Leese and back to the photos. His mouth was working as though to speak but no words were coming out.

Leese again: "We have video evidence of five of your liaisons. I believe your wife only knows of three at this point. And these aren't Geldered, Mr. Bahr, these are the real thing. Are you aware that the young lady of whom you are so fond, the one who works in the Mexican place, is seventeen?"

Bahr's eyes widened but Leese didn't let him speak. "That's right, Mr. Bahr, she's a minor. And in this state you go to jail for that." Leese glanced at the black-suited man. "You can put those away for now."

Bahr's head sagged. I thought he might be crying but couldn't tell from where I was sitting.

After a couple of circuits along the table, Leese swung around to look at him again. His face was pinched and his eyes were hot. "I cannot, Mr. Bahr, adequately express to you the depth of my anger at this moment. It is immense. It is a white-hot raging anger. And it is directed at you, Mr. Bahr. At your gross stupidity. At your mindless activities that now threaten the very core of this institution."

Leese did another circuit along the table. "Your wife paid us a visit yesterday," he said. "Did you know that?"

Bahr shook his head but remained silent, his eyes cast down toward his lap.

"And she delivered a threat. Either you stop—we make you stop—or she goes public. Nice, isn't it? Can you imagine how much I like being threatened by some trailer-trash moron like that? Can you?"

A beat of silence in the room. Everyone except Leese was looking at the top of the table. Leese's eyes were on Bahr. "No, I imagine you can't. Do you know how I react when I'm threatened? Have any idea?"

Silence again.

"I'm walking along and a snake rears up and starts hissing. Know what I do? I club that snake to death, that's what I do." Leese was almost spitting the words, his mouth a narrow dark gash in his angry face. "To death. I club that snake to death. No one threatens me." Leese paused and collected himself, straightening his jacket and running a hand across his black tie.

"You, Mr. Bahr, are a dime a dozen, a paid clown, a ventriloquist's dummy. You are as replaceable as a handkerchief. You're in breach of your contract—the morals clause—and you could be out this door in a second. If you walked out this door, I could have the police standing there to meet you with an arrest warrant for having sexual congress with a minor. What do you think of that?"

Bahr raised his eyes. "Anything you say, Mr. Leese." His face looked broken.

"But I don't need the grief," said Leese. "This show is too successful right now to allow a load of garbage like you to poison it. So here's the way it's going to be. Are you listening?"

Bahr sat up a little straighter and nodded.

"Good. Get rid of the girlfriends. All of them. Now. Is that clear?"

Bahr nodded.

Leese glanced at the black-suited man who had presented the photographs. "Mr. Thomas."

The man put on a pair of gold-rimmed glasses, opened another file and started reading, his voice a flat and emotionless monotone: "Pursuant to the order of the Fifth District Court, State of Texas, issued this date so on and so forth, Mr. Iso Bahr, also known as Gordon Donald Barton, moves to formally dissolve his marriage from Barbara Bahr, nee Barbara Williams, on the grounds of irreconcilable differences. Mrs. Bahr, with a known history of psychological trauma and treatment, is enjoined by this order from either approaching the filee, Mr. Bahr, or from speaking in any form with the press, either print or electronic, and is liable to contempt and jail if she so attempts."

Bahr's face was a mask of disbelief. Leese was looking at the wall.

The black-suited man continued. "And, by decree, also this date, of the Tarrant County Court, Judge David Boyd, Mrs. Barbara Bahr, nee Barbara Williams, is remanded for immediate transfer to the Fort Worth Medical Center for evaluation and treatment, as needed, for what is suspected to be psychotic depressive behavior that is a possible threat to herself and her offspring. Petition filed by and for Mr. Iso Bahr, also known as Gordon Donald Barton, and granted on this, the thirteenth day, etc. etc." The man closed the file and removed his glasses.

Leese turned back to the room. "You have some papers to sign, Mr. Bahr. I suggest you arrange child care promptly. I believe the court intends to have her picked up this afternoon. Do you have any questions?"

Bahr looked from face to face around the room, his eyes hollow, and brought his gaze back to Leese. "No, sir."

"Good," said Leese, his voice as precise as the edge of a knife. "She'll be in a day or two. I expect the experience will be enough to convince her of the folly of taking her story public. If not, and if she does ultimately take this public, she will be discredited as certifiably psychotic. Let's get back to work."

Chapter Twenty-two

I FELL hard that night. Very hard. At first I pretended to myself—I was alone in my apartment so there wasn't anyone else to pretend to—I pretended to myself that I wasn't getting drunk. I had a couple of beers and jumped around the TV channels, then tried reading but couldn't keep the sentences straight so I switched back to the TV. I told myself I was relaxing after a tough day. A tough day? Castrating a man and institutionalizing his wife was a tough day? I needed a vacation. Maybe I needed a life.

After the beers I started on the Scotch. That's where the pretending came in. I was pretending that the drinking was social, acceptable. Unwinding. Coming down. I'd learned the pretense well after the fire. I could pretend with the best of them that I wasn't a drunk.

I made a ceremony of it, pretending it was a special occasion, something like that. A nice crystal glass with ice in it, a splash of Scotch and a topper of bottled French water. Very fancy. Social. I wasn't a drunk. I was having a drink. Late news on the tube. America was bombing someone again. I switched to something about polar bears. On the next drink, I mixed in more Scotch than water. By the third, I'd abandoned the water—just Scotch—and found a smutty movie. Not hard-core but a lot of T&A, as they said in my business. Tits and ass. My business? Jesus, my business. What exactly was my business now? After a while I gave up on the ice and stopped counting the drinks. Fuck pretense.

I had not said a word. As Bahr sat there having his little

pecker chopped off on the shiny tabletop, I had not said a word. My own ears heard Leese say he was throwing the man's wife into an asylum. And I had not said a word.

I poured the glass full and took a slug from the bottle itself as extra measure. It burned my throat going down and I switched to a golf match. But what could I say that would have made a difference? Leese and the threats from a trailer-trash moron. Leese clubbing his snake to death. Is it conceivable that anything I could have said at that point would have made a difference? Obviously the deal was done long before I'd walked into that room and just as obviously there wasn't a chance in hell that anything I could have said would have changed it one iota. Jesus Christ. The power was awesome.

Between our final call at one in the morning and the meeting—what? ten, eleven hours later—in that time he'd bought two judges, started a divorce proceeding and railroaded a woman into a mental institution for a couple of days of "observation and evaluation." Golf is the dullest spectator sport on the face of the earth. I switched back to the movie where the man and woman were pretending to have sex.

The photos on the table. I'd tried not to look after I'd realized what they were. A whole stack of pictures of Bahr and his girlfriends doing it. They hadn't gotten those overnight, had they? There hadn't been time. So they'd been watching him. Leese said they had video evidence. Did that mean they'd been taping him? How? Cameras in the ceiling? I looked up at my own ceiling. Taping me, too? Fuck you, Clare Leese. I made a clumsy finger at the ceiling. "Tape that, you Blender Tycoon little cross-eyed fuck wit." I took another drink and stared malevolently at the ceiling. "I hope you're getting this all on fucking video fucking tape. Huh? Are you? Talk to me, huh! Are you taping me, too?" The ceiling stared back, silent, unanswering.

Then I lost my nerve. I went into the bedroom and sat on the edge of the bed in the darkness taking short nips from the bottle. It was pitch dark but I felt like somebody was watching me. It wasn't particularly cold but I was shivering. I must have jumped a foot when the phone rang and I managed to knock it to the floor scrambling for it in the dark.

"It's me," said a woman's voice.

At first I thought it was Wares. Christ, the dinner I never took her to. What happened with that? Was I too busy, or was I a coward? It took me a beat or two before I figured out the voice belonged to Jolene. I realized I was too drunk to talk without slurring.

"You okay?" she asked.

Was she one of Leese's spies? Checking up on me? "Asleep," I managed to say.

"Sorry. I thought you'd be up. I heard something bad went down today. You sure you're okay?"

"Just sleeping. Let's talk in the morning."

"You're sure you're okay?"

"Dead tired," I lied. "I'll call you in the morning."

I managed to hang up the phone, wondering if I'd sounded drunk. I took a long pull on the bottle. Jolene, too? Fuck. Cornered. Like an animal cornered. Leese and his snake. *I club that snake to death that's what I do.* I'd never heard Leese like that before. Another pull from the bottle. The phone started whining. A moment of intense panic before I realized that I'd failed to get the receiver on right. I fumbled with it and the whining stopped. I looked back at the ceiling. Fuck you, Clare Leese, and every single fucking blender you rode in on.

I lurched back into the living room and sat down heavily next to the other phone. I had trouble reading the numbers from the phone book but managed somehow to dial them.

It seemed to ring a long time and I'd just about decided to hang up when I heard it picked up.

"Hello." Margaret Wares's voice was husky with sleep.

I sat there staring at the receiver, trying to imagine what she looked like right then. Were her eyes as blue as I remembered? I wondered what she was wearing. What do women wear to bed when they're alone, when they're not trying to please a man?

"Hello?" she said again, her voice sharper this time. "Is there somebody on here?" A pause. I could hear her breathing.

How I wished at that moment I wasn't drunk. I wanted to talk to her. To reach out through the dark night and the fear and Clare Leese and dirty photos and creepy lawyers and talk to someone removed from it all, someone sane, someone level. But what could I say that she'd hear? That would make sense to someone who wasn't in the middle of it?

"Go to bed," she said gently, and the receiver went dead in my ear.

Chapter Twenty-three

. . . AND IT is almost unprecedented," John Sinclair was saying, "that an American government would set out to kill its own people. To recap the main, the only story of this sad day, federal authorities"—Sinclair's face was replaced by a videotape of a helicopter hovering over a squat two-story apartment building, its rotors slapping the air—"federal authorities under the command of the FBI today ended a siege in Pittsburgh"—the chopper suddenly dived and a satchel the size of a suitcase fell from its belly—"by bombing an apartment house"—a huge ripping explosion—"where an extended family of up to eight adults and more than twenty children had been holed up for more than two weeks." The building now totally obscured in welling smoke and flying debris. "The citizen's group inside claimed it was a religious order. The police—and the FBI—claimed it was a subversive organization involved in drug smuggling and that there had been incidents of child abuse on the property, though they've offered not a single strand of evidence to back up their charges."

The camera's eye came down to a ground-level shot that pushed into the very heart of the fiery bier and held it there, the screen consumed completely with the violent oranges and reds of the inferno. "No count yet on the casualties but it's clear few could have lived through this bombing. That's the news you need to know. I'm John Sinclair. Elvis is next. Good day."

". . . and fade to black," snapped Jolene. "And—roll commercial."

"One minute," said a voice from the front of the control room.

I watched in a preview monitor as a woman daubed at Bahr's face. On the other monitor, exactly the same thing was happening to the face of John Sinclair—which changed in midstroke to the face of Elvis. Technicians were removing the desk to transform Sinclair into Elvis. I keyed the intercom. "How's it going?"

"It's going," said Bahr vacantly.

"You're Elvis in forty-five seconds. Remember to keep referencing the bombing tape. It's good stuff. Better since we Geldered it. Nobody else has anything like it so hit it hard. Knock 'em dead."

Jolene called the countdown and the Elvis animation rolled across the theater as the audience began clapping and cheering.

I took a call from an Oregon station that was having satellite-reception problems. When I put the phone down, Bahr-Elvis was already well into his opening monologue.

". . . no one can have any doubt about just exactly how this tragedy happened. John Sinclair reported at the top of this hour"—Jolene rolled the tape again and the helicopter appeared over the building—"about the involvement in this sorry mess of the attorney general and the head of the FBI. You're watching the pictures, you're seeing the truth with your own eyes. Look at that, just look at that." Slow motion this time as the satchel hit the roof and the translucent shock line of the explosion coned outward. "I think it's clear to everyone what the fate should be of the attorney general and the FBI director. If there's any justice on this good green earth, their time in office is over, or should be over. When you get to the end of this show, I think you'll realize along with millions of others out there that those two have no place in public office. They're killers." The camera zoomed into the inferno and the shot dropped into black.

Elvis looked out at the audience with a sweeping glance and then appeared to look down at his hands, though the large monitor had framed him in a tight shot that cut him off about midchest and his hands weren't visible. He looked back up at the audience. "I'm feeling ashamed right now to be an American. I look at those pictures—we're going to show them again here in just a minute—I look at those pictures and I'm ashamed to be an American." Elvis paused to wipe his eyes. "We're back in sixty seconds."

The first commercial rolled and Bahr looked up at the camera, his eyes flat, his expression neutral.

I keyed the intercom. "I think it's working. Let's keep it simple. The politicians are liars. The people die and the politicians lie."

"The people die and the politicians lie." No change of expression as he said the words. He seemed okay on the air. Off it, though, he was hollow and lifeless. Could I blame him? If the events of the day before had happened to me, I wouldn't even be there. I wondered briefly if they'd come for his wife. BB, the homemaker.

"Thirty seconds," said a voice on the speaker.

"Tape first," I said, "then we'll get to the guest."

I switched off the intercom and rubbed my eyes. One of the most vicious hangovers I'd ever given myself. Even my hair hurt. I'd come to that morning lying naked on the living-room floor, the phone off the hook, the Scotch bottle empty, the television and all the lights on. If Clare Leese was surveiling me, he at least had some interesting videotape. My stomach knotted up and I tried to push the image away.

An assistant was counting backward from ten. Jolene watched the monitors. "And—take camera one," she said quietly. Elvis appeared on the central screen.

"We're back and we've got some amazing stuff to show you. Some of this is the government's—how we got it has to remain a secret—and some of it is ours. By way of background, what we did is we took all the tape from all the available sources—there were cameras everywhere—we took that tape and in a computer we recreated everything we were seeing, everything that was happening on a second-by-second basis to give you a fuller appreciation of what happened this morning in Pittsburgh."

Elvis looked off-camera. "Can we roll that tape now? Are we ready?"

With that, the house lights dimmed, and Elvis's image on the big screen was replaced by an aerial shot with the apartment house highlighted in a round moving circle, the rest of the neighborhood obscured in shadow.

The early-morning scene was deceptively quiet. As the shot pushed in, though, the audience could see that things already had been happening. One entire corner of the building was collapsed. Another wall had a giant hole driven into it.

"It's about seven in the morning now. You can see that a big battle tank the army loaned the FBI has already been busy. For those of you old enough to remember, it is almost identical to the government assault in Waco when the feds went in and killed the Branch Davidians and their children. So here we have the walls busted down and the yard in back flattened and cleared to give the government snipers a clear field of fire. You'll see in a minute that they used that to good effect."

The shot pulled out wider to the tape Gelder had manufactured less than an hour before. We'd borrowed a lot of it from a documentary of Waco that had had a brief run in theaters years earlier. "Now here's a key point, a piece of tape the government will pray you never see." The video changed to a wide shot of the apartment house, a tank backing out of the picture to the lower right. "If you look closely there at the top of the apartment complex, right there next to that alley, you'll see three figures come out. Here, let's zoom in." The shot enlarged and three people could be seen walking out of the structure, their arms in the air. "Those are children. Look at them. They're kids. They're trying to surrender. Now watch

with me to see what happens." The forms took a dozen or so
steps out into the yard, their hands clearly above their heads,
when suddenly tracer fire from automatic rifles started streak-
ing in. One figure crumpled, then the other two were literally
blown backward and fell like rag dolls. Elvis let it play a beat
or two. "Those are dead kids, ladies and gentlemen. And your
tax dollars bought the bullets that cut them down. The people
die, the politicians lie. You hear me: the people die, the politicians lie."

"Mr. Upton . . ." I was so wrapped up in the show I'd lost
track of where I was. A voice from the front console told me I
had a phone call.

I picked up the receiver. "Upton here."

"Wares."

Silence.

"Nick? Are you there?"

The voice from last night. "Hi," I managed, wondering with
scalding embarrassment if she had someone figured out it was
my drunken breathing on the other end of the phone during
the night.

"Hi," she said, and then paused, as though waiting for me
to pick up the threads and begin to knit a conversation. I
couldn't manage it.

"Are you busy? I mean, is this a bad time?"

I looked at the monitor. Elvis had brought out his first
guest. "We're in a show," I said.

"Oh, sorry. Look, maybe you could give me a call when
you're free?"

"No, I can talk."

Another short run of silence. "Look, I . . ." She paused again.

"How are you?" I said.

"Good. Actually, I'm really good. Look, Nick, the reason I
called is I'm making some pasta tonight. Nothing special. I
remember we'd said we'd have dinner and I was cooking up
this big pot of food and I was wondering . . ." A short pause.
"Can I feed you tonight?"

I grinned inwardly. "I'd like that a lot."

"Sevenish?"

"Sevenish," I said. "What can I bring?"

"Yourself would be fine."

On the screen, the picture had changed to a wide aerial and Elvis and his guest were talking about infrared-radar images and rifle shots coming from FBI-sniper positions.

A LATE-MODEL pickup was pulling out as I turned into the narrow lane that led to Margaret Wares's house. We had to inch down to a crawl to pass each other and in the dusk I could make out a guy about my age, in a baseball cap, a rifle slung on a rack in the rear window. I returned his nod.

Margaret was standing at the kitchen door. She waved as I pulled up and parked.

"Found your way back to this old place all right?" she asked, the odd off-center smile I remembered from before spreading across her lips.

I handed her a bunch of flowers wrapped in cellophane. "For my spectacular host," I said with what I hoped was a flourish.

"Hostess," she corrected, dipping her nose into the bouquet. "Lovely. And welcome. Glad you could get away. Come inside."

The kitchen, as we passed through it, smelled distinctly Italian, and the formica and chrome table I had seen through the window on my first visit was set for two. She arranged me on a sofa and disappeared to put the flowers in water, reappearing with two glasses of wine.

"I hope you like it," she said, handing me a glass. "It's homegrown. My cousin has a vineyard in Oregon. He ships me cases of the stuff every Christmas." She held the glass to her nose. "I don't drink much so it has quite a good chance to age. And age. And age." She touched my glass in a casual toast.

"To aged wine," I said. The wine was good even on top of

the hangover and I complimented her on it. Which led into a discussion of her cousin. He'd been a commodities broker in Chicago, had gotten heavily into drugs, burned out, fried out and dropped out for a number of years. Had reappeared sober and clean with a small vineyard in Oregon. Which led to a discussion of her other relatives. There weren't many. Dad was long dead, mom long remarried and moved away to Florida. Her closest relative was her brother. That was him in the pickup when I drove in. Owned a small fabricating plant in Fort Worth. Stainless steel. Which led to a discussion of her carpentry and how the last time I visited she was building a floor or something like that.

"Greenhouse," she said. "Still working on it. There's never enough time in a day. And I guess there hasn't been enough time for that dinner we talked about?" She said it with a gentle, mocking look on her face that put the words about dead center between a question and a statement of fact.

"Yeah. Dinner. Guess something came up." I smiled lamely. Elvis had come up, is what happened. "I guess I got busy."

"I saw the show today."

That surprised me and I said so.

"Natural curiosity," she said. "I turned it on after I called you. I dip in from time to time."

I groaned out loud. "Here we go again. Perverting the minds of all those poor benighted souls out there and all that, huh? At least we're not killing people like the government."

She shot me a mysterious look and her smile faded. "Actually, it's the first time I've watched for a while. I figured I should see what's happening—after your call last night."

My wineglass paused halfway up the arc toward my mouth. After my call last night? I felt an instant flush bloom across my face and had to make a conscious effort to steady the wineglass in my hand. After my call last night? For one of the few times in my life, I felt what had to be total humiliation. Humiliation that I'd been drunk, that I'd been so frightened. I managed to get the wineglass back to the tabletop, steadying my eyes on it so I wouldn't have to look up and meet her gaze.

"My phone tells me what number's calling," she said simply.

I groped around in my mind for something—anything—to say, but there was nothing there. I'd been lonely when I made that phone call. Drunk as a proverbial skunk. And now caught in the middle of the sad, hopeless act by my own complete stupidity. There was no answer to it. I stood up and started for the door.

She jumped up and took my arm. "Look, buster," she said, forcing a lightness to her voice that neither of us felt, "you sit right back down. I didn't cook all this food to give it to the cat."

We stood for a moment arm in arm as I struggled with my own emotions.

"Don't be a pig-headed male just because YOU ARE a pig-headed male." She steered me slowly back toward the sofa. "So you had a bad night. Sit. Talk."

I did as I was told, feeling like a child who's been scolded and given a reprieve. "I'm sorry," I managed to say. "It was stupid."

Margaret arranged herself in a chair and looked at me across the coffee table. "It's no big deal." She gave me a long look. "We all do stupid things once in a while. It sounded to me like you needed to talk to somebody. So here I am."

I remained silent, trying to get my senses back under control, trying to figure out what I could possibly say that would retrieve the situation.

Margaret reached across the table and topped up the wine and then settled back, eyeing me over the rim of her glass. The off-center smile had crept back onto her lips. "Maybe we should start again here," she said. "So, Nick Upton, glad you could come by for dinner tonight. I had all this pasta and nobody to feed it to." She waited for a response from me. I nodded but didn't say anything, still uncertain of my footing.

She continued as though I'd spoken. "You're right, Nick. The last time you were here I was actually building a new floor for the greenhouse. Maybe you'd like to see how it's coming after dinner?" I nodded, feeling myself begin to relax as she continued with her game of words.

"And we were supposed to have dinner. But something came up, right?" An edgy, challenging smile. "Abraham Lincoln? No, let's see. It wasn't Lincoln. Was it . . . ? Oh, I know. It was Charlie Chaplin. Chaplin, right? No? It wasn't Chaplin? But something came up, right? Some person came up? I mean you said we'd have dinner and then I didn't hear from you and it's been a long time, so something had to have come up." She paused, fluttering her eyelashes at me in a silly, exaggerated way. "I remember," she said, drawing out the "I." "It was Elvis Presley." She grinned broadly and fluttered her eyelashes again.

I couldn't hide my own smile. The woman could be disarming. "Yeah, Elvis," I said. "Things got pretty intense pretty quickly."

"Must have," she said. "I'm not usually that easily forgotten."

"You weren't forgotten."

"Just overlooked, huh?"

I shrugged.

"Apology accepted," she said. "I was busy, too."

"How's your book?"

She laughed out loud. "That old thing? It's doing okay, I guess. More work selling the darned thing than it was writing it." The conversation eased back into normal channels as she launched into a series of tales about trying to flack the book through the small-market radio and television stations of Texas, Oklahoma and New Mexico. Some of the stories made her awkward experience with Iso Bahr the first time I met her seem downright civilized.

Somehow the talk veered to childhoods. I didn't offer much. There's little entertainment value in a story of a father dead before you've turned ten, and a mother remarrying so casually down through the years that you stopped bothering to learn the last names of the new stepfathers. I picked up the tale well out of college—the small stations, moving up through the dial, Los Angeles. I didn't talk about the fire, didn't tell her I literally and figuratively helped bury the woman I was engaged to marry.

Margaret's stories about growing up in west Texas led us to the dinner table. Italian bean soup and some sort of truly good baked-pasta dish. She'd been raised in a town so small it didn't get its first traffic light until the seventies. The drugstore still had a hitching post for horses and people still used it. Not foo-foo tourists, she said, but real cowboys on real horses. It was all picturesque and Western, but even towns that small had another side of the tracks, and that's where she lived. Dad sold cars. Not new ones. And in the unspoken caste system of small-town America, there wasn't much lower to go.

Not that she knew it at the time. Well, she knew she didn't have the best clothes, and their house wasn't the biggest, but their situation wasn't remarkable in the least as far as she could tell. The one thing she knew, though, was that the town didn't offer anything in the way of a future. At least not the kind of future she wanted. Girls did not go to college. Girls did get married and raise families. She left town the summer after high school for a community college in San Antonio, then the University of Texas. They liked her there. Gave her a teaching assistant's job to help her get through graduate school. And the rest, she said, is history—which took us back into the living room over dainty little glasses of some sort of chilled lemon liqueur which went down too well and too fast. She apparently realized it and before long we had switched to heavy black coffee.

"Nice meal," I said. "Thank you."

"Sounds like an exit line."

"It's late."

Margaret looked at her watch. "Midnight. Want more coffee?"

I shook my head. "Coffee-ed out." But I made no move to get up. There was something about the place that I didn't want to leave. It wasn't sexual, though in the presence of this woman the notion could never be too far from the surface. It was more a feeling of warmth—and comfort. It was nice to sit and talk with someone about something other than what I do for a living, and to sit and talk without another agenda. It was almost a feeling of being in the right place. I enjoyed this woman. She was interesting to talk to, to talk with. She had opinions and attitudes and didn't bother to offer patronizing niceties. She was—human. It felt good to be around another human. Maybe it was a measure of how far I'd gotten away from my own tribe.

"Before you go, I thought I'd show you something?" She offered the words shyly, looking off toward the side as she said them. "Maybe you already know about it?" The same tone of voice again—somewhere between statement and question.

"Know about what?"

"You know how you said earlier that you're not like a politician, you're not killing anyone?"

"Right?"

"I guess you don't know about the woman in Utah?"

"What woman in Utah?"

"The one who died?"

I shook my head. I didn't have a clue what she was talking about.

"Let me get it," said Margaret, rising and disappearing into another room. She came back a moment later, a piece of paper in her hands. "I thought maybe you should see this." She handed the paper to me tentatively, almost as though she wasn't sure she wanted to.

It was a clipping from a Salt Lake City paper. A couple of months old. I moved it around so I could see it better.

"I found it on the web during an Elvis search," said Margaret.

"'Elvis Fire Leaves One Dead.'" I looked from the paper to Margaret and she shrugged. I looked back at the paper.

SALT ROCK, UTAH: AP: Police say they've recovered the body of a fifty-three-year-old woman from the rubble of a flower shop that was razed Tuesday night in a fire which authorities now believe was deliberately set. It is the same shop which featured prominently the day before in the nationally syndicated *Elvis Live at Five* show.

I glanced at Margaret. "That's the show we did about the little boy. The Dufour boy."

She nodded.

Police say the body of Lucinda Buckalew, the shop manager, was found in a rear lavatory. An autopsy is pending, but authorities say they suspect she died of smoke inhalation.

I looked up from the paper. What was it I had said to myself when I left the newsroom and took over the Elvis show? No more pallbearers? "I didn't know about this."

"I figured you didn't. I didn't know if I should show it to you."

The shop, Rose Buds, became a center of controversy when it was charged in the *Elvis Live at Five* show that the establishment was paying "slave wages" to a local employee. The employee is the mother of one of the two children killed a week earlier in a school shooting in the town. Police reported that after the broadcast of that show, they received what they called several telephone threats against the shop and its owner. An investigation continues.

I laid the paper on the table.

"I thought it was something you should know about," said Margaret gently, busying her hands and her eyes with her coffee cup as though she didn't want to meet my gaze. "You—"

But I interrupted her. "I'm glad you showed me this." I looked back down at the piece of paper. "I thought I was out of the pallbearer business."

Margaret glanced at me with a question in her eyes.

"Long story," I said, rising and squaring my shoulders.

"You can drive all right?"

I tried a smile but it caught about halfway. "Yeah, I can drive all right."

She took my arm as we walked to the door.

"Thank you," I said. "This evening's meant a lot to me."

"To me, too," she said, and then, searching my eyes: "Look, sorry about the clipping. I thought it was important you see it. If you're the man I think you are . . ." She didn't finish the sentence. She didn't need to finish the sentence.

I shrugged.

She looked away, and then looked back at me. "Nick, I need to say something here. I don't know what kind of demons you're dealing with. But we all have demons. You're not alone. And it helps if there's somebody on the other end who will pick up the phone. Next time, talk to me. I'll listen." With that, she gave me a gentle push into the night.

CHAPTER TWENTY-FOUR

FOR THE effort it took to get there, Salt Rock, Utah, wasn't much of a place. I'd called the show early the next morning to say I'd be out a couple of days. No explanation, no excuse—they could make of it what they would.

I wasn't sure myself what to make of it. After the dinner—after the news story—I'd gone home to an almost sleepless night, punctuated by grotesque nightmares of dead children and women burning. Somewhere in there BB Bahr did a walk-on cameo. Dawn found me sweaty and spooked—and determined to find out for myself if I had played a part in whatever had happened at the flower shop.

I caught an early flight to Salt Lake, took a twin-engine prop plane to a smaller town in the mountains and drove a rental car three hours on a twisting two-lane road through an edgy landscape of sandstone canyons and deep river valleys.

The local booster club's faded 1950s-style sign on the outskirts of Salt Rock had been spray-painted by kids to welcome people to Tall Cock, Utah, home of the fighting barn owls. An old garage that was a restaurant advertised the best steaks west of Colorado, and a hand-painted sign invited travelers to Whiskey Joe's Rock Shop. It didn't look like a setting for murder—but I was beginning to realize just how little appearance actually has to do with reality.

A few lights were beginning to come on as I turned into the main street, which featured a combination gas station and convenience market and one short block of buildings, some of them abandoned and boarded up. At the far end of the street, I pulled up in front of a pile of burned timber and charred concrete blocks. Rose Buds. It hadn't been much of a building to start with: single story by the looks of the rubble, maybe twenty- or twenty-five-feet wide, wood-frame with cinder-block supports. Now it was even less. A thin plastic line of black and yellow police tape was the only guard on the site.

I found a motel about a half mile out of town. A thick and unfriendly woman let me know that the only place in town to eat was Best Steaks, but I'd better hurry because supper was early in these parts. Have a real nice day.

Best Steaks was all but deserted and actually pretty good. A mother-and-son place—she cooked, he talked. He'd escaped Utah as a young man and worked in Hollywood for a while, a grip or best boy or something like that. Utah pulled him back, but not before he'd learned to tango at an Arthur Murray dance course. He'd come back and tangoed his way through every bar and dance hall in the eastern part of the state and told me proudly he was the Tango King of Utah.

The steak was the size of a laptop with a mountainous side of mashed potatoes and a red-plastic quart cup of spring water and ice. Son hovered and mother sat with me to make sure I ate it all. Been a heck of a year, they both agreed, what with the school shootings—the school was actually about three miles out of town, more or less a central magnet that drew kids from four surrounding valleys, but they still called it Salt Rock—really too bad about the Dufour family, remember them on TV, that new Elvis show. That's quite a show, isn't it. Amazing what they can get away with these days, huh? Must be some kind of technology. But yeah, it's been a heck of a year with the school shootings and Rose Buds and Lucinda Buckalew. The woman was a piece of work, but dead's dead and it's still a tragedy even if she was trash.

I didn't want to push too hard, and I didn't have to. The tales of Salt Rock poured out of them without prompting: the history of the Dufour family who'd lost the little boy—they were new to the area, been here only two, maybe it was three years, then with the Elvis money and all, they moved away to the coast or something—Rose Buds wasn't a very nice shop even if it did sell flowers, and most of its business was funerals anyway and that's depressing.

How'd it burn? Rumors. Maybe the sheriff knew something but he wasn't talking, and he was up in Hanksville anyway and almost never got down here unless something really bad happened, which it had, come to think of it. Rumors? Insurance money, mostly—some said the place was about to go out of business and the owner didn't even live here anymore, did he? But there'd been threats after the Elvis show, hadn't there? Yeah, that, too. People were real upset with the way the shop treated the Dufour woman, slave wages and all, but nobody here's getting rich, that's for sure. People watch Elvis? Sure. We put it on in the afternoons. A little bit racy for Mormons, but the church is changing you know. Dessert was coconut-cream pie.

The owner of Whiskey Joe's Rock Shop was just about as talkative, though the clipped sentences and contracted words he used made him tough to follow. I found him the next morning sitting in the sunshine on a cane-bottom chair outside a dusty window choked with a lifetime's collection of nondescript rocks and chunks of fossil bone and shell. He looked like part of the collection: a narrow and dusty face under a full beard, tangled white hair and a frame so thin it was almost skeletal. His given name was Howard, he said, but Whiskey Howard's didn't sound quite right so I should call him Joe. His delight at having a visitor indicated the rarity of the experience.

The old man walked me through his shop, explaining that Salt Rock was in the middle of some of the best fossil limestone in North America, and the Anasazi Indians had been here, too, so it was almost impossible to take a step up in the mountains without tripping over a T-rex or a thousand-year-old Indian pot. Illegal as hell to keep anything like that, he said, and he'd certainly never do such a thing. I realized he was worried I might be some sort of federal fossil cop or something, so I gave him about half an explanation of why I was there.

"Elvis, huh?" he said. "Haven't seen it. Don't own a TV. Complete goddamned waste of time, ask me. Better things to do." He gave me a disbelieving look. "You all the way from Dallas for a flower-shop fire?"

I nodded.

He smiled at the thought of it. "More money than sense. Sure I knew the Buckalew woman. Too goddamned bad, ask me. Never be homecoming queen but she was a decent sort, get to know her."

"What'd you hear about the fire?"

"All sorts of things town like this. Pretty goddamned simple. Somebody got irate after that TV show, burned the place down."

"She live at the shop?"

The old man shook his head. "Shouldn't have been there."

"I heard it might be an insurance scam."

He let out a wheezy chuckle. "Bullshit. Place wasn't worth the matches."

"Hear who might have done it?"

"Enough goofballs around here fill the goddamned football field. Your pick."

"But you think it was the TV show, the Elvis show?"

The man seemed to study the question and slowly nodded his head. "Think people's feelings was hurt, ask me. Didn't see this Elvis thing, but the way I hear made us out to be shit-kickers and hillbillies. Lot of irate folks. And real irate at the shop. Just a goddamned flower shop but people are funny, huh?"

"Why'd people get mad at the flower shop?"

A long pause again. Finally: "Ask me, I think they got real confused about those killings at the school. People mad, scared. Needed somebody to take it out on. Along comes this fuss about Rose Buds and, bingo, goddamn, there's a target.

Dead kids. Vengeance is mine sayeth the Lord. Burn the god-damned thing down. Just opinion but I'm born and starved these parts so I know people pretty good." The old man paused at that and seemed to be weighing a thought in his head. "Perception's funny thing. Everybody knows Lucinda didn't kill that little boy. But it got twisted all around. All around. Ended up killing her. You talk to her brother. Name's Lewis. Draw you a map so you can find it. Can or two shy of a six-pack but I s'pect he knows up from down on this. Use my name."

The old man hunted down a scrap of paper and wrote out directions. Then, with an odd look I couldn't decipher, he guided me wordlessly to a small room at the rear of the shop where he pulled back a tarp to reveal a bone that had to be at least six feet long and almost a foot thick. The fossil had been painted a shiny brick red and rested in a handmade wooden cradle.

"T-rex," he said. "When monsters walked the land."

I waited for him to elaborate but he was silent. "Nice bone," I offered.

His glance lingered on the fossil for several long seconds before he covered it back up and turned to me. "You go talk with Lewis, son."

As I drove away, the old man was taking his cane-bottom chair back inside the shop.

Lucinda Buckalew's brother didn't actually live in a double-wide, as I'd expected. That would have been a step up from the squalid log-and-plywood shack where I found him. Three wild-looking dogs barked and bit at my tires as I pulled into the dirt lot. A sheer limestone cliff rose up on one side of the shack and I could see toward the back a cave someone had dug into the soft rock.

I waited in the car and after a while a man appeared and called the dogs back. The man was tall and thin with a pro-nounced bulge around his waist and brown hair that spilled greasily down onto his shoulders.

He approached the car as though it was booby-trapped and I realized with a small sense of shock that the bulge around his waist was actually an old-fashioned gun belt with a pistol holstered on his right hip. In any other circumstance, the get-up would have looked comical. Here, amid the limestone cliffs, caves, log shacks and mangy dogs, it seemed precisely appropriate. There was little in the way of friendliness in his greeting.

Using Whiskey Joe's name in every other sentence, I explained some of who and why I was. That only seemed to make things worse.

"Elvis?" he said, as though the word was vinegar. He rocked back on his heels and gave me a hard look, his right hand resting casually on the grip of the pistol. "Would that by any chance be the same Elvis that accused my sister of being a slave owner?"

"I don't think that was the intention," I said, though even as I said them, the words sounded feeble and ineffectual. How do you sensibly argue with a man with a pistol on his hip? How do you ever win such an argument?

The man fingered the leather snap that held the pistol in the holster. "Sounded that way to me," he said. "Sounded that way to a lot of people who live around here. Sounded enough like it that it was a death sentence. Might as well have stuck up a dead-or-alive poster with her face on it after that happened."

"But I heard in town there might have been something about insurance? That it might have been the owner burning the place down to get the money?"

The man actually laughed and spit on the ground. The gesture seemed so outlandish, so predictable, that I thought for an instant he was putting me on, that this was all some scene he'd copied from a bad Western and that now we'd both get the joke, slap each other on the back and get on with a civilized conversation. But if it was a joke, only one of us was getting it. "Tell you what, you fancy piece of dog shit. The only thing stopping me killing you right now is at least one other person knows where to look for the body."

It was like someone had hit me with a hot wire. This psychopath wasn't kidding.

He took a step toward me and I backed toward the car. "You give that motherfucker Elvis a message for me. You've got my word on it. He's a motherfucking dead man."

A couple of cute retorts occurred to me—like he didn't know how right he was—but I got in the car and backed out of the lot without saying another word. Through forty-odd years, I've been able to duck and weave my way through life without ever being at a real loss for words, and I've seldom left an argument without getting in at least one good parting shot. This time was different. Through those forty-odd years, I had never come up against another human who would actually rather kill me than look at me, and who was prepared to do it. Standing there in that miserable dirt lot, I'd suddenly figured out that there was another world out there, a world that didn't make it into our precious television sitcoms and East Coast editorials. It was a world of blinding ignorance and casual violence where all my cherished little notions of fair play, civilization and goodwill were so much dust in the wind. And it was a world I didn't care to see again.

I got in my car and did a quick U-turn back the way I'd come. It astonished me that people like this guy actually existed out there. And it made me furious with myself that I'd turned tail so quickly. Fury and adrenaline were combining in potent mixture as I made my way back toward town, and I had to almost physically will myself to bring things back under control—and to remind myself that the brother might be a psychopath, but the sister was, as far as I could tell, an innocent victim. An innocent victim of something much larger, and much more dangerous, than a half-witted shit-kicker in a Utah canyon.

I finally brought my system down to nearly normal and figured my next step would be to drive to Hanksville to try to find the sheriff. I stopped off at Best Steaks for lunch. Tango King wasn't around but mom was solicitous as ever and served up a hamburger with grilled onions. She turned on the television to catch the news and I watched as I chewed. The audio was off but I didn't need sound to figure out the pictures. There was a story about Iraq—old file pictures of Saddam Hussein and an exterior of the UN building in New York. An item about stocks. They'd dropped significantly: the screen said three and a half percent with a red arrow pointing downward. Then a tape of what appeared to be the aftermath of a bad fire. Trucks with flashing lights, firemen rolling hoses, the open doors of ambulances spilling light across a background of smoking rubble. A graphic on the lower edge of the shot said nineteen killed. The tape ended and the anchorman came back on. Over the anchorman's shoulder was a picture of Elvis Presley—our Elvis Presley—and below it the logo of the Leese Broadcasting Network. I swallowed hard and jumped up to turn the sound on.

"Fucking thing," I yelled as the sound came up slowly with a green arrow superimposing itself across the center of the screen. ". . . are denying the broadcast in any way encouraged acts of aggression or violence against the American gay community." The Elvis picture dissolved into a headshot of Clare Leese. "The owner of the Elvis program admits the nightclub that burned last night in Seattle was one of twelve homosexual clubs the show displayed during its broadcast about homosexuality in America. But he firmly denies any direct responsibility for the fire. In other news . . ."

I stood there staring at the television, paralyzed by the shock of what I'd just seen. What was that? We hadn't planned any gay shows. Nineteen people? I reached for my wallet to pay the bill. What the fuck had Leese gotten himself into? Gotten me into?

CHAPTER TWENTY-FIVE

LEESE WAS in his office at the theater, his feet on the desk, his hands webbed behind his gray hair as I burst through the door the next afternoon. He didn't seem particularly surprised to see me, though I hadn't told him I was returning.

"Enjoy your vacation?" he asked. His voice had an edge of smugness to it I hadn't heard before.

I ignored his question: "What's with the show?"

"The show?" he smiled and brought his feet down from the desk. "You must learn to be more precise, Mr. Upton. To what show do you refer? Today's show? That's well in hand, no thanks to you. We're doing the border crisis. Maybe you'll drop by to watch?"

"You know the show. The gay show."

Leese pursed his lips as though deep in thought. "Let's see. We did alter programming somewhat when you dashed away for your precious rest? How was Utah, by the way?"

I recoiled inwardly, as one would recoil from a hot stove. I hadn't told Leese where I was headed. The dirty photos of Bahr flashed through my head.

Leese didn't wait for an answer. "The day you left our plans fell apart. The guest got cold feet. So we simply went in another direction, exposing to the light one of the uglier aspects of this culture. Bad for some, I'll admit, but quite good for us. Some of the highest numbers we've ever had. Mr. Bahr's idea, actually. Really quite remarkable numbers." Leese's gray eyes were alive. "One out of four households, in fact. It seems, Mr. Upton, that our fortunes truly are the misfortunes of others." He spread his hands before him. "What's a person to do, huh?"

"But you actually ran a list of gay nightclubs?"

"A public service. Some are quite close to schools and other public structures, you know."

"It's like drawing a bull's-eye."

"No, Mr. Upton, a spotlight. We simply chose the dozen worst and threw the spotlight of public awareness on them." Leese shook his head sadly. "And what that spotlight revealed is almost too base for human contemplation. Actual dens of sodomy. Can you imagine?"

"But nineteen people are dead. People who shouldn't be dead."

"It's actually twenty-three," said Leese. "They found four more bodies this afternoon. Twenty-three."

"You should have talked to me first."

Leese looked at me quizzically. "But you weren't here, Mr. Upton. Everyone is entitled to their rest. Entitled to recreate without interference. We did just fine in your absence. Really, we did just fine. One out of four households. You can't argue with the numbers. That's very good television."

I leaned back against the wall and rubbed my eyes, exhaustion sweeping across me like a dark wave. I'd gotten out of the news business so I'd never have to carry another casket. Good God. They were stacking up like cordwood.

So many things had occurred to me on the flight back, things I wanted to tell Leese, things I wanted to get straight with him. I'd gone through it over and over in my head. I'd make a scene, set the man straight. I'd tell Leese that you can't treat people the way you treated BB Bahr, the way you treated the senator's son, the way you treat the whole world. You can't do that. You can't twist reality around to serve your own little power-hungry purposes. I'd tell him the truth. I'd tell him once and for all that I wasn't in the business to hurt people. But as I looked into his gray eyes all I felt was emptiness and exhaustion. And shame. Leese didn't understand what he'd done. "We need to talk, Clare. We need . . ."

The small man cut me off in midsentence. "I'm late for a meeting," he said briskly, shooting a cuff to look at his watch and rising from his chair. "You need some rest. And it's almost showtime."

"CONGRESSIONAL HEARINGS are set to begin today in Washington to look into the growing problem of illegal immigration across the U.S.-Mexican border."

John Sinclair tilted his head slightly as the shot changed to a different camera and a boxed picture of a barbed-wire fence appeared in the upper right of the screen. "The move comes after last week's gang-rape of a ten-year-old San Diego girl by a group of illegals who had crossed over from Tijuana." Sinclair's face was replaced by a tape of the president and first lady emerging from the White House and waving to a knot of reporters. "The president himself has taken the lead on this, promising legislation within days to stamp out what he calls 'this menace from the south.'"

I hurried into the control room late to find Leese sitting in my chair at the rear console. He glanced at me as I entered but made no move to get out of my seat.

"And ready animation," said Jolene from the front of the room. "And—let's take it."

The opening theme poured from the speakers as the tape rolled.

Leese keyed the intercom—my intercom: "Let's keep it brisk," he said.

On the twin monitors at the front of the control room, the Sinclair face had been transformed into Elvis. Bahr-Elvis looked up at the camera and nodded.

"I want to keep this lively," said Leese, "lively and moving. Real quick into the guests. Got it?" Another simultaneous nod from the two heads.

"And—cue Elvis," said Jolene softly into her mike.

Elvis came to life on the main screen in the studio and the audience cheered and clapped. He let it run for a few seconds and quieted them with a movement of his arms. "You're great people," he said, "great people, all of you." Another eruption of applause and he waved it away. "We need to get down to business quick today because we have so much ground to cover."

Someone in the audience shouted out "You the man!" and laughter rippled across the crowd. Elvis smiled. "You're good folk, good folk, all of you. God did good when he turned out this lot, but let's get down to business now. You just saw the news with John Sinclair. You saw the thing about Congress holding hearings about the border problem. You saw how the president is getting involved. God did good when he turned out this president, let me tell you." A thick burst of applause at that and Elvis moved again to quiet them. "And you saw the item from San Diego and the absolutely hideous, awful, gut-wrenching rape of that poor dear ten-year-old girl. I know God works in mysterious ways. I know that. But a little part of me died inside when I heard that news."

Elvis paused briefly to collect himself and the camera switched to a wide shot of the audience, as though to give Elvis some privacy to deal with his emotions. He cleared his throat, and the shot came back on him, this time up close, his face all but filling the screen. "So let's get to it, good people. Stay right here, because in ninety seconds, that's just a minute and a half, we're going to talk about the monsters in our back-yard. And you, ladies and gentlemen, you are going to meet that little girl. Ninety seconds, starting—now."

I turned to Leese, startled. "You got the girl?"

He was on the intercom to Bahr and didn't pay any attention to me. "I want tears, big guy, tears. You hear that?"

"She's pretty young," said Bahr as the makeup woman wiped the sweat from his face.

"Tears," snarled Leese. "I want tears and I want them fast. Got that?"

Bahr nodded. In the monitor next to him, Elvis nodded, too.

I raised my voice. "The girl's only ten."

Leese was looking at the screens. "Ten, twenty. Rape's rape."

Jolene glanced back over her shoulder at the two of us, a look of uncertainty in her eyes.

"But she's a baby," I said. "You can't do that."

Leese turned and looked me full in the face, fixing me with a hard stare. "I can't do that, Mr. Upton? Who says I can't do that, Mr. Upton?"

"The law says you . . ."

He didn't let me finish. "This transcends the law."

"Thirty seconds," said Jolene from the front of the room, her words clipped and anxious.

"But she's a juvenile."

"Makes it a better story," snapped Leese. He keyed the intercom to Bahr. "Don't fuck this up." A grim nod from Bahr and Elvis.

"Clare," I said, standing up from my chair, "we can't do this. You can't even name a juvenile victim, let alone put her on national TV."

"And—fifteen," said Jolene.

"Quiet, Mr. Upton, or I'll have you removed."

Have me removed? Have me removed from a fucking show I created? I felt the blood rush to my face.

"And—ten, nine, eight . . ."

Like some zombie, I sat back down, dumbly watching the screens come to life, my mind short-circuiting with anger and confusion—have me removed from a show I built?

"And we're back," said Elvis. "We're going to bring our guests on-stage now. This is a tough moment, tough for all of us. We have a little girl—remember, she's only ten—and she's been brutally violated, raped, by a pack of jackals so we need to understand her pain. She has her mom and dad here to help her through this. And we've brought her minister in as well." Elvis looked from side to side in the screen, as though looking around the studio. "Are we ready? Okay, I think we're ready. Let's bring them on now."

The applause grew as a small parade filtered in from off-stage led by a statuesque blond woman in a silver gown: a portly white-haired man in black with a clerical collar at his throat and behind him, walking slowly and uncertainly, a little girl in a knee-length white dress gripping the hand of her mother on one side, her father on the other. The small procession arranged themselves on two sofas, the mother and father sandwiching the girl on one, the minister sitting alone on the other. The blonde disappeared back into the wings.

The girl looked even younger than ten. Her brown hair was tied back in twin ponytails and she was wearing black strap-on little-girl shoes and bobbysocks with pink and blue flowers embroidered into them. She demurely tucked her hands into her lap and dropped her gaze.

Mom—mid-thirties, attractive—fussed with the girl's hair. Dad—forties probably, Italian suit, hair moussed back—was staring out at the audience with a stiff-necked look of anxiety. The minister was checking out the Elvis screen.

"A welcome to our guests," said Elvis. "The Right Reverend Nigel Stains of the First Methodist Church of Rio del Plata, California." The camera moved slowly from face to face as Elvis spoke. "Mr. and Mrs. Richard Evans and their daughter, Jenny. Folks, thank you for coming. I know this is a hard, painful thing but God tests us in hard and painful ways. Jenny"—the shot moved to a tight closeup of the girl's face—"we're all your good friends here. You know that, don't you?

The girl brought her eyes up to the screen and nodded to Elvis.

"We're not going to do anything to hurt you. Now, we want you to tell us what happened on that bad day two weeks ago. Can you do that?"

The girl looked from Elvis to her father, and then to her mother, who nodded and took her hand. She took a breath as if to speak but hesitated and looked around again uncertainly.

"It's okay, Jenny. I'll help you along here a little bit. We've talked to your mom and dad and so we know a lot of what happened that day. You were out with a bunch of your friends, right?" The little girl nodded shyly. "You'd been to a 7-Eleven, right? It was hot and the bunch of you got Slurpies. What flavor'd you get, Jenny? Cherry. Did you get cherry?"

"Lime," said the girl.

"Ah, my favorite," said Elvis. "Nothing like a lime Slurpie on a hot summer day. There just is nothing like it. Don't you agree out there, audience?" A sprinkle of applause and the girl seemed to relax a little.

"So you were out getting lime Slurpies at a 7-Eleven with a bunch of friends. And then you got separated, right?" The girl nodded. "Some of your friends went one way, another group went another way and you started walking home alone? Can you tell us the story from there, Jenny?"

Back in the control room, Jolene ordered the head-on camera to go very tight on the girl and her face now completely filled the screen. I sat there feeling the outrage grow, my blood boiling.

"Go ahead, Jenny. We need to know what happened to you. We need to know so we can make sure it doesn't happen to any other little girls."

"Well," said the girl, "we got the Slurpies and then, like, I was supposed to be at home." She looked at her mother as though for permission to continue. Her mother nodded softly and the girl resumed. "Well, then my friends and me sort of split up."

"My friends and I," whispered her mother.

"My friends and I," said the girl, hesitating again and looking around uncertainly.

"You're doing great. So you and your friends got the Slurpies and you had to get home so you split up. Go ahead, Jenny, tell us what happened then."

"Well, I guess I shouldn't of done it. There's these railroad tracks I cut across. And I saw these boys following me."

"How many boys, Jenny?"

"A whole bunch, I guess."

The shot of the little girl dissolved to a video of her walking alone down a deserted railroad track. The pictures had been Geldered—there was no way cameras could have been there for the actual event—and she was wearing the same little girl's dress she had on today.

"Did you know them?" Elvis asked over the top of the tape. A group of young men had fallen into step fifteen or twenty yards behind the girl.

The girl shook her head. "No. I mean it's like they . . . I mean I didn't see them before." The girl paused and the camera came back on her. She looked confused.

"It's okay, Jenny. So you didn't know these men. Do you remember what color they were Jenny?"

The girl looked at Elvis uncertainly.

"Were they like you, Jenny? Were they white men? Or were they brown?"

"They were really tan."

Elvis paused for a long, telling beat, fixing the audience with a knowing look. "They were really tan. Okay, Jenny. We're with you now. You're going down the railroad tracks, minding your own business, just a little kid headed for home, and this pack of tan men starts following you. So then what happened?" The video came back on the wall monitors. The group of young men was closing in on the little girl.

"Well, they started catching up so I started running. But they were really fast and they caught up with me and one of the men tripped me and I fell down." On the monitors, the girl lay sprawled on her back on the ground and the men were in a circle around her. The tape faded to black and the girl was unconsciously rubbing her knees as though reliving the violence of that day. Her mother took her hands, but the girl wrenched them free and started rubbing her knees again. "And then they were all on top of me but it wasn't any fun. They were . . . I mean . . . they were hurting me."

Her mother took the girl's hands again and squeezed them. On the other side, her father was staring off into the distance above the heads of the audience, a stricken look on his face.

"I know, Jenny, I know." Elvis paused, looked around at the audience, seemed to study his own hands for a moment and looked back to the side as though he was looking at the girl.

"Hold the shot," said Jolene in the control room. "Nobody even twitch."

Elvis cleared his throat nervously. "Jenny, have you ever seen boys naked?"

"This is fucking outrageous!" I shouted, jumping from my chair and turning on Leese. "Stop this!"

Leese barely glanced my way. "Jolene, you hold that shot. Somebody else up there, call security. Now."

"You can't do this!" I said. "You've just fucking ruined that kid's life."

Leese keyed the intercom to Bahr as though I wasn't even there. "Have her show us how they pulled up her dress."

Bahr-Elvis looked at the screen uncomprehendingly.

"Show us how they pulled up her dress," Leese hissed. "Now!"

Jolene stood up and started taking off her headset.

Leese glanced at her. "Take that off, you don't work again. Ever."

Jolene sat back down.

I looked from the monitors to Leese to Jolene, back to the monitors and back to Leese. Elvis was saying something but I couldn't hear it for the blood pounding through my brain. I couldn't stop it. Like a nightmare I couldn't wake from, I couldn't stop it. "Clare," I said, "please, listen to me. Can't you see what you're doing. You're branding that little girl. She's always going to be the little raped girl. Clare, do you . . ."

Suddenly, an arm came around my neck and my head was jammed down into my chest and I felt myself being lifted off the floor. Something was choking my throat and I was gagging and then I was being physically carried out of the control room. I didn't even have a chance to see if Leese was watching before I was out in the hall, like a sack of garbage half-carried, half-dragged to a side door, where they gave me a toss and I landed on the asphalt of the parking lot, tiny stars of light exploding in my eyes and my knees erupting in pain.

I sat up, trying to collect myself, trying to marshall my dignity, but there was very little of it left. Two guards I knew very well were standing in front of the door, their muscled arms crossed on their chests in a posture of almost incidental threat.

"Fuck you," I spat. "Fuck both of you."

They said nothing, their eyes flat, hard and expressionless.

I struggled to my feet, my knees protesting in pain, and straightened my clothes. "Go fuck yourselves. And tell that scrawny little midget-fuck Leese to go fuck himself, too."

I limped across the lot to my car and unlocked the door, my hands shaking so badly I could barely manage the key. I slammed the door and sat there trying to bring the trembling under control—and unconsciously rubbing my knees.

CHAPTER TWENTY-SIX

THE NEXT couple of days were some of the worst I'd ever known—what I can remember of them. I went home that afternoon and drank until I simply passed out. No pretense. No excuses. I simply drank until I passed out. I awoke in a daze the next morning to a man in a black suit pounding on my door. He thrust some papers in my face and told me I no longer worked for the Leese Broadcasting Network. He threatened me with prison if I violated the confidentiality terms of my severance. And he threw a check at my feet. I didn't look at it. Fuck Clare Leese. I drank some more and fell into darkness.

Somewhere in there Margaret phoned a couple of times but I let the machine take the calls. And I drank some more.

It was three days before I started sobering up. The bottom came when I staggered into the bathroom to vomit and caught a reflection of myself in the mirror. I barely recognized the man. My eyes were bloody and baggy, my clothes wrinkled and stained, my hair matted on my head like the fur of some abandoned mongrel, and I had a three-day growth of beard. I made myself clean up—slowly. My hands trembled so much I could barely shave. After a while, I gagged down some scrambled eggs and sat at the table taking stock of myself and my situation.

The downsides seemed like a black pit with no bottom. I was out of work and had no prospects. I'd made an enemy of Clare Leese and in the process cut myself off from ever hoping to find a job in Dallas, probably in most other big cities. I'd been out of the news business long enough that I probably couldn't get back in—at least not at the level I'd been at. And my most recent experience, as they liked to say on resumes, was in a line of work I vowed never to touch again as long as I lived. I was single, alone and without an identifiable future.

Hopeless, but maybe not completely hopeless, I realized—and the prospect cheered me up a little—I had a good pot of money stashed away. That could keep me going for four or five years, more if I scrimped. I was healthy enough—if I could get away from the Scotch. And I was away from Clare Leese. Thank God for little courtesies. I was done with the poison that had become Clare Leese. The last scenes from the rape show rolled through my mind and I shuddered. But I was pulling myself together, and it was beginning to feel good.

After a week or so, I made contact with Margaret, telling her I'd left the show and giving her some of the details. She sounded pleased and we made a date to make a date for dinner. That was good enough for me. I didn't want more commitment than that. More than my knees had been skinned on the asphalt.

I stayed low, and worked on recovering. Rule one was no more booze. None at all. I even threw out a couple of beers I had in the refrigerator. And I started jogging. Well, not really jogging—more like walking faster than usual. I did a lot of it. Miles and miles of long solitary conversations with myself.

Funny, the ambivalence losing a job can create. In some respects it was like going into mourning. I missed it the way I'd miss somebody who died and disappeared from my life. I missed the regularity and pattern it gave to the days, the sense of purpose—even if the purpose in this case had become distorted and ugly. It had been a reason to get up in the morning and to go to bed at night—I went to bed because I had to get up. Now that was all gone, and it was like somebody had stolen my clock: I didn't get up in the morning, I didn't go to bed at night. My soul didn't know what time it was.

On the other hand, it was like a mist was lifting and I was beginning to see things around me that I hadn't known were there. For the first time that I could remember, I actually saw people walking down the street. Not people I knew: just people. People walking down the street. Somehow I hadn't noticed them before, locked away as I was in my own metronomic world where everything was rushed, where the only thing that mattered was the next show, where the only people I noticed were people who were important to my work, important to the next show.

And the colors: I started seeing colors as though for the first time. It hit me when I realized that the hedge outside my apartment building was actually two hedges: one olive green, the one behind it a blue-green. I don't think I had ever even seen the hedges before. It was almost as though they had sprouted into life in the course of three or four days.

What I saw most profoundly, though, was what I had been living through. I traced it out in my head day after day: Marilyn, Gelder, the early fun with the show, and then Leese's arrival—the money, the high-wire excitement of it all, the new car, life lived large, so large. I'd been too busy—too high—to see it as it crested and began to slide toward a nightmare. Or maybe I had gotten a glimpse of it but hadn't cared: the ugly outline had been obscured by the come-on curves of dollar signs.

At any rate, I'd emerged from the literal bum's rush out of the Elvis show into a new existence. Some parts of it were good, some parts bad. On balance, though, it seemed to me I'd come through okay. I think Margaret agreed.

After more phone calls back and forth, we finally worked out a time and place for dinner. A small Mexican restaurant tucked away in a tatty strip mall but rumored to have good food. I'd gotten through a bowl of chips by the time she rushed in, all apologies for being late.

I hadn't seen her since I'd gone to Utah—before the mists had started to clear—and was surprised again at what a spectacular human being she was. This night she seemed radiant.

The blue eyes set against the red of her hair fairly sparkled with intelligence and life. She'd added a touch of makeup and her lips gleamed in the soft light. She pulled off her jacket as she sat down to reveal a silver satin blouse that did nothing to conceal the very prominent outline of her nipples. I had to consciously force my eyes away to avoid embarrassing myself.

"You look spectacular," I said.

"And you look thin," she said. "Being a man of leisure obviously agrees with you."

I smiled. "No complaints. How's school?"

A waiter interrupted and she ordered a margarita, I another iced tea.

"School's school," she said, shaking her head in mock disgust. "Sometimes they're with me, sometimes they're not."

"And you're teaching what?"

"Umberto Eco."

"And he's . . . ?"

". . . an extraordinary Italian writer. *Foucault's Pendulum?*" A gentle, challenging smile shown in her eyes and on her lips.

"Sorry," I said. "Guess I have some catching up to do, huh?"

She nodded, trying to help me along. "*The Name of the Rose?*"

"What rose?"

She laughed out loud. "You ARE hopeless, aren't you? It's a book. *The Name of the Rose.* They made it into a movie. Sean Connery, I think."

"That rose."

"Umberto Eco wrote the book."

"Cool."

She studied me for a time, the smile on her face gradually fading into a look of concern. "So tell me how you're doing, Nick."

The waiter brought the drinks. "I'm doing pretty well, actually. I had a couple of rough weeks but I got over them. Pulling myself up by the bootstraps and all that."

"Have you talked with Leese?"

I shook my head. "There's nothing to say."

"Was it bad?"

My mind flashed on the control room and the two men throwing me into the headlock. At least it had taken two of them. "It was ugly."

"Want to talk about it?"

I shrugged. "There's not much to talk about, really. I didn't like what he was doing and told him so. He had me thrown out."

"It was the rape show, wasn't it?"

"You know about that?"

"It's been in the papers for days."

"I haven't been reading them." I didn't tell her that I'd decided I would never read another newspaper again.

"It's causing a lot of outrage. It was quiet for a week or so after the show, but Elvis came back to it and things have been getting worse. Even the president's gotten involved now."

"The president?"

Margaret nodded. "They've passed some sort of emergency legislation and they're building a wall through San Diego."

"A wall?"

"It's worse than that."

I looked at her with a question in my eyes.

"Vigilantes," she said. "They're calling themselves something else, border-watch volunteers or something, but they're vigilantes. They've been rounding up illegals and turning them in. A lot of them are pretty bloody and bruised."

"I didn't know." I looked away, thinking about the ten-year-old girl. Leese certainly knew how to cut things to the quick. Goon squads rounding up illegals. A hundred people dead in a nightclub fire. What's next?

"I'm sorry, Nick. I thought you knew."

I leaned back in my chair and rubbed my eyes, trying to

blot out a pain I felt growing there. "I haven't been watching much news."

Margaret pulled some money from her purse and laid it on the table. "Come on," she said, "I'll make you a taco at my place." Her nipples were hard and the look on her face was serious and unmistakable.

We were barely through her front door before we were in each others arms. Without preface and without words, our lips came together in an urgency and precision that surprised both of us, our bodies locking into each other like two steel plates fusing under the heat of an electric arc. Piles of clothing marked a trail to the bedroom where we twisted against each other in a disarray of dim lights and discarded sheets. She seized me in her hand as I roughly kissed across her silken skin, her back arching out and presenting her breasts to my mouth. I rolled to lie upon her, but she suddenly stopped me with her hands and a movement of her shoulders.

"Wait," she said, gasping for breath, "wait a minute. There's something I need to do."

I lay back, fondling my erection as I watched her dim form roll naked from the bed and walk to the window. She pulled down the shade and moved across the room and switched on the light.

I flinched backward. "Bright," I managed to say, shading my eyes with my arm.

"It's something that I need to do."

I brought my arm down. She stood at the foot of the bed surveying me, her face serious, her ribs and her breasts moving with the heaviness of her breath. I started to pull up the sheet.

"Don't," she said. "Please. Let me say this." She looked away for a brief instant and then looked back. "I don't want this to be trivial. I won't allow it to be casual." She moved slightly to widen her stance. "I want you, Nick. I very much want you inside me." She came around the bed and lay down next to me, her legs apart. "I want us both to see this. I want this to be two humans giving everything to each other and being witness to the gift."

I swung over her and felt myself enter. She closed her eyes as I plunged deeply into her and her eyes came open and she gazed at me long and hard as her muscles contracted around me like a vise. I could feel her spasms stirring inside and I drove in deep, impossibly deep, and we hit the edge at the same time and poised there, arched against each other, my chest against hers, neither of us daring movement, her eyes wide and hard on mine, and then just the hint of a movement and I felt myself losing control, and a small enigmatic smile spread on her face and I smiled back, and we drove against each other hard and harder and even harder, and suddenly the wave broke over us as though we were one body, consuming, devouring, extinguishing, forgiving.

CHAPTER TWENTY-SEVEN

NICK, WAKE up. I think you need to see this."

My eyes opened to a shaft of bright sunshine cutting diagonally across the bed.

Margaret's voice again from the other room. "Nick, are you awake?" I could hear the television in the background.

"I hate TV," I yelled good-naturedly.

"You're going to hate this more. Come."

I padded into the living room wrapped in a sheet. Margaret in a white-cotton robe was huddled on the couch watching the television, a mug of coffee untouched in front of her. She turned as I walked in and her eyes looked frightened. "Trouble in LA."

". . . started before midnight," an announcer was saying over pictures of squad cars with flashing lights and screaming sirens rushing down a smoky street. "Police called to the scene of a hit-and-run accident discovered a badly injured Hispanic man lying in the street. As they called in an ambulance, an angry crowd began to gather. Police say it was mostly white and mostly young. Okay, we're going upstairs now to NewsEye Two for an eye-in-the-sky view of the situation.. Roberta, are you there?"

A woman came on, almost shouting to be heard over the roar of helicopter rotors. "We're looking now at Sepulveda Boulevard, Ross, and things are obviously out of control, things are obviously spreading. We're over the Century City area right now. This is where it started." Three tall buildings—they looked like office towers—were burning fiercely. "We don't see any fire apparatus here. I think they can't get through the lines of rioters. Let's pan up the street now." The camera pulled away from the buildings and moved slowly up the broad street where dozens and dozens of smaller buildings were ablaze and giving off thick clouds of black smoke. "It's a war zone, Ross. The LA police and sheriff's department are on a full emergency mobilization, and the mayor is talking to the governor about help from the National Guard. Ross."

"We'll stay with your pictures for a moment, Roberta. Once again, this began as a routine hit and run, police discovering a badly injured Hispanic man near the intersection of Century and Sepulveda Boulevards shortly before midnight. By the time the ambulance arrived, an angry crowd of young whites had gathered. Police say they were chanting 'Jenny' just before the attacks began."

I felt my stomach contract at the sound of the name. My breathing grew shallow, almost as though I was afraid to hear what might be coming next. "Now we're not sure," said the announcer, "mind you, we're not sure, but we think that is probably a reference to the young girl so brutally raped several weeks ago by a gang of Hispanic illegals in San Diego. I think it is fair to say we have a race riot in LA."

"Turn the sound down," I said quietly.

"What?" said Margaret, glancing toward me.

"Please turn the sound down."

Margaret killed the sound and looked at me. "The little girl, huh?"

"I guess so." I looked around for something else to say but there was nothing. One way or another, the trail to the pictures on TV led back to me.

"Maybe it wasn't the show," Margaret offered, but her tone was unconvincing.

"It was the show. One way or another, it was the show." I got up and headed for the bedroom.

"What are you doing?" Worry and fear in her voice. "Nick, what are you doing?"

"I don't know," I said over my shoulder. "Talk to Leese. Talk to somebody. He has to be stopped."

But I couldn't get into the theater. Leese's pickup was there so he had to be inside. But they'd apparently changed the locks on the side entrance and my key card didn't work. The two guards who'd thrown me onto the asphalt were at the lobby entrance. They barred my way as I tried to push through.

"Sorry, Mr. Upton," said one of them, "but you're not allowed in."

"Mr. Leese told me to come by," I said, smiling, casual. "I'm supposed to pick up a check."

The guard was shaking his head. "Sorry. Mr. Leese thought you might stop by and told us under no circumstances were you to be allowed inside. I'm instructed to say that if you have a message for Mr. Leese, you should write him a letter. Sorry Mr. Upton."

"Tell him I stopped by?" I said, turning on my heel and marching back to the parking lot. The two made no move to follow me.

I drove around the city for a while trying to figure things out. Everything led back to Leese. I cruised past his house but the gate was closed and a car with a security guard in it sat outside.

Back at my apartment I turned on the TV. Rioting had spread to San Diego and the governor of California was calling on the president to send in federal troops. Jesus Christ. I had to find Leese. He started it. He could do something to stop it.

I called the theater, disguising my voice as well as I could, and asked for Leese. The operator said he was tied up. No surprise. I asked for Bahr and was told he wasn't available. Frustrated, I asked to be put through to Jolene Pool. I knew she could be counted on to take a phone call even if she was in the middle of a tornado—and this was feeling a lot like a tornado.

The operator put me on hold for a minute and came back to say Jolene Pool was no longer employed there. No longer employed there? That was impossible. If anyone was central to Elvis, to the show, it was Jolene with her detached calm and her extraordinary precision. I told her to check again but she said there was no mistake, there was no Jolene Pool currently working at the theater or at the Leese Broadcasting Network. The ground under my feet was feeling decidedly shaky.

One last shot. "Could you connect me with Duncan Gelder, please."

"I'm sorry," said the operator, efficiently. "He is not employed here."

"That's Duncan Gelder. G-E-L-D-E-R."

"Yes, sir. We have no one employed here by that name."

I mumbled a thanks and hung up the phone, looking at it as though it was somehow the phone's fault that the world was turning upside down. Jolene and Gelder gone? He couldn't put on a show without Jolene and Gelder. Could he?

I found my address book and tried Gelder's home phone number. It rang and rang with no answer. I tried Bahr's home number but a metallic voice on the line said it had been changed and the new number was unlisted. Jolene's message machine picked up on the third ring.

"It's Nick," I said into the device. "What's happening?"

I'd no sooner put the phone down than it rang, startling me enough that I actually jumped at the sound. I picked up the receiver.

"Nick, it's Margaret."

"Hi."

"You've been on the phone?" That tone of voice again that wedged the words somewhere between a declaration and a question.

"Yeah. Weird things at the show."

"That's why I called," said Margaret. "Turn on the show."

"The show?" I said vacantly.

"Turn on the show, Nick. It's on now. Turn it on."

I laid the phone down and switched on the TV. The face of Elvis Presley came on full screen, staring into my eyes. I recoiled inwardly: it was the first time I'd seen the image since the Jenny day. It was a face I'd hoped never to see again.

". . . the situation in Los Angeles and San Diego. We need to stay calm, and we need to stop the rioting. Hear me out there. This is Elvis speaking, and you know this is real, you know I speak the truth. Rioting's not going to do us any good, any one of us. There are other ways to deal with the Mexican problem in this country. If they don't pay taxes, their kids shouldn't go to our schools, they shouldn't get our welfare or our medicine. We can put them in camps, we can toss them back over the border and put up a wall that a possum couldn't climb. But rioting isn't the right thing. There, wait, hold on a second. . . ."

Elvis put his right hand up to his ear, obviously trying to hear something on the miniature earpiece that I knew was connected to Leese's—to my—intercom set.

"I'm sorry," said Elvis, "but this is just coming in to me as we're speaking. Stay with me folks." Elvis looked to his side and back into the camera, a frown of confusion on his face. "Do we have him or not, is what I asked?" He held his hand to his ear, still looking directly into the camera. "Okay, all right. Thank you. Ladies and gentlemen, it's a rare privilege. I think it may be unique in the history of television, but I'm joined now from Washington by the president of the United States."

At that the screen split into two boxes, Elvis on one side, the president on the other seated at his Oval Office desk. I sat back in shock. If it was real, it was the coup of the century. Astonishing, if it was real. If it was Geldered, it was the most reckless stunt in the history of the business. There was no way to tell which it was.

"Sir, it's an honor that you'd join the Elvis show today."

I grabbed the remote and frantically switched through the other channels. Bahr-Elvis was right. This was unique. The president—or what appeared to be the president—was appearing on the Elvis show and on the Elvis show alone. The other nets didn't have him.

". . . developments on the ground," the president was saying. "Governor Nelson called me a couple of hours ago, Elvis, and asked for help and I consented. By executive order effective immediately, I'm sending in a number of units from the Eighty-second Airborne Division in North Carolina. The lead elements should be arriving on the ground in both LA and San Diego within eight hours. I'm also dispatching units of heavy armor from the First Armored Division at Fort Hood, Texas. Lead elements should be arriving in six hours."

I switched quickly through the other channels again. One had already swallowed its pride and was running the shot of Elvis and the president boxed side by side. What were Leese's words? "Give me a place to stand"?

I switched back to Elvis. The president looked down and cleared his throat and then looked back into the camera. "Elvis, I want to tell the American people that we will get through this. It will take common sense and courage, but those are two qualities found in abundance across this great land. And also, let me assure the American people we will deal with this nation's border problem. It has festered too long, and when the fires are out, we will move aggressively to put it behind us. And a personal note to you, Elvis, that I want the American people to hear. You're doing the Lord's work. Thank you from me and from the nation I lead for allowing me to appear on your show. God bless you."

Elvis looked like he was weeping. "On behalf of all Americans, I thank you, Mr. President. I want to thank you as well for joining us today. I know this is a difficult time. And I want to extend an invitation, Mr. President. Anytime you'd like to come on and talk to us—and to America—about our problems, and about triumphs, we'd be proud to have you here, sir."

The president smiled and nodded his head. "You have my

promise, Elvis, and it's a promise to the American people as well: I'll make sure we aren't strangers."

The shot switched back to a single full-frame facial of Elvis Presley. "Our president, ladies and gentlemen. We're going to break now for a commercial."

I switched off the set and looked around the room dazed. Whether it was real or Geldered, the effect was the same: the president of the United States had just established a public political alliance with a computer-generated electronic image. I realized the phone was still lying on the table and scooped it up. "You still there?"

"I'm here," said Margaret. Her voice was shaky and uncertain.

"Fuck me."

"That makes two of us," she said.

"I can't believe that just happened."

"I can't believe any of it's happened. What do we do?"

"Find a hole and climb in?"

"I'm frightened," said Margaret.

"Want some company?"

"I do," said the woman.

"On my way," I said, forcing more energy and optimism into my voice than I felt. Leese and the president of the United States? My stomach turned at the thought. Leese had proven his power for the world to see. There wasn't much that could get in his way now. He'd stopped a Senator and created enough hatred that the attorney general and the head of the FBI would probably lose their jobs. He'd caused arson. He'd caused riots. He'd managed to get the U.S. military called out. And now he'd summoned the president of the United States to appear on his network, and the president had obeyed.

As I started to climb into my car, I spotted a piece of paper folded beneath the windshield wiper. I grabbed it and slid inside the car, opening and smoothing the paper against the steering wheel. It was in a tight hurried longhand in blue ink on white unlined paper.

Dear Nick,

A friend's delivering this and by the time you read it I'll be three two one long gone. Don't look for me as you won't find me and I don't want to be found. Ever. They tapped my phone and my computer and I think they were following me. They know everything about me, except my plan to fade to black.

I talked to BB Bahr and I know what they did to her. She said you were there and that you were part of it. I didn't believe that then and I don't now, especially after what they did to you, too. After they fired you, Leese and his people wanted me to take a lie-detector test and sign a secrecy pledge. They showed me dirty photos of me having sex with some woman I'd never even met. Me with a woman? Yuck! Gross! But how do you prove a photo is faked, huh? I figured it was only a matter of time so I slipped out the back, Jack.

I don't know what's happened to Duncan. I know he's disappeared. They must have scared him, too, though I can't imagine how. Anyway, he's as long gone as I am and they have some whiz kid from Seattle running the computers.

I'm going to miss you, Nick. You're not a great man but you've had your moments. You're a good man. I'm gone now, like a live shot that never got the signal up. No trace of me, no trace I ever existed. Someday, though, maybe when you have a free second or two, you'll think of me, your friend the director, and smile for what could have been.

With My Love,
Jolene

I sat there and read it three times through before folding it carefully and putting it in my pocket.

CHAPTER TWENTY-EIGHT

MARGARET WAS standing in the driveway and greeted me with a hollow, haunted look. "Leese called," she said. "I just hung up from him. He says he'll see you. How'd he know about me?"

"He called here?"

"A few minutes ago," she said.

"I don't know how he knew about you," I said, but even as I said it I realized it was foolish: Leese made it his business to know everything he needed to know. "How was he? Was he rude?"

"No. He was okay, I guess. Brief. To the point. He said he'd heard you'd stopped by. Sorry he missed you but they had a big show today. I told him I saw it and he asked what I thought. I told him it was repulsive."

I smiled. "I bet he hated that. Good for you."

"He wants to see you."

"He say why?"

"He says you called him. Seven o'clock at his house."

THE SECURITY guard was still sitting in his car when I pulled up a few minutes after seven. I'd chosen to arrive late. There were few things in the world that angered Clare Leese more, and it would be a good reminder that he no longer owned me.

The guard eyed me in the mirror and the main gate swung open silently at my approach. Leese appeared at the front door and watched me walk up.

There was no handshake, no greeting. We exchanged guarded looks and he led me through to the same austere room where he'd told me about staging the shooting in his own theater.

That had been a turning point for me, I realized now, and I'd taken the wrong road. I should have seen it then, seen the ugliness and deceit that was starting to take root in the Elvis enterprise. The evidence was there—and I'd known it. But I'd chosen to ignore it.

People were dead now because of my choice. Everybody was paying for that stupidity. Or was I flattering myself that I could have made a difference even then? Could I have stood up to him, or would I have been flushed away like a scrap of toilet paper and replaced by someone more malleable and more easily corrupted? Though it turned out I was pretty malleable and easily corrupted myself, wasn't I? All it took was a pep talk and an eye-popping check or two. Life lived large, huh?

"Sit down, Mr. Upton," said Leese. It was less an invitation than an order. He took a seat in the rocking chair across from me and smoothed the lapels of his gray suit. "I understand you came by the theater?"

"I did."

"For what reason?"

Good question, I thought to myself. Because I had some misplaced notion he might make everything all right? I didn't answer him.

"Mr. Upton?"

"I came by because I was pissed off."

"'Pissed off,' huh? A vulgar colloquialism coming from you. And what exactly was the cause of your anger?"

I thought about the Jenny show, the riots, the nightclub fire and realized for the first time that my anger was over something else. "I was pissed off, Clare, that I didn't stop you when I could. I should have killed you when you were a baby."

Leese laughed bitterly and shook his head. "Young men and their delusions of power. You never had the power to stop the inevitable."

"I should have tried."

"You perplex me, Nick. I'm serious. Perplex and vex. What is it about *X* words, huh? You are a perplexity and a vexation. You knew from the beginning what this was all about. Remember the day in my office early on when we talked about Hearst? About the Maine? You knew what this was about and you were happy to be a part of it. You were avid to be part of it, if I recall correctly. You took the checks. What happened to change that?"

I sat silent for a few moments considering the response. He was right. I was happy to be part of it for a long time. But it started to sour for me. Had Leese somehow changed? No. He was then as he is now. Had the game changed? Not really. It was always about manipulating public emotion. The stakes had gotten higher, the techniques more refined, but the fundamental game had remained the same. "Maybe I changed," I said simply.

"That's precious," said Leese. "You changed. Got in touch with your feelings, maybe? Got centered? Got some other little bit of psychoanalytical nonsense? You changed. Well, bully for you."

Leese stood up and walked to the mantel where he inspected the red peace pipe for a moment before turning on me suddenly. "You didn't change, Mr. Upton. You just chickened out. You spent all your life in this pissant little world of yours and when you got moved up to the big leagues you didn't have the stomach for it. That's all it was. You didn't have the stomach for it. That's not change, that's cowardice and there's no room in my world for a coward."

I rose from the chair.

"I'm not through," Leese said sharply.

"I'm not either."

"Fine. As I said earlier, you called. What's on your mind? Let's get this meeting over with quick, huh?"

"Why are you doing it?" I said. "The rape show, the riots? The gay clubs? Why do you hate these people so much?"

I could read it on his face—the question seemed to genuinely surprise him. "I don't hate anybody," he said. "You think I hate these people? You think that? Good Lord, Mr. Upton, I gave you more credit than that."

"Then why do you do it?"

Leese looked at me hard for a beat or two before he answered. "They're blenders, Mr. Upton. They're just blenders. You think I have any emotion for the blenders I sell? Don't be absurd. Blenders are a commodity. You don't hate a commodity. The gays are blenders, they're commodities. The Mexicans are blenders. That little ten-year-old girl's a blender. The president himself's a blender. I don't hate them—I use them. I thought you understood that."

"But it's killing people."

"Sometimes people have to die to make the world a better place."

"A better place?" I felt the bile rising in my throat. "A better fucking place? You're killing people. That's a better fucking place?"

Leese fixed me with a disbelieving look. "I very severely overestimated you, didn't I? You think Hearst didn't understand it? You think Teddy Roosevelt didn't know people had to die when he charged up that hill? They both did what they did to make the world a better place. That's all I'm doing."

"You have enough power. So stop."

Leese smiled. "There is never enough of that, I'm afraid."

"I called to ask you to stop," I said simply. "So I'm asking you face-to-face, as one who's been there from the start. Stop it. Too many people are getting hurt. It's time to end it."

Leese shook his head. "Mr. Upton, I invited you here this evening because I thought you might have had a change of heart, that we might be able to reach some sort of working understanding. I'm sure it pains you to hear it, but you're very good at the sort of television I like to do, and I'd still rather have you with me than against me. Now I see, though. You haven't had a change of heart. So be it. But understand this:

you can't stand in my way. I am a tool of the inevitable. And even the all-seeing God can't stop the inevitable." He held my gaze for a long moment. "I tried teaching you about inevitability, but apparently the lesson didn't stick."

I remained silent.

Leese walked back to the peace pipe and examined it for a few moments before turning to me. "You know what they say about weapons? How man never invented a weapon he didn't use? It's the same here, Mr. Upton. A weapon's just a fancy name for a tool—and you happened to stumble on one of the most powerful new tools to come along in thirty or forty years. The continuous manipulation of visual reality. You have no idea, Mr. Upton, how powerful that is. With that little tool, you can literally change the face of the world. Imagine that, Mr. Upton. CHANGE THE FACE OF THE WORLD. But you, sir, don't get it. You're like a caveman looking at a sharp rock. You don't have the imagination to see that some-day that rock will be a nuclear bomb. I have that imagina-tion. I know what sharp rocks can become. I recognize tools of power when they're put in my hand.

"Now, the thing about tools, Mr. Upton, is you can't unin-vent them any more than you can uninvent weapons. This tool is here. It's now. It's inevitable. And it will be used for the accumulation of power; it will be used to change the face of the world. That's what it does. If I walked away from it now—if I were to do as you say and walk away from it, throw up my hands and say 'Oh, this is too evil' and walk away from it—someone else would pick it up. It's that way with tools, Mr. Upton. For better or worse, you can't uninvent them, you can't unimagine them and wish them away. It's like the sharp rock: somebody's going to figure it out. There's no going back."

Leese turned away. "This thing is now beyond you," he said over his shoulder. "I won't threaten you. There's no reason to. If you ponder on it good and long, you will see that you are utterly and completely without power. You are face-to-face with the inevitable. And the inevitable is in my hands. Now, go away. You are no longer good for me."

I took a final long look at the man in the crisp gray suit—there was nothing left to say—and let myself out of his house.

Chapter Twenty-nine

THE RIOTS were wall-to-wall on television when I turned on the news back at the apartment—and things were getting worse. A large part of a Hispanic neighborhood near downtown Los Angeles had been torched. Running gun battles between whites and Hispanics were reported in parts of San Diego, and a column of the California National Guard was stuck in a giant traffic jam in Orange County.

The Elvis interview with the president was everywhere. Most networks were using the original pictures broadcast by Leese: the president—or what appeared to be the president—in a box on the right side of the screen, Elvis listening on the other side. One enterprising network had put its computers on the case and erased the Elvis side completely, expanding the picture of the president to fill the screen. You could hardly tell the picture had been altered—Geldered—except for a small widening of the president's already ample nose. A few minutes later the same picture popped up on a twenty-four-hour-news network.

As I watched the pictures pour in, I realized that if I'd been running a newsroom, I would have done the same thing. I would have stolen the picture, altered it and made it my own. If I'd been running a newsroom. The thought brought me up short and the sound and fury of the riots retreated into the background. If I'd been running a newsroom. In the world of "what ifs" that was a big one.

If I'd been running a newsroom. Pictures washed through my mind: Jolene with her air controller's headset and her reliable studied calm in a crisis. Felicity the assignment editor with the changing hair color running across the newsroom screaming out orders.

If I'd been running a newsroom. That day so long ago when I'd heard Marilyn Monroe in the edit bay. Gelder sitting there with an ice-cream bar in his hand—jumping as I interrupted his session with a dead movie star. Gelder, whose computers created the man up there on the TV talking to the president.

If I'd been running a newsroom, there wouldn't be an Elvis Presley in a box next to the president. There wouldn't be pallbearers.

The hard gray face of Clare Leese swam into my mind. Uninventing an idea. Maybe he was right. Maybe I was just a hapless fool who'd stubbed his toe on a sharp rock and didn't have the sense to know what it was. But I realized sitting there in front of the pictures that Leese had at least some of it wrong. The small gray man who knew so much didn't know he had me figured wrong when he'd called me a coward. I was a coward all right, but not in the way he thought. I wasn't afraid of the big leagues. I wasn't afraid of the power. Wrong, Clare Leese. I was afraid of looking too closely at what I had become. Afraid of looking too closely at what I had created. And when things had finally gotten too tough to stand, I'd thought I could somehow take the easy way out—the coward's way out—by turning my back and pretending it all away, pretending I didn't have the responsibility to end it. I was wrong.

On the television, a fat man in a dirty white T-shirt was spraying a machine gun back and forth down a city street. The cameraman dove for cover and the picture jarred and lurched and came to rest with a shot of the open sky. Incongruously— almost surreally—a yellow biplane flew into the picture trailing a banner advertising a beach concert. Leese's words floated through my head again—as an idea formed in my mind. Utterly and completely powerless? We'd see about that.

"PLUG IT in here," I said, pulling out the phone jack and offering the socket to Margaret. "You need power?"

She shook her head as she got the computer hooked up. "Tell me what we're doing?"

"I'm not sure," I said, honestly. I'd called her after I'd seen the man with the machine gun and the biplane in the sky and asked her to bring over her computer. Mine was in an office I no longer inhabited. "I need to talk to Duncan Gelder."

Margaret shot me a questioning glance. "You said he's disappeared. From what you've told me about this guy, I bet he can cover his tracks pretty well."

"I've got something in mind but I need to get on the Internet."

Margaret keyed in some commands and we watched as the machine chirped and hissed and came up with a net browser. "Tell me what you're looking for?" she said over her shoulder, her eyes on the screen.

"I don't know. Try '3-D' and 'animation.'"

Margaret entered the search words and the screen changed to a page-long list.

"If he's hiding, he won't be on here," said Margaret.

"That's not what I'm doing. Bring the cursor down to that one, the third one."

Margaret moved the arrow down to a line that read "www.hotresin.com/video-scantech.htm" and double-clicked. The screen digested the orders for a few seconds and popped up the image of a white plastic human trunk revolving on a pedestal. A line of lasers passed over it and an identical trunk scanned in next to it.

"Right technology," I said. "Is there a chat room or something like that on the page?"

"Nick, you've lost me."

"This is the kind of stuff Duncan does. Hi-tech animation and reanimation."

"And . . . ?"

"And . . . I don't know. I saw something today that gave me an idea. I'm thinking maybe we can get a message to him." I told her about the man with the machine gun and

how the airplane flew into the shot trailing the banner. "I figure we need to wave a banner at him. Somewhere where he
can see it."

"Gotcha," said Margaret. "We need a news group for that."

It was my turn to be lost.

"Sort of a party line," said Margaret. "I use them at school.
It's a chat room that moves through a whole bunch of ISPs
and URLs."

I gave her an uncomprehending gaze and she smiled, the
first smile I'd seen on her face that day. "Trust me," she said.
"It's like an electronic conversation that goes everywhere. If
he's looking at any of this stuff, he might see it."

"So let's converse."

It took her three tries before "www.hessem.com/redbus.htm"
flashed onto the screen, a news group icon prominent on its
home page. "I think we're there," said Margaret. "It's in the
right discipline, it's a big site. If he's looking at this stuff at all
he might see it. What do you want to say?"

I'd been thinking about that ever since the plane with the
banner. The message would have to be innocuous enough
that it wouldn't draw the attention of others, but specific
enough that Gelder would recognize I was talking to him and
him alone. "Why don't you try this," I said: " 'Duncan. Marilyn's in trouble. Phone Nick.' "

CHAPTER THIRTY

THOUGH I knew better than to expect an instant reply, hope triumphed over logic and I remained through that night and the next day like a prisoner in my own apartment, watching the telephone for a sign that Duncan Gelder was out there and had seen my electronic banner in the sky. Maybe the phone was tapped—but it was a chance I'd have to take.

Margaret packed up her computer after a while and went home.

I checked in with the TV from time to time to follow the West Coast riots. The arrival of federal troops had stopped the looting. No calls. I made an omelette and gulped it down quickly, as though that could somehow hurry things along— and the phone rang, but it was Margaret checking in. I kept the conversation short and gave her my cell phone number. Sometime past midnight I reluctantly went to bed and read for a long time, finally falling into a troubled sleep filled with odd electronic dreams. No calls.

The next morning, I called the phone company and arranged for a service that could forward the phone to my cell phone. At least that way I could get out of the apartment, which was fast taking on the feel of a well-appointed prison cell. But then I had nowhere to go and sat through the day watching the riots end on TV.

By the third day it was becoming preposterous. There was no sign of Duncan Gelder and I was beginning to believe there never would be. I realized the chances of him actually stumbling across the message were so slim as to be almost absurd. And I wondered whether he'd do anything if he did see it. He had gone silent and gone deep. And I had no idea whether he would care enough to respond even if he did happen across a message from a past he had chosen to abandon.

I also started second-guessing the whole idea of trying to reach him. I'd originally reasoned that since he had developed the technology to make Elvis, he would know how to unmake him. The more I thought about it, though, the less promising it seemed. In fact it was beginning to look stupid. Even if Gelder could do something to sabotage the show, it would only be a disruption, not a destruction. Elvis would be back on the air in the time it took to fix the system. That would be almost no time at all given the resources and money Leese could throw at the problem.

The realization threw me into my own dive. I had to have a new plan. But what in the fuck was the plan? Could it be that Leese really did have me checked at all sides? What were his words? "You are utterly and completely without power"? I realized the only way I could make him eat those words was if I could somehow publicly discredit him—make him so wholly unbelievable that he became an object of derision and ridicule. If I could expose the artifice and evil, maybe people might begin to listen. But how?

Margaret and I spent the better part of two days talking about it. She suggested a letter campaign to the major newspapers. We realized, though, that wouldn't get to the right people: the people who watched Elvis—the people who believed in him—weren't the people who read the *New York Times* and the *Washington Post*. We talked about trying to get to the major television networks—maybe on their morning shows—but I knew they probably wouldn't go for it. The network philosophy was to ignore the competition completely, realizing that even bad publicity for the competition would still be publicity and, in essence, free advertising. They might, just might, take Elvis's wife—but they'd never take me.

By Saturday evening, we'd all but talked ourselves out and had adjourned to iced tea and tacos on her patio when my cell phone went off. We looked at each other cautiously over the first two rings and came to the mutual but silent agreement that it couldn't be Gelder. I hit the button.

A voice that sounded clear enough to be calling from the next room said simply, "Gelder."

I took a deep breath, darting a quick glance and nod at Margaret. "How are you?"

"You sent me a message about Marilyn?" He sounded nervous and suspicious. There was little in the way of friendliness in the tone.

"I did. I need to talk to you. Are you okay?"

"What'd you want to talk to me about?"

"Listen, Duncan. I don't know what you may think but I'm not your enemy." I paused, looking around for the right words. "I'm Leese's enemy and I want to stop him. I thought maybe you could help."

"You can't do it," said Gelder.

"I've got to try."

"I already tried."

"And . . ."

"I pulled the plug when I left, screwed up the system so bad I thought they'd never be able to fix it." A slight pause. "They didn't even miss a show."

"Shit."

Margaret gave me a questioning look and I shrugged.

"Yeah," said Gelder. "I think Leese had things figured out and had everything ready. They didn't even miss a show. He must've had new gear just sitting there somewhere. I heard they brought in a guy from Seattle. Just like that." There was sadness in his voice.

"So there's no way to sabotage it?" I asked, looking at Margaret as I spoke the words into the phone.

"No way," said Gelder. Another long pause. "Ask you a question?"

"Sure."

"You hear anything about Jolene?"

The question surprised me. "I had a note from her, Duncan. She was disappearing. She didn't say where."

"Oh." His voice sounded hollow.

"If I hear from her again, I'll tell her you asked."

"Tell her to post a note the way you did. That was slick."

"Are you okay?"

"I'm okay. It's not like they can ever find me."

"Did they threaten you?"

It was a moment before Gelder answered. "No," he said, drawing out the word as though he was considering its meaning. "But I overheard Leese doing that to Mr. Bahr and I figured I was next."

"Doing what?"

"Threatening him. At least it sounded like it."

"Why Bahr?"

"I think he was thinking about leaving, too. Everybody had a bad reaction when you got kicked out. That, and the show about the rape. It was pretty depressing around there."

"Bahr was upset, too?" It hadn't occurred to me that Bahr might be on the outs with Leese.

"I guess," said Gelder. "Nothing major. I mean it was nothing like your scene in the control room. That was really something. Did they hurt you?"

I unconsciously rubbed my knees. "A few scratches is all. So Bahr was upset?"

"He said a few things later that were pretty anti-Elvis and that's when I overheard Leese going at him."

"Bad?"

"Heavy. Things like 'I pay you to talk not think so shut up.' Things like that."

"And you thought he was depressed by it?" An idea was beginning to form in my head. Maybe not a great one—but it was the only possible chance I might have. "Did he say anything to you? Like he was ready to leave, too? Anything like that?"

Gelder was slow to answer. "No. Not really. But yeah, I think he was pretty depressed. I was only there for two or three shows after you left so I probably didn't see much. Why the questions?"

"I'd rather not say on the phone."

Gelder didn't respond.

"So are you okay?" I asked. "Is there anything I can do for you, anything you need?"

"I'm fine," said Gelder. "Into another project, working for myself this time and it's pretty cool. I'm not in Dallas anymore so that's cool, too."

"What kind of project?"

"Computers, what else, huh?" Gelder paused for a moment. "I've got to go," he said. "You'll tell Jolene if you hear from her?"

"I will, Duncan. I promise. Look. If I need to find you, how do I do it?"

"Why would you need to find me?" His voice had become guarded again, the tone suspicious, and I realized he didn't trust me, couldn't trust me. In his mind I would always be one of the bosses. A "them" not an "us."

"Not find you, Duncan. That's not what I meant. Get in touch with you. Is there a way I can get in touch with you if I need to? You know the show inside and out, you know it better than anyone. I might need that knowledge. I don't want to know where you are. I just want to be able to get to you quick."

Gelder was silent for a few moments. "All right," he said finally, reluctantly. "Got a pencil?"

I fumbled at my pockets, mouthing "pencil" to Margaret who jumped up from the table and came back with a pen and a scrap of paper. "Got one," I said and listened as Gelder spelled out a long e-mail address. I repeated it back to him.

"It's a computer pager," said Gelder. "If you send that, I'll call you back in a minute or two."

"Got it."

"And you can give that address to Jolene, too."

"I will, Duncan. If I hear from her."

The line went dead and I turned the phone off.

"So?" said Margaret.

"So, he's okay. Moved, working in computers. He tried sabotaging the set and they fixed it so fast they didn't miss a show." I took a sip of the tea. "He said Bahr was in trouble, or having troubles, with Leese."

"Bahr?"

"Bahr."

"I thought Bahr was a wholly owned commodity?"

"Seems not. Gelder said Bahr had problems with the way I was treated and problems with the rape show, too. That he and Leese had words."

"Interesting," said Margaret. "I wonder . . . ?"

"I'm wondering the same thing," I said. "Guess I need to have a chat with a weatherman."

CHAPTER THIRTY-ONE

THE DAWN air seemed almost alive with the fragrance of freshly mown grass and the clocklike ticking of irrigation sprinklers washing back and forth over the fairways. The sun was just beginning to edge above the forest of pecans and oaks that shielded the golf course from the highway and the ground was still cool and dew-covered though the empty sky promised a hot day ahead.

I worried as I climbed from the car that I might be too late: the parking lot was already more than half full and I could see knots of men gathered at the first tee swinging their clubs and stretching their arms and legs as though they were preparing for some serious physical exercise rather than a round of golf. I walked past the pro shop and along the first tee but there was no sign of Bahr.

Back in the shop I got a cup of coffee and stationed myself at a table where I could see people coming in. My concern that I'd somehow miscalculated increased with every new arrival that wasn't Bahr. I knew golf was a religion to the man, knew the old Bahr at least wouldn't miss a Sunday morning. But maybe something had happened to change his pattern, or maybe he'd gone by and I hadn't spotted him.

I waited for almost forty-five minutes and was beginning to think about giving up when I saw him and smiled inwardly to myself—I need not have worried about missing him in his custard-colored slacks, electric-green shirt and a bright-red tam on his head that looked like some sort of surgical accident. I waited for him to get to the cashier's counter before I came up beside him. "Hey there, Iso, how's the game?"

Bahr turned and a look of surprise and fear washed through his eyes but he recovered quickly. "Nick. Didn't know you played."

"I don't. You got a minute?"

Bahr looked at me uncertainly, glancing at the cashier and back at me, and it was as though I could read his mind: No, he didn't have a minute for me, but he also didn't have a polite way of refusing it. "Sure."

We sat down at the table where I'd been watching the crowd. "Buy you a coffee?"

Bahr shook his head and gestured toward the course. "Thanks, but I'm meeting some friends. So what's up?"

I sized up the small man and his silly little hat and wondered if I could ever really communicate with him. Though I'd rehearsed the scene dozens of times in my head, I realized sitting there that we inhabited different universes—and I really didn't have more than a small clue that he might be unhappy in his. I decided to toss out the script and hit it head-on.

"Leese has to be stopped. I need your help."

Bahr's eyes registered the comment without expression but his body slumped in the chair as though someone had opened a valve and let the air out. He put his head back and stared at the ceiling for a time, then steadied himself and brought his gaze back to me.

"Iso," I said, pressing it home, "I can make a list for you if that's what you want but we both know what's happening. The rape show, the riots, the president. That little girl should have never been on TV. He destroyed her—and he built it into a race war. The club fire? He killed a lot of innocent people."

"Twenty-three," said Bahr in a voice so low it was barely more than a mumble. His eyes were in his lap.

"Pardon me?"

Bahr looked up. "Twenty-three. They visit me sometimes."

I remained silent.

"They come and stand by my bed." His eyes were back down again. "Sometimes I can't see them but I can smell them—they're on fire." He trailed off into silence.

"That's rough," I said.

"I miss my wife," he said. "I miss the kids." He looked up and I could read the pain in his eyes.

"How is she?"

He gave me a bitter smile. "A divorced mommy raising a bunch of little kids by herself? How do you expect she is? A divorced mommy with a medical record that says she's crazy? How do you expect she is?"

"I'm sorry."

Bahr didn't seem to hear it. "The court lets me visit every two weeks. Every two fucking weeks. But I've been sneaking over to the house. I don't think Leese knows. Fuck it. Maybe he does." His voice trailed away and he sat in silence for a time before he started up again, his words a low whisper. "Some nights the people on fire don't come. And it's funny because those are the worst. I lie there and wait for them to come, and they don't come and I panic because I know they'll be back the next night and it'll be worse than it was the time before." He shook his head. "Sometimes I think it'll pass. And sometimes I think I'm losing my mind."

"We've got to stop him."

Bahr went on as though I hadn't spoken. "And sometimes I think maybe I'll quit and go away, go somewhere where the dead people can't find me. But another part of me says I'm a two-bit weatherman and I'll never have another gig like this the rest of my life. I mean there have been some good times, too. And the money. God, the money. But the nightmares keep coming and I go back to thinking about just leaving, getting away somewhere where those people can't find me." He lapsed into a thoughtful silence, studying his hands.

"I think you have to make a choice, Iso," I said carefully.

The small man shook his head softly. "Not easy."

"I know."

"He'd make sure I never work again."

"Maybe you could teach."

Bahr shrugged. "I don't even have a college degree. Not much call out there for a ventriloquist's dummy. What's next for you?"

The question caught me off-guard, without an answer. I'd thought about it from time to time but in a hazy, general way. I'd have to get a job sooner or later. But I hadn't thought about specifics. "I don't know," I said, honestly. "I suppose something will come up."

"I wouldn't be the King anymore," said Bahr.

"You're not the King," I said, as gently as I could. "Clare Leese is the King. You're his mouth. You know that."

"I talked to the president, you know."

"Elvis talked to the president, Iso. Not you."

Bahr glanced away, and it was as though even more air was escaping from his frame. "I know," he said, avoiding my eyes. He looked out the open door toward the first tee and let his gaze idle there for a time. Finally, he turned back to me, his eyes hardening even as he spoke. "Tell me what you want me to do."

Chapter Thirty-two

. . . you could be with us here today," Elvis was saying as the applause faded, "because we have a truly special show for you. It's the kind of show, the kind of topic, we think we have a real responsibility to present, because it goes right to the heart of what it is to be an American. And it exposes a group in this country that aren't Americans, at least in the way we have come to understand and love that word. It's a group we need to look at closely. And I think it's a group we need to do something about, something radical." Elvis paused and looked out over the audience from the large central screen. "Ladies and gentlemen, you saw the headlines in the news. Now you're about to meet the people behind those headlines. Stay tuned because we're back in sixty seconds with the story of a little boy murdered in cold, cold blood."

I leaned across the front seat of the car and kissed Margaret lightly on the cheek. She put her arms around me—the move in the cramped space felt clumsy and awkward—she put her arms around my neck and held me tightly. "I love you," she whispered into the skin below my ear.

I gave her a last long look and climbed out of the car, walking across the parking lot toward the theater as casually as my screaming senses would allow. The lot was filled with cars but empty of people.

At the stage door, I pulled out the key card Iso Bahr had given me and swiped it through the machine. The door gave off a soft mechanical hiss. So much adrenaline was pumping through my system that I was light-headed and my legs felt rubbery. I pulled the door open and, with a last furtive look around the parking lot, ducked inside.

The hallway was empty and I could dimly hear the sounds of applause from the direction of the main studio. Halfway down the hall, I let myself into a small makeup room and checked my watch: Three minutes to my last contribution to *Elvis Live at Five*. In a monitor in front of me, the man himself was introducing a sofa-full of guests. I felt my guts twist as his face came on to the screen.

". . . Mr. and Mrs. Loch's son can't be here today," he was saying, an exaggerated look of sadness on his face, "and I think we all know why, don't we? Because he is dead." The view cut to a reverse shot of the audience nodding in agreement, then switched back to a wide shot of the stage—Elvis in the screen, two young children and a man and woman beside him on the sofa. "Homer and Elizabeth Loch ran a drugstore in a small Nebraska town. A nice town—a couple of thousand people, Little League baseball, Fourth of July parades, high-school proms. It was the kind of place we're all from, the kind of place we all want to get back to. It was a good town with good neighbors. But then bad things started happening in Brickens, Nebraska."

I stared at the screen. Brickens? I'd heard that name before.

"There's no other way to say it except that one day a couple of years ago Satan came to Brickens. He wasn't dressed in a hood with horns and carrying a pitchfork or anything like that. No, he was in a business suit, carried a briefcase, looked just like you and I. Who was this Satan? He was none other than the leader of the Oh Som cult."

The words sent a chill through my body. The cult, Brickens, the dead kid—the story we'd looked at but passed on because there was nothing there. It was just a kid who'd committed suicide. Sad, but meaningless. But I realized it wouldn't be meaningless for long now, not when Leese got his teeth into it, not when he got through using the bag of tricks I'd given him. The realization sent a wave of anger through me—anger and cold, hard resolve. If I'd ever doubted the man had to be stopped, that doubt was now gone. I checked my watch. Two minutes. Two minutes to the last broadcast of *Elvis Live at Five.*

"Now I know you've all heard of the Oh Soms. There are millions of them around the world, tens of thousands right here in the United States." Video of a knot of shaven-headed young people dressed in saffron robes dancing wildly down a city street. "You see them in the airports banging on their tambourines and making a general nuisance of themselves getting in your face about buying their books or their incense. What you probably don't know is they are really big business." A picture in the monitor of a dark-haired man, early fifties, conservative business suit, smiling at the camera. "This," said Elvis, "is Nandini Patel. He's the brains, the bucks, the drive behind the Oh Soms. He calls himself the Guru Sartori, the Enlightened One, and claims a spiritual lineage back to the earliest days of Hinduism. The truth is a lot different. The truth is he's a fraud—a fraud and a killer."

Thirty seconds. I wiped the sweat from my face and reminded myself that my part was simple. All I had to do was push a button. Bahr had the tough job.

"Now you ask what any of this has to do with Mr. and Mrs. Loch and their lovely children seated here? The answer is simple. They come from Brickens, Nebraska, which also happens to be home to the largest single settlement of Oh Som cult members anywhere in the United States. Twelve thousand of them. Imagine it: twelve thousand. Look at Mr. and Mrs. Loch here and understand this—the Oh Soms murdered their little boy. In the small American town of Brickens, Nebraska, a cult of Satan-worshipping foreigners cut the throat of a young American child."

Like hell they did. Just push the button, Nick. I cracked open the door. Applause was welling from the main studio. The hallway was still deserted. With a last look at the screen, I edged through the door and crept noiselessly out. At the end of the hallway, I turned into another that led toward the rear of the studio. It too was deserted. Near the end of it, I slipped through a door into an equipment maintenance room. Tall racks of cabling and connectors lined the walls. I made my way silently to the rear and listened at a metal door. Beyond I could plainly hear Bahr's voice giving orders to the makeup woman. Taking a deep breath, I turned the knob and pushed into the room.

Bahr was sitting on his stool bathed in the crosshatches of the scanning lights. He turned toward me with a serious look. Two technicians sitting at a row of computers glanced up, startled, and rose warily to their feet. The makeup woman backed away uncertainly. The three cameramen stood at their machines, watching me intently. Above us, a large monitor gazed blindly down—the face of Elvis filling it from side to side.

I locked the door behind me and moved quickly to the main door and threw the bolt, locking it from the inside. Overhead, a man's voice on a speaker announced fifteen seconds. Otherwise, the room was quiet as a coffin. Both computer techs were on their feet now.

"Nobody's going to get hurt," I said, keeping my voice calm but forceful. "Keep your hands at your sides."

The light-headedness and shortness of breath were gone, replaced by an almost crystalline clarity of thought and purpose. Gelder's concise instructions floated in my mind like a road map. The main override to take the show back from the control room was a silver panel the size of a cake pan on the far right side of the console. Slide the second black lever from the left up to the top and push the green button.

Above me, the speaker came to life with a man's voice: "Five, four, three . . ."

I slid the black lever all the way to the top and pushed the green button. Elvis's face instantly disappeared on the monitor, replaced there by the face of Iso Bahr. I looked at Bahr. He gave me a shallow nod and turned to face the camera.

"Hello," he said calmly. "We've had a slight change of programming. Let me introduce myself to you. I'm the person you know as Elvis Presley . . ."

The overhead speaker erupted in the screaming voice of Clare Leese. "What the fuck is happening in there . . . !"

". . . been watching me for more than a year now," Bahr was saying, his voice still calm, his words matter-of-fact and measured. "I've taken the electronic mask off so I can speak with you directly and without tricks or deceit. This has all gotten out of control."

". . . this fucking minute," Leese was screaming, "or you're dead. You're fucking dead . . ."

Bahr looked up at the speaker and back at the camera. "The screaming you're hearing is coming from Clare Leese. He's the one who owns Elvis. It's his ideas that come out of the mouth the Elvis—out of my mouth. I'm just the ventriloquist's dummy. We had a good idea once, a long time ago. We thought we could bring you something that was fun, that you hadn't seen before, that would make television more accessible to everyone."

Someone was pounding on the main door. I looked at it uncertainly but the bolt was holding.

The noise didn't seem to faze Bahr. "But now it's gotten out of control. It's been twisted and perverted and allowed to become a kind of social pornography that has no place in this society. We should never have put the ten-year-old girl who had been raped on the air. I apologize for that. I apologize to her and her family. We shouldn't have put the gay clubs on the air. To those who lost friends and loved ones, I apologize with all my heart and soul. To those who died, if you can somehow hear me, please understand how deeply, deeply sorry I am for what I did, for what we did. We shouldn't have . . ."

A crash erupted from the side of the studio, then another—

they were hammering at the door and the frame was beginning to bend.

Bahr didn't seem to notice. He was square-on to the camera, his eyes intense, his mouth in a hard set. ". . . to apologize for all of us. Most of the images you see on this broadcast are fake. They're phoney, they aren't real. We build them in the computer. That's the genius of this broadcast. We take a little slice of what's out there—the bad slice—and we exaggerate it, magnify it, then we create our own pictures. We didn't have pictures of the little ten-year-old girl walking across the railroad tracks . . ."

Another crash from the side door and the wood frame around the knob was cracking.

". . . created those pictures so you'd watch, so you'd get outraged. This cult today. The one in Nebraska. It's just a bunch of normal people. They didn't have anything to do with this little boy's death. WE'RE the ones who are linking this . . ."

The door burst open and before I could even move, a security guard hit me with a full-body block that sent me reeling backward across the room. At the same time another man lunged for the control panel and Bahr's face disappeared from the monitor.

A black-leather boot came down hard on my neck and I spun to the side and brought my foot up into the man's crotch and sprang to my feet as he bent over with a surprised cry of pain. Even as I rose, two other men were coming through the door, one swinging a baton wildly at my head. I ducked the blow and caught the man full in the face with my fists, hammering him backward across the room until he crumpled to the floor.

Out of the corner of my eye, I could see two men pulling Bahr from his chair and throwing him into the same headlock that had ended my days at the Theater of the United States. I turned and lunged and got one of the men in the side of the head with my balled fists but then he was on me and we did a clumsy violent shuffle across the room, knocking over one of the cameras and falling together backward across the tripod. I wrestled with him as he gouged a thumb into my eye and I managed to get his wrist and bend it back. I heard it snap and the man cursed and I scrambled to my feet, but before I could even get my balance, a blinding impact took me in the side of my head and the room spun as light exploded behind my eyes and I dropped into darkness.

I came to choking for air under a black boot crushing into my windpipe. "Ladies and gentlemen," a man's voice was saying smoothly from the speaker, "we apologize for a slight technical difficulty. We're going to pause now for a commercial break and we'll be back in ninety seconds."

"Get him up!" snarled a familiar voice and I felt myself being lifted into the air and slammed face first into the wall, the cartilage in my nose crushing under the impact and blood gushing into my mouth. Two guards twisted my arms painfully behind me and I gagged on the blood. From the corner of my eye I could see Leese glaring at me, his narrow lips curled into a black worm of hatred and anger. "Hold both of them," he snapped and climbed into Bahr's chair and hooked the mike into his lapel. He barked at the makeup woman and she came over and started dusting powder onto his face, her hands shaking, her face white as a linen sheet. I tried turning my head slightly to watch and the guard shoved me harder into the wall. I could hear Bahr gasping for breath on the other side of me.

Leese straightened up and looked into the camera. Then he slowly looked over at me, a small nasty smile forming on his lips. "How do I look, Mr. Upton? You like it? You like your Elvis show?"

The monitor came back to life with the face of Elvis on it.

"Ten seconds," said a voice from above.

"You did me a favor," Leese said, glancing from me to Bahr. "Now I don't have to fire the stupid little fuck."

254 • JOHN PAXSON

"And five, four, three . . ."

"And, by the way, Mr. Upton. You lose."

The red tally light on the camera blinked on. Leese started talking, and Elvis started speaking. "We're back folks, and we apologize for those technical problems. I checked with our boys in the back and it turns out somebody rolled a tape that shouldn't have been rolled. We'll investigate it, but we think it's probably a prank or a hoax or something like that. So let's get back to business. No matter how you look at this, the Oh Soms cult is killing Americans. We have some truly extraordinary videotape to show you today—it's exclusive, it's ours and it's real. It's the last few violent, fatal minutes of this little boy's life. It will be like nothing you have ever seen. First, before we get to that, a question for Mrs. Loch: I wonder if you'd share with us your thoughts when police told you your little boy had been murdered. How did it feel?"

*T*HE SUN *is going down in an unexpected burst of orange brilliance across the squat brick-chimney skyline of south London and the river is falling back into shadow. The heron pokes through a tidal pool. The bridge is clogged with commuters and a red double-decker bus inches through the traffic.*

I finally managed the nerve to turn on the BBC a few minutes ago. Nebraska is still a top story. The U.S. Army is still in Brickens, still hunting down the cult members and marching them off through the snow to holding pens outside town. One picture showed a line of more than a dozen television satellite trucks parked along the main street. Refugees always make good TV. Another showed the internment camp in Iowa where the people are being sent: rows and rows of austere barracks surrounded by barbed-wire fences with watchtowers. It looked frozen and inhuman under the cold blue lights of the cameras and reminded me of scenes from a war. And they showed the shot again from last night, the one that spooked me so badly—refugees huddled around bonfires in the heavy snow, the soldiers pushing into the crowds with their rifles, the dark-haired reporter talking earnestly into the camera, steam pouring from her mouth as she spoke. I knew a reporter like that once.

The second item on the report was a shoot-out between white and Vietnamese shrimp fishermen in Brownsville, Texas. A protest had descended into rocks and bullets on the arrival of the KKK. A dozen people were wounded and one man—a Vietnamese—was dead. The Texas National Guard had been called out and the president had called for calm. Elvis wasn't mentioned. But I could sense his presence in the pattern; a local story growing like a tropical vine under the hothouse lights of the cameras, the president coming on television—coming on the Elvis show—to try to calm tensions, and unwittingly playing directly to the twisted script that Clare Leese was writing for the world.

I switch the TV to video and slide a cassette into the machine. The face of Marilyn Monroe swims up from the black depths. "Well, hi there, Duncan." Her eyes are shining with sexuality. "What brings you by today?"

I look out the window, thinking about my life in Dallas, about the people I knew, the times I lived through. I opened this by promising to tell you a story. That story is now almost told.

That the final day in the studio did no good must be obvious by now. Bahr's noble gesture was in the end no more than a ripple on a pond, a ripple that washed against a couple of shores but died away quickly and was just as quickly forgotten.

Clare Leese rode the cult like a strong horse, as he was so fond of saying. I watched it for almost a week from a hospital bed after surgeons reconstructed my face. It was slow to develop, but when it did, there was no other story in America. Leese played the Geldered tape of the dead boy like a fine violin, driving the public and the politicians to frenzies of fear and outrage and generating such paranoia that the final executive order to send in the army— fully three months after the first Brickens broadcast—nearly doubled the president's popularity ratings.

I play Bahr's painful—and pointless—soliloquy from time to time to give myself courage. A studio tech got a copy to me. It lies now on my desk next to a black frame which holds the final uncashed check from Claire Leese. I keep it as a signpost to remind myself where I've been—and where I will never go. Near it is the note from Jolene which is rumpled and discolored around the edges. I find myself wondering occasionally where she is and if she's all right. I will probably never know.

There are many things I will never know, though I've been able to piece together some, and recall others. As Leese became Elvis on that final fruitless day, his guards methodically set about beating me into unconsciousness. I remember, even as they started with *their fists and clubs, thinking about Leese's words, how if a snake threatened him he would beat that snake to death. I was his snake. When I came to later I was surprised I wasn't dead. The images were confused and blurred—I know now I was in the back of an ambulance—and I remember seeing Margaret's face and feeling her hands holding my cheeks.*

She took me back to her homemade house after the stay in the hospital and started the process of rebuilding my skin and my soul. Sometime there in the pain and the sweats I told her about the woman in the canyon and the wall of fire. I don't remember what she said or did but in the quiet moments now when I survey who I am and what I stand for—when I tally the ledger of my life—the woman in the fire is no longer a guilty entry, only a sad memory.

I know now that Bahr was in the same hospital though I never saw him, never heard from him until much later. He wasn't beaten as thoroughly as I. Within a week, he, his wife and kids were gone. I had an e-mail from him later and we still correspond. He and BB moved about as far away from Texas as they could get and remarried. He's working toward finishing his degree. He's going to teach grade-school science.

I still hear from Duncan Gelder, too. I don't know where he is— he's never said—and I don't know exactly what he's doing, though I can guess. Hollywood is advertising the Christmas release of a mixed-media blockbuster starring a reanimated John Lennon with cameos by Richard Nixon and J. Edgar Hoover. PBS is Geldering Winston Churchill to narrate a documentary series on a reanimated Adolf Hitler, and there's talk in the trade magazines that one of the networks is creating a Geldered anchor clone like John Sinclair for a prime-time news magazine. I suspect Gelder's back in the thick of it, and I don't begrudge him that. When it was time to do the right thing, he did. That he would return to his passion is no betrayal.

As I write these words, the sunset loses its brilliance and fades toward a purple dusk. Behind me, I hear stirrings from the kitchen. Without turning to look, I imagine Margaret's slender hands and shining blue eyes. My mind paints a quirky, enigmatic smile across her lips—and I feel such an overwhelming tenderness and love that my own eyes sting with tears. Through my pain and nightmares, it has been Margaret's hands that have kept me tended, Margaret's eyes that have kept me sane. It has been Margaret's gentle smile that has given me the will and the courage to tell this story.

I admit I was ready to give up. In my mind, and in my heart, Leese had won. When the last day in the studio failed so spectacularly, I saw no other path. I believed Leese had me checked at every turn. Margaret, though, never accepted that, never believed it—and I slowly came to see that she was right. A fight is never over, a battle never truly lost, as long as the will to carry on remains. That will not only remains, but gets stronger every day—for both of us.

Margaret left her teaching job to join me in London and spends her time making a meticulous record of every lie, falsity and ugly fantasy that Leese and the others in his burgeoning trade try to pass off on the public. Her column cataloging the deceit syndicates to nearly a hundred newspapers. They're not the big papers yet, but that will come. She's also on radio and TV now and again, talking about the difference between myth and reality in the age of media convergence. We both draw enormous hope from the fact that some people out there seem to care. It's a small number—but it's growing.

My nights are still troubled, the bad dreams still there, but with these last few words I have now managed the first step in trying to make things right, and it is as though a great iron clamp has been taken off my chest. I have told the story of how this all came to be. It's a simple story, actually: I created a TV show and Clare Leese created a monster. Your response to this story is yours and yours alone. If you see no reason for fear or concern—if you're content with the world as it seems to be—I wish you peace and health on your blind journey. But if you're troubled by a Geldered world—frightened by the monsters now walking among us—give this book to a friend and tell him to pass it on. And tell your friend that Elvis is dead.

Signed, this 11th day of January,
Nicholas Upton
London